"Francis, As We All Know, Is One of the Best."
—*The New York Times*

"One of the greatest living suspense writers"
—*CBS Radio*

"When violence strikes, Francis describes it with the authority of a writer who has taken his share of painful falls: a tumble over a balcony here hurts worse than the ritual beatings most fictional private eyes undergo."

—*Newsweek*

"No one has ever been cheated by a Dick Francis novel . . . this story is packed with action."
—*The Miami Herald*

"An exciting tale . . . horribly plausible."
—*The Atlantic Monthly*

Winner of the Mystery Writers of America Award for Best Novel of the Year, Dick Francis is the bestselling author of *Enquiry, Knockdown, For Kicks, Nerve, Forfeit, Dead Cert, Blood Sport, Odds Against, Flying Finish,* and *Slayride* —all published by Pocket Books.

I was cleaning the brushes when Donald came back. I heard the scrunch of the car, the slam of the doors, and,

Books by Dick Francis

Blood Sport
Dead Cert
Enquiry
Flying Finish
Forfeit
For Kicks
High Stakes
In the Frame
Knockdown
Nerve
Odds Against
Slayride

Published by POCKET BOOKS

Dick Francis
In The Frame

PUBLISHED BY POCKET BOOKS NEW YORK

**POCKET BOOKS, a Simon & Schuster division of
GULF & WESTERN CORPORATION
1230 Avenue of the Americas, New York, N.Y. 10020**

Copyright © 1976 by Dick Francis

Published by arrangement with Harper & Row, Publishers, Inc.
Library of Congress Catalog Card Number: 76-47255

ISBN: 0-671-81883-X

First Pocket Books printing September, 1978

Trademarks registered in the United States and other countries.

Printed in the U.S.A.

For Caroline
sound asleep

My thanks to two professional artists:
Michael Jeffery,
of Australia,
and
Josef Jira,
of Czechoslovakia,
who generously showed me their studios, their methods,
their minds, and their lives.

Also to the many art galleries whose experts gave me information and help, and particularly to Peter Johnson, of Oscar & Peter Johnson, London, S.W. 1, and to the Stud & Stable Gallery, Ascot.

D.F.

In The Frame

CHAPTER 1

I stood on the outside of disaster, looking in.

There were three police cars outside my cousin's house, and an ambulance with its blue turret light revolving ominously, and people bustling in seriously through his open front door. The chill wind of early autumn blew dead brown leaves sadly onto the driveway, and harsh scurrying clouds threatened worse to come. Six o'clock, Friday evening, Shropshire, England.

Intermittent bright white flashes from the windows spoke of photography in progress within. I slid my satchel from my shoulder and dumped both it and my suitcase on the grass verge, and with justifiable foreboding completed my journey to the house.

I had traveled by train to stay for the weekend. No cousin with car to meet me as promised, so I had started to walk the mile and a half of country road, sure he would come tearing along soon in his muddy Peugeot, full of jokes and apologies and plans.

No jokes.

He stood in the hall, dazed and gray. His body inside his neat business suit looked limp, and his arms hung straight down from the shoulders as if his brain had forgotten they were there. His head was turned slightly toward the sitting room, the source of the flashes, and his eyes were stark with shock.

"Don?" I said. I walked toward him. "Donald!"

He didn't hear me. A policeman, however, did. He came swiftly from the sitting room in his dark blue uniform, took me by the arm, and swung me strongly and unceremoniously back toward the door.

"Out of here, sir," he said. "If you please."

The strained eyes slid uncertainly our way.

"Charles . . ." His voice was hoarse.

The policeman's grip loosened very slightly. "Do you know this man, sir?" he asked Donald.

"I'm his cousin," I said.

"Oh." He took his hands off, told me to stay where I was and look after Mr. Stuart, and returned to the sitting room to consult.

"What's happened?" I said.

Don was past answering. His head turned again toward the sitting-room door, drawn to a horror he could no longer see. I disobeyed the police instructions, took ten quiet steps, and looked in.

The familiar room was unfamiliarly bare. No pictures, no ornaments, no edge-to-edge floor covering of Oriental rugs. Just bare gray walls, chintz-covered sofas, heavy furniture pushed awry, and a great expanse of dusty wood-block flooring.

And, on the floor, my cousin's young wife, bloody and dead.

The big room was scattered with busy police, measuring, photographing, dusting for fingerprints. I knew they were there; didn't see them. All I saw was Regina lying on her back, her face the color of cream.

Her eyes were half open, still faintly bright, and her lower jaw had fallen loose, outlining brutally the shape of the skull. A pool of urine lay wetly on the parquet around her sprawled legs, and one arm was flung out sideways, with the dead white fingers curling upward as if in supplication.

There had been no mercy.

I looked at the scarlet mess of her head and felt the blood draining sickeningly from my own.

The policeman who had grabbed me before turned round from his consultation with another, saw me swaying in the doorway, and took quick annoyed strides back to my side.

"I told you to wait outside, sir," he said with exasperation, stating clearly that my faintness was my own fault.

I nodded dumbly and went back into the hall. Donald was sitting on the stairs, looking at nothing. I sat abruptly on the floor near him and put my head between my knees.

"I . . . f . . . found . . . her," he said.

I swallowed. What could one say? It was bad enough for me, but he had lived with her, and loved her. The faintness passed away slowly, leaving a sour feeling of sickness. I leaned back against the wall behind me and wished I knew how to help him.

"She's . . . never . . . home . . . on F . . . Fridays," he said.

"I know."

"S . . . six. S . . . six o'clock . . . she comes b . . . back. Always."

"I'll get you some brandy," I said.

"She shouldn't . . . have been . . . here. . . ."

I pushed myself off the floor and went into the dining room, and it was there that the significance of the bare sitting room forced itself into consciousness. In the dining room, too, there were bare walls, bare shelves, and empty drawers pulled out and dumped on the floor. No silver ornaments. No silver spoons or forks. No collection of antique china. Just a jumble of table mats and napkins and broken glass.

My cousin's house had been burgled. And Regina— Regina, who was never home on Fridays—had walked in.

I went over to the plundered sideboard, flooding with anger and wanting to smash in the heads of all greedy, callous, vicious people who cynically devastated the lives of total strangers. Compassion was all right for saints. What I felt was plain hatred, fierce and basic.

I found two intact glasses, but all the drink had gone. Furiously I stalked through the swing door into the kitchen and filled the electric kettle.

In that room, too, the destruction had continued, with stores swept wholesale off the shelves. What valuables, I wondered, did thieves expect to find in kitchens? I jerkily made two mugs of tea and rummaged in Regina's spice cupboard for the cooking brandy, and felt unreasonably triumphant when it proved to be still there. The sods had missed that, at least.

Donald still sat unmoving on the stairs. I pressed the

cup of strong sweet liquid into his hands and told him to drink, and he did, mechanically.

"She's never home . . . on Fridays," he said.

"No," I said, and wondered just how many people knew there was no one home on Fridays.

We both slowly finished the tea, I took his mug and put it with mine on the floor, and sat near him as before. Most of the hall furniture had gone. The small Sheraton desk, the studded leather chair, the nineteenth-century carriage clock . . .

"Christ, Charles," he said.

I glanced at his face. There were tears, and dreadful pain. I could do nothing, nothing, to help him.

The impossible evening lengthened to midnight, and beyond. The police, I suppose, were efficient, polite, and not unsympathetic, but they left a distinct impression that they felt their job was to catch criminals, not to succor the victims. It seemed to me that there was also, in many of their questions, a faint hovering doubt, as if it were not unknown for householders to arrange their own well-insured burglaries, and for smooth-seeming swindles to go horrifically wrong.

Donald didn't seem to notice. He answered wearily, automatically, with long pauses sometimes between question and answer.

Yes, the missing goods were well insured.

Yes, they had been insured for years.

Yes, he had been to his office all day, as usual.

Yes, he had been out to lunch. A sandwich in a pub.

He was a wine shipper.

His office was in Shrewsbury.

He was thirty-seven years old.

Yes, his wife was much younger. Twenty-two.

He couldn't speak of Regina without stuttering, as if his tongue and lips were beyond his control. "She always s . . . spends F . . . Fridays working . . . in a f . . . friend's . . . f . . . flower . . . shop."

"Why?"

Donald looked vaguely at the Detective Inspector sitting opposite him across the dining-room table. The matched antique dining chairs had gone. Donald sat in a garden armchair brought from the sunroom. The Inspector, a constable, and I sat on kitchen stools.

"What?"

14

"Why did she work in a flower shop on Fridays?"

"She . . . she . . . I . . . likes—"

I interrupted brusquely. "She was a florist before she married Donald. She liked to keep her hand in. She used to spend Fridays making those table-arrangement things for dances and weddings and things like that." And wreaths, too, I thought, and couldn't say it.

"Thank you, sir, but I'm sure Mr. Stuart can answer for himself."

"And I'm sure he can't."

The Detective Inspector diverted his attention my way.

"He's too shocked," I said.

"Are you a doctor, sir?" His voice held polite disbelief, which it was entitled to, no doubt. I shook my head impatiently. He glanced at Donald, pursed his lips, and turned back to me. His gaze wandered briefly over my jeans, faded denim jacket, fawn polo-neck, and desert boots, and returned to my face, unimpressed.

"Very well, sir. Name?"

"Charles Todd."

"Age?"

"Twenty-nine."

"Occupation?"

"Painter."

The constable unemotionally wrote down these scintillating details in his pocket-sized notebook.

"Houses or pictures?" asked the Inspector.

"Pictures."

"And your movements today, sir?"

"Caught the two-thirty from Paddington and walked from the local station."

"Purpose of visit?"

"Nothing special. I come here once or twice a year."

"Good friends, then?"

"Yes."

He nodded noncommittally. Turned his attention again to Donald and asked more questions, but patiently and without pressure.

"And what time do you normally reach home on Fridays, sir?"

Don said tonelessly, "Five. About."

"And today?"

"Same." A spasm twitched the muscles of his face. "I saw . . . the house had been broken into. . . . I telephoned . . ."

15

"Yes, sir. We received your call at six minutes past five. And after you had telephoned, you went into the sitting room, to see what had been stolen?"

Donald didn't answer.

"Our sergeant found you there, sir, if you remember."

"Why?" Don said in anguish. "Why did she come home?"

"I expect we'll find out, sir."

The careful exploratory questions went on and on, and as far as I could see achieved nothing except to bring Donald ever closer to all-out breakdown.

I, with a certain amount of shame, grew ordinarily hungry, having not bothered to eat earlier in the day. I thought with regret of the dinner I had been looking forward to, with Regina tossing in unmeasured ingredients and herbs and wine and casually producing a gourmet feast. Regina with her cap of dark hair and ready smile, chatty and frivolous and anti-bloodsports. A harmless girl, come to harm.

At some point during the evening, her body was loaded into the ambulance and driven away. I heard it happen, but Donald gave no sign of interpreting the sounds. I thought that probably his mind was raising barriers against the unendurable, and one couldn't blame him.

The Inspector rose finally and stretched kinks caused by the kitchen stool out of his legs and spine. He said he would be leaving a constable on duty at the house all night, and that he himself would return in the morning. Donald nodded vaguely, having obviously not listened properly to a word, and, when the police had gone, still sat like an automaton in the chair, with no energy to move.

"Come on," I said. "Let's go to bed."

I took his arm, persuaded him to his feet, and steered him up the stairs. He came in a daze, unprotesting.

His and Regina's bedroom was a shambles, but the twin-bedded room prepared for me was untouched. He flopped full-length in his clothes and put his arm up over his eyes, and in appalling distress asked the unanswerable question of all the world's sufferers.

"Why? Why did it have to happen to *us?"*

I stayed with Donald for a week, during which time some questions, but not that one, were answered.

One of the easiest was the reason for Regina's premature return home. She and the flower-shop friend, who had been repressing annoyance with each other for weeks, had erupted into a quarrel of enough bitterness to make Regina leave at once. She had driven away at about two-thirty, and had probably gone straight home, as it was considered she had been dead for at least two hours by five o'clock.

This information, expressed in semiformal sentences, was given to Donald by the Detective Inspector on Saturday afternoon. Donald walked out into the autumnal garden and wept.

The Insepctor, Frost by name and cool by nature, came quietly into the kitchen and stood beside me watching Donald with his bowed head among the apple trees.

"I would like you to tell me what you can about the relationship between Mr. and Mrs. Stuart."

"You'd like *what?*"

"How did they get on?"

"Can't you tell for yourself?"

He answered neutrally after a pause: "The intensity of grief shown is not always an accurate indication of the intensity of love felt."

"Do you always talk like that?"

A faint smile flickered and died. "I was quoting from a book on psychology."

" 'Not always' means it usually is," I said.

He blinked.

"Your book is bunk," I said.

"Guilt and remorse can manifest themselves in an excess of mourning."

"Dangerous bunk," I added. "And as far as I could see, the honeymoon was by no means over."

"After three years?"

"Why not?"

He shrugged and didn't answer. I turned away from the sight of Donald and said, "What are the chances of getting back any of the stuff from this house?"

"Small, I should think. Where antiques are involved, the goods are likely to be halfway across the Atlantic before the owner returns from his holidays."

"Not this time, though," I objected.

He sighed. "Next best thing. There have been hundreds of similar break-ins during recent years and very little has been recovered. Antiques are big business these days."

"Connoisseur thieves?" I said skeptically.

"The prison library service reports that all their most requested books are on antiques. All the little chummies boning up to jump on the bandwagon as soon as they get out."

He sounded suddenly quite human. "Like some coffee?" I said.

He looked at his watch, raised his eyebrows, and accepted. He sat on a kitchen stool while I fixed the mugs —a fortyish man with thin sandy hair and a well-worn gray suit.

"Are you married?" he asked.

"Nope."

"In love with Mrs. Stuart?"

"You do try it on, don't you?"

"If you don't ask, you don't find out."

I put the milk bottle and a sugar basin on the table and told him to help himself. He stirred his coffee reflectively.

"When did you visit this house last?" he said.

"Last March. Before they went off to Australia."

"Australia?"

"They went to see the vintage there. Donald had some idea of shipping Australian wine over in bulk. They were away for at least three months. Why didn't their house get robbed *then*, when they were safely out of the way?"

He listened to the bitterness in my voice. "Life is full of nasty ironies." He pursed his lips gingerly to the hot coffee, drew back, and blew gently across the top of the mug. "What would you all have been doing today? In the normal course of events?"

I had to think what day it was. Saturday. It seemed totally unreal.

"Going to the races," I said. "We always go to the races when I come to stay."

"Fond of racing, were they?" The past tense sounded wrong. Yet so much was now past. I found it a great deal more difficult than he did to change gear.

"Yes . . . but I think they only go—went—because of me."

He tried the coffee again and managed a cautious sip. "In what way do you mean?" he asked.

"What I paint," I said, "is mostly horses."

Donald came in through the back door, looking red-eyed and exhausted.

"The press are making a hole in the hedge," he said leadenly.

Inspector Frost clicked his teeth, got to his feet, opened the door to the hall and the interior of the house, and called out loudly, "Constable? Go and stop those reporters from breaking into the garden."

A distant voice replied, "Sir," and Frost apologized to Donald. "Can't get rid of them entirely, you know, sir. They have their editors breathing down their necks. They pester the life out of us at times like these."

All day long, the road outside Donald's house had been lined with cars, which disgorged crowds of reporters, photographers, and plain sensation-seekers every time anyone went out the front door. Like a hungry wolf pack, they lay in wait, and I supposed that they would eventually pounce on Donald himself. Regard for his feelings was nowhere in sight.

"Newspapers listen to the radio on the police frequencies," Frost said gloomily. "Sometimes the press arrive at the scene of a crime before we can get there ourselves."

At any other time I would have laughed, but it would have been far from amusing for Donald if it had happened in his case. The police, of course, had thought at first that it more or less had happened, because I had heard that the constable who tried to eject me forcibly had taken me for a spearheading scribbler.

Donald sat down heavily on a stool and rested his elbows wearily on the table.

"Charles," he said, "if you wouldn't mind heating it, I'd like some of that soup now."

"Sure," I said, surprised. He had rejected it earlier as if the thought of food revolted him.

Frost's head went up as if at a signal, and his whole body straightened purposefully, and I realized he had merely been coasting along until then, waiting for some such moment. He waited some more while I opened a can of Campbell's condensed, sloshed it and some water and cooking brandy into a saucepan, and stirred until the lumps dissolved. He drank his coffee and waited while Donald disposed of two platefuls of soup and a chunk of brown bread. Then, politely, he asked me to take myself off, and when I'd gone he began what Donald afterward referred to as "serious digging."

It was three hours later, and growing dark, when the

19

Inspector left. I watched his departure from the upstairs-landing window. He and his attendant plainclothes constable were intercepted immediately outside the front door by a young man with wild hair and a microphone, and before they could dodge round him to reach their car, the pack on the road were streaming in full cry into the garden and across the grass.

I went methodically round the house drawing curtains, checking windows, and locking and bolting all the outside doors.

"What are you doing?" Donald asked, looking pale and tired, in the kitchen.

"Pulling up the drawbridge."

"Oh."

In spite of his long session with the Inspector, he seemed a lot calmer and more in command of himself, and when I had finished Fort Knoxing the kitchen-to-garden door he said, "The police want a list of what's gone. Will you help me make it?"

"Of course."

"It'll give us something to do."

"Sure."

"We did have an inventory, but it was in that desk in the hall. The one they took."

"Damn silly place to keep it," I said.

"That's more or less what *he* said. Inspector Frost."

"What about your insurance company? Haven't they got a list?"

"Only of the more valuable things, like some of the paintings, and her jewelry." He sighed. "Everything else was lumped together as 'contents.'"

We started on the dining room and made reasonable progress, with him putting the empty drawers back in the sideboard while trying to remember what each had once contained, and me writing down at his dictation. There had been a good deal of solid-silver tableware, acquired by Donald's family in its affluent past and handed down routinely. Donald, with his warmth for antiques, had enjoyed using it, but his pleasure in owning it seemed to have vanished with the goods. Instead of being indignant over its loss, he sounded impersonal and, by the time we had finished the sideboard, decidedly bored.

Faced by the ranks of empty shelves where once had stood a fine collection of early-nineteenth-century porcelain, he balked entirely.

"What does it matter?" he said drearily, turning away. "I simply can't be bothered. . . ."

"How about the paintings, then?"

He looked vaguely round the bare walls. The site of each missing frame showed unmistakably in lighter oblong patches of palest olive. In this room they had mostly been works of modern British painters: a Hockney, a Bratby, two Lowrys, and a Spear, for openers, all painted on what one might call the artists' less exuberant days. Donald didn't like paintings that he said "jumped off the wall and made a fuss."

"You probably remember them better than I do," he said. "You do it."

"I'd miss some."

"Is there anything to drink?"

"Only the cooking brandy," I said.

"We could have some of the wine."

"What wine?"

"In the cellar." His eyes suddenly opened wide. "Good God, I'd forgotten about the cellar."

"I didn't even know you had one."

He nodded. "Reason I bought the house. Perfect humidity and temperature for long-term storage. There's a small fortune down there in claret and port."

There wasn't, of course. There were three floor-to-ceiling rows of empty racks, and a single cardboard box on a plain wooden table.

Donald merely shrugged. "Oh, well . . . that's that."

I opened the top of the cardboard box and saw the elegant corked shapes of the tops of wine bottles.

"They've left these, anyway," I said. "In their rush."

"Probably on purpose," Don smiled twistedly. "That's Australian wine. We brought it back with us."

"Better than nothing," I said disparagingly, pulling out a bottle and reading the label.

"Better than most, you know. A lot of Australian wine is superb."

I carried the whole case up to the kitchen and dumped it on the table. The stairs from the cellar led up into the utility room among the washing machines and other domesticities, and I had always had an unclear impression that its door was just another cupboard. I looked at it thoughtfully, an unremarkable white painted panel merging inconspicuously into the general scenery.

"Do you think the burglars *knew* the wine was there?" I asked.

"God knows."

"I would never have found it."

"You're not a burglar, though."

He searched for a corkscrew, opened one of the bottles, and poured the deep red liquid into two kitchen tumblers. I tasted it, and it was indeed a marvelous wine, even to my untrained palate. Wynn's Coonawarra Cabernet Sauvignon. You could wrap the name round the tongue as lovingly as the product. Donald drank his share absentmindedly, as if it were water, the glass clattering once or twice against his teeth. There was still an uncertainty about many of his movements, as if he could not quite remember how to do things, and I knew it was because with half his mind he thought all the time of Regina, and the thoughts were literally paralyzing.

The old Donald had been a man of confidence, capably running a middle-sized inherited business and adding his share to the passed-on goodies. He had a blunt uncompromising face lightened by amber eyes that smiled easily, and he had considered his money well spent on shapely haircuts.

The new Donald was a tentative man shattered with shock, a man trying to behave decently but unsure where his feet were when he walked upstairs.

We spent the evening in the kitchen, talking desultorily, eating a scratch meal, and tidying all the stores back onto the shelves. Donald made a good show of being busy, but put half the tins back upside down.

The front doorbell rang three times during the evening but never in the code prearranged with the police. The telephone, with its receiver lying loose beside it, rang not at all. Donald had turned down several offers of refuge with local friends and visibly shook at the prospect of talking to anyone but Frost and me.

"Why don't they go away?" he said despairingly, after the third attempt on the front door.

"They will, once they've seen you," I said. And sucked you dry, and spat out the husk, I thought.

He shook his head tiredly. "I simply can't."

It felt like living through a siege.

We eventually went again upstairs to bed, although it seemed likely that Donald would sleep no more than the night before, which had been hardly at all. The police surgeon had left knock-out pills, which Donald wouldn't take. I pressed him again on that second evening, with equal non-results.

"No, Charles. I'd feel I'd deserted her. D . . . ducked out. Thought only of myself, and not of . . . of how awful it was for her . . . dying like that . . . with n . . . no one near who 1 . . . loved her."

He was trying to offer her in some way the comfort of his own pain. I shook my head at him, but tried no more with the pills.

"Do you mind," he said diffidently, "if I sleep alone tonight?"

"Of course not."

"We could make up a bed for you in one of the other rooms."

"Sure."

He pulled open the linen-cupboard door on the upstairs landing and gestured indecisively at the contents. "Could you manage?"

"Of course," I said.

He turned away and seemed struck by one particular adjacent patch of empty wall.

"They took the Munnings," he said.

"What Munnings?"

"We bought it in Australia. I hung it just there . . . only a week ago. I wanted you to see it. It was one of the reasons I asked you to come."

"I'm sorry," I said. Inadequate words.

"Everything," he said helplessly. "Everything's gone."

CHAPTER 2

Frost arrived tirelessly again on Sunday morning, with his quiet watchful eyes and noncommittal manner. I opened the front door to his signal, and he followed me through to the kitchen, where Donald and I seemed to have taken up permanent residence. I gestured him to a stool, and he sat on it, straightening his spine to avoid future stiffness.

"Two pieces of information you might care to have, sir," he said to Donald, his voice at its most formal. "Despite our intensive investigation of this house during yesterday and the previous evening, we have found no fingerprints for which we cannot account."

"Would you expect to?" I asked.

He flicked me a glance. "No, sir. Professional housebreakers always wear gloves."

Donald waited with a gray patient face, as if he would find whatever Frost said unimportant. Nothing, I judged, was of much importance to Donald any more.

"Second," said Frost, "our investigations in the district reveal that a removal van was parked outside your front door early on Friday afternoon."

Donald looked at him blankly.

"Dark-colored, and dusty, sir."

"Oh," Donald said meaninglessly.

Frost sighed. "What do you know of a bronze statuette of a horse, sir? A horse, rearing up on its hind legs?"

"It's in the hall," Donald said automatically; and then, frowning slightly, "I mean, it used to be. It's gone."

"How do you know about it?" I asked Frost curiously, and guessed the answer before I'd finished the question. "Oh, no—" I stopped, and swallowed. "I mean, perhaps you found it . . . fallen off the van?"

"No, sir." His face was calm. "We found it in the sitting room, near Mrs. Stuart."

Donald understood as clearly as I had done. He stood up abruptly and went to the window, and stared out for a while at the empty garden.

"It is heavy," he said at last. "The base of it."

"Yes, sir."

"It must have been . . . quick."

"Yes, sir," Frost said again, sounding more objective than comforting.

"P . . . poor Regina." The words were quiet, the desolation immense. When he came back to the table, his hands were trembling. He sat down heavily and stared into space.

Frost started another careful speech about the sitting room being kept locked by the police for a few more days yet, and please would neither of us try to go in there.

Neither of us would.

Apart from that, they had finished their inquiries at the house, and Mr. Stuart was at liberty to have the other rooms cleaned, if he wished, where the fingerprint dust lay grayish-white on every polished surface.

Mr. Stuart gave no sign of having heard.

Had Mr. Stuart completed the list of things stolen?

I passed it over. It still consisted only of the dining-room silver and what I could remember of the paintings. Frost raised his eyebrows and pursed his lips.

"We'll need more than this, sir."

"We'll try again today," I promised. "There's a lot of wine missing, as well."

"Wine?"

I showed him the empty cellar, and he came up looking thoughtful.

"It must have taken hours to move that lot," I said.

"Very likely, sir," he said primly.

Whatever he was thinking, he wasn't telling. He suggested instead that Donald should prepare a short statement to read to the hungry reporters still waiting outside, so that they could go away and print it.

"No," Don said.

"Just a short statement," Frost said reasonably. "We can prepare it here and now, if you like."

Frost wrote it himself, more or less, and I guessed it was as much for his own sake as Donald's that he wanted the press to depart, as it was Frost who had to push through them every time. He repeated the statement aloud when he had finished. It sounded like a police account, full of jargon, but because of that so distant from Donald's own raw grief that my cousin agreed in the end to read it out.

"But no photographs," he said anxiously, and Frost said he would see to it.

They crowded into the hall, a collection of dry-eyed fact-finders, all near the top of their digging profession and inured from sensitivity by a hundred similar intrusions into tragedy. Sure, they were sorry for the guy whose wife had been bashed, but news was news and bad news sold papers, and if they didn't produce the goods they'd lose their jobs to others more tenacious. The Press Council had stopped the brutal bullying of the past, but the leeway still allowed could be a great deal too much for the afflicted.

Donald stood on the stairs, with Frost and myself at the foot, and read without expression, as if the words applied to someone else.

". . . I returned to the house at approximately 5 P.M. and observed that during my absence a considerable number of valuable objects had been removed. . . . I telephoned immediately for assistance. . . . My wife, who was normally absent from the house on Fridays, returned unexpectedly . . . and, it is presumed, disturbed the intruders."

He stopped. The reporters dutifully wrote down the stilted words and looked disillusioned. One of them, clearly elected by prearrangement, started asking questions for them all, in a gentle, coaxing, sympathetic tone of voice.

"Could you tell us which of these closed doors is the one to the room where your wife . . ."

Donald's eyes slid briefly, despite himself, toward the sitting room. All the heads turned, the eyes studied the uninformative white painted panels, the pencils wrote.

"And could you tell us what exactly was stolen?"

"Silver. Paintings."

"Who were the paintings by?"

Donald shook his head and began to look even paler.

"Could you tell us how much they were worth?"

After a pause Don said, "I don't know."

"Were they insured?"

"Yes."

"How many bedrooms are there in your house?"

"What?"

"How many bedrooms?"

Donald looked bewildered. "I suppose . . . five."

"Do you think you could tell us anything about your wife? About her character, and about her job? And could you let us have a photograph?"

Donald couldn't. He shook his head and said, "I'm sorry," and turned and walked steadily away upstairs.

"That's all," Frost said with finality.

"It's not much," they grumbled.

"What do you want—blood?" Frost said, opening the front door and encouraging them out. "Put yourselves in his position."

"Yeah," they said cynically; but they went.

"Did you see their eyes?" I said. "Sucking it all in?"

Frost smiled faintly. "They'll all write long stories from that little lot."

The interview, however, produced to a great extent the desired results. Most of the cars departed, and the rest, I supposed, would follow as soon as fresher news broke elsewhere.

"Why did they ask about the bedrooms?" I said.

"To estimate the value of the house."

"Good grief."

"They'll all get it different." Frost was near to amusement. "They always do." He looked up the stairs in the direction Donald had taken, and almost casually said, "Is your cousin in financial difficulties?"

I knew his catch-them-off-guard technique by now.

"I wouldn't think so," I said unhurriedly. "You'd better ask him."

"I will, sir." He switched his gaze sharply to my face and studied my lack of expression. "What do you know?"

I said calmly, "Only that the police have suspicious minds."

27

He disregarded that. "Is Mr. Stuart worried about his business?"

"He's never said so."

"A great many middle-sized private companies are going bankrupt these days."

"So I believe."

"Because of cash-flow problems," he added.

"I can't help you. You'll have to look at his company's books."

"We will, sir."

"And even if the firm turns out to be bust, it doesn't follow that Donald would fake a robbery."

"It's been done before," Frost said dryly.

"If he needed money, he could simply have sold the stuff," I pointed out.

"Maybe he had. Some of it. Most of it, maybe."

I took a slow breath and said nothing.

"That wine, sir. As you said yourself, it would have taken a long time to move."

"The firm is a limited company," I said. "If it went bankrupt, Donald's own house and private money would be unaffected."

"You know a good deal about it, don't you?"

I said neutrally, "I live in the world."

"I thought artists were supposed to be unworldly."

"Some are."

He peered at me with narrowed eyes, as if he were trying to work out a possible way in which I, too, might have conspired to arrange the theft.

I said mildly, "My cousin Donald is an honorable man."

"That's an out-of-date word."

"There's quite a lot of it about."

He looked wholly disbelieving. He saw far too much in the way of corruption, day in, day out, all his working life.

Donald came hesitantly down the stairs, and Frost took him off immediately to another private session in the kitchen. I thought that if Frost's questions to Don were as barbed as those he'd asked me, poor Don was in for a rough time. While they talked, I wandered aimlessly round the house, looking into storage spaces, opening cupboards, seeing the inside details of my cousin's life.

Either he or Regina had been a horder of empty boxes. I came across dozens of them, all shapes and sizes,

28

shoved into odd corners of shelves and drawers: brown cardboard boxes, bright gift-wrapped boxes, beribboned chocolate boxes, all too potentially useful or too pretty to be thrown away. The burglars had opened a lot but had thrown more unopened on the floor. They must, I thought, have had a most frustrating time.

They had largely ignored the big sunroom, which held few antiques and no paintings, and I ended up there, sitting on a bamboo armchair among sprawling potted plants, looking out into the windy garden. Dead leaves blew in scattered showers from the drying trees, and a few late roses clung hardily to thorny stems.

I hated autumn. The time of melancholy, the time of death. My spirits fell each year with the soggy leaves and revived only with crisp winter frost. Psychiatric statistics proved that the highest suicide rate occurred in the spring, the time for rebirth and growth and stretching in the sun. I could never understand it. If ever I jumped over a cliff, it would be in the depressing months of decay.

The sunroom was gray and cold. No sun, that Sunday.

I went upstairs, fetched my suitcase, and brought it down. Over years of wandering journeys, I had reversed the painter's traditional luggage: my suitcase now contained the tools of my trade, and my satchel clothes. The large toughened suitcase, its interior adapted and fitted by me, was in fact a sort of portable studio, containing besides paints and brushes a light collapsible metal easel, unbreakable containers of linseed oil and turpentine, and a rack that would hold four wet paintings safely apart. There was also a dust sheet, a large box of tissues, and generous amounts of white spirit, all designed for preventing mess and keeping things clean. The organization of the suitcase had saved and made the price of many a sandwich.

I untelescoped the easel and set out my palette, and on a middling-sized canvas laid in the beginnings of a melancholy landscape, a mixture of Donald's garden as I saw it, against a sweep of bare fields and gloomy woods. Not my usual sort of picture, and not, to be honest, the sort to make headline news a century hence; but at least it gave me something to do. I worked steadily, growing ever colder, until the chillier Frost chose to depart; and he went without seeing me again, the front door closing decisively on his purposeful footsteps.

Donald, in the warm kitchen, looked torn to rags.

When I went in, he was sitting with his arms folded on the table and his head on his arms, a picture of absolute despair. When he heard me, he sat up slowly and wearily, and showed a face suddenly aged and deeply lined.

"Do you know what he thinks?" he said.

"More or less."

He stared at me somberly. "I couldn't convince him. He kept on and on. Kept asking the same questions, over and over. Why doesn't he believe me?"

"A lot of people lie to the police. I think they grow to expect it."

"He wants me to meet him in my office tomorrow. He says he'll be bringing colleagues. He says they'll want to see the books."

I nodded. "Better be grateful he didn't drag you down there today."

"I suppose so."

I said awkwardly, "Don, I'm sorry. I told him the wine was missing. It made him suspicious. . . . It was a good deal my fault that he was so bloody to you."

He shook his head tiredly. "I would have told him myself. I wouldn't have thought of not telling him."

"But . . . I even pointed out that it must have taken a fair time to move so many bottles."

"Mmm. Well, he would have worked that out for himself."

"How long, in fact, do you think it would have taken?"

"Depends how many people were doing it," he said, rubbing his hand over his face and squeezing his tired eyes. "They would have to have had proper wine boxes in any case. That means they had to know in advance that the wine was there, and didn't just chance on it. And that means—Frost says—that I sold it myself some time ago and am now saying it is stolen so I can claim fraudulent insurance, or, if it was stolen last Friday, that I told the thieves they'd need proper boxes, which means that I set up the whole frightful mess myself."

We thought it over in depressed silence. Eventually I said, "Who *did* know you had the wine there? And who knew the house was always empty on Fridays? And was the prime target the wine, the antiques, or the paintings?"

"God, Charles, you sound like Frost."

"Sorry."

"Every business nowadays," he said defensively, "is going through a cash crisis. Look at the nationalized industries, losing money by the million. Look at the wage rises and the taxes and the inflation. . . . How can any small business make the profit it used to? Of *course* we have a cash-flow problem. Whoever hasn't?"

"How bad is yours?" I said.

"Not critical. Bad enough. But not within sight of liquidation. It's illegal for a limited company to carry on trading if it can't cover its costs."

"But it could . . . if you could raise more capital to prop it up?"

He surveyed me with the ghost of a smile. "It surprises me still that you chose to paint for a living."

"It gives me a good excuse to go racing whenever I like."

"Lazy sod." He sounded for a second like the old Donald, but the lightness passed. "The absolutely last thing I would do would be to use my own personal assets to prop up a dying business. If my firm was that rocky, I'd wind it up. It would be mad not to."

I sucked my teeth. "I suppose Frost asked if the stolen things were insured for more than their worth?"

"Yes, he did. Several times."

"Not likely you'd tell him, even if they were."

"They weren't, though."

"No."

"Underinsured, if anything." He sighed. "God knows if they'll pay up for the Munnings. I'd only arranged the insurance by telephone. I hadn't actually sent the premium."

"It should be all right, if you can give them proof of purchase, and so on."

He shook his head listlessly. "All the papers to do with it were in the desk in the hall. The receipt from the gallery where I bought it, the letter of provenance, and the customs and excise receipt. All gone."

"Frost won't like that."

"He doesn't."

"Well . . . I hope you pointed out that you would hardly be buying expensive pictures and going on world trips if you were down to your last farthing."

"He said it might be *because* of buying expensive pictures and going on world trips that I might be down to my last farthing."

Frost had built a brick wall of suspicion for Donald to

batter his head against. My cousin needed hauling away before he was punch-drunk.

"Have some spaghetti," I said.

"What?"

"It's about all I can cook."

"Oh . . . " He focused unclearly on the kitchen clock. It was half past four and long past feeding time, according to my stomach.

"If you like," he said.

The police sent a car the following morning to fetch him to his ordeal in the office. He went lifelessly, having more or less made it clear over coffee that he wouldn't defend himself.

"Don, you must," I said. "The only way to deal with the situation is to be firm and reasonable, and decisive, and accurate. In fact, just your own self."

He smiled faintly. "You'd better go instead of me. I haven't the energy. And what does it matter?" His smile broke suddenly and the ravaging misery showed deeply like black water under cracked ice. "Without Regina . . . there's no point making money."

"We're not talking about making money, we're talking about suspicion. If you don't defend yourself, they'll assume you can't."

"I'm too tired. I can't be bothered. They can think what they like."

"Don," I said seriously, "they'll think what you let them."

"I don't really care," he said dully; and that was the trouble. He really didn't.

He was gone all day. I spent it painting.

Not the sad landscape. The sunroom seemed even grayer and colder that morning, and I had no mind any more to sink into melancholy. I left the half-finished canvas on the table there and removed myself and trappings to the source of warmth. Maybe the light wasn't so good in the kitchen, but it was the only room in the house with the pulse of life.

I painted Regina standing beside her cooker, with a wooden spoon in one hand and a bottle of wine in the other. I painted the way she held her head back to smile, and I painted the smile, shiny-eyed and guileless and unmistakably happy. I painted the kitchen behind her as I literally saw it in front of my eyes, and I painted Regina herself from the clearest of inner visions. So easily did I see her that I looked up once or twice from her face on the canvas to say something to her, and was disconcerted to find only empty space. An extraordinary feeling of the real and unreal disturbingly tangled.

I seldom ever worked for more than four hours at a stretch, because for one thing the actual muscular control required was tiring, and for another the concentration always made me cold and hungry; so I knocked off at around lunchtime and dug out a tin of corned beef to eat with pickles on toast, and after that went for a walk, dodging the front-gate watchers by taking to the apple trees and wriggling through the hedge.

I tramped aimlessly for a while round the scattered shapeless village, thinking about the picture and working off the burst of physical energy I often felt after the constraint of painting. More burnt umber in the folds of the kitchen curtains, I thought; and a purplish shadow on the saucepan. Regina's cream shirt needed yellow ocher under the collar, and probably a touch of green. The cooking stove needed a lot more attention, and I had broken my general rule of working the picture as a whole, background and subject pace by pace.

This time, Regina's face stood out clearly, finished except for a gloss on the lips and a line of light along inside the lower eyelids, which one couldn't do until the underpaint was dry. I had been afraid of seeing her less clearly if I took too long, but because of it the picture was now out of balance and I'd have to be very careful to get the kitchen into the same key, so that the whole thing looked harmonious and natural and as if it couldn't have been any other way.

The wind was rawly cold, the sky a hurrying jumbled mass of darkening clouds. I huddled my hands inside my anorak pockets and slid back through the hedge with the first drops of rain.

The afternoon session was much shorter because of the light, and I frustratingly could not catch the right mix of colors for the tops of the kitchen fitments. Even after years of experience, I found that what looked right on the palette looked wrong on the painting. I got it wrong three times and decided to stop.

I was cleaning the brushes when Donald came back. I heard the scrunch of the car, the slam of the doors, and, to my surprise, the ring of the front doorbell. Donald had taken his keys.

I went through and opened the door. A uniformed policeman stood there, holding Don's arm. Behind, a row of watching faces gazed on hungrily. My cousin, who had looked pale before, now seemed bloodlessly white. The eyes were as lifeless as death.

"Don!" I said, and no doubt looked as appalled as I felt.

He didn't speak. The policeman leaned forward, said "There we are, sir," and transferred the support of my cousin from himself to me; and it seemed to me that the action was as much symbolic as practical, because the policeman turned immediately on his heel and methodically drove off in his waiting car.

I helped Donald inside and shut the door. I had never seen anyone in such a frightening state of disintegration.

"I asked about the funeral," he said.

His face was stony, and his voice came out in gasps.

"They said . . ." He stopped, dragged in air, tried again. "They said . . . no funeral."

"Donald . . ."

"They said . . . she couldn't be buried until they had finished their inquiries. They said . . . it might be months. They said . . . they will keep her . . . refrigerated. . . ."

The distress was fearful.

"They said . . ." He swayed slightly. "They said . . . the body of a murdered person belongs to the State."

I couldn't hold him. He collapsed at my feet in a deep and total faint.

CHAPTER 3

For two days Donald lay in bed, and I grew to understand what was meant by prostration.

Whether he liked it or not, this time he was heavily sedated, his doctor calling morning and evening with pills and injections. No matter that I was a hopeless nurse and a worse cook, I was appointed, for lack of anyone else, to look after him.

"I want Charles," Donald in fact told the doctor. "He doesn't *fuss*."

I sat with him a good deal when he was awake, seeing him struggle dazedly to face and come to terms with the horrors in his mind. He lost weight visibly, the rounded muscles of his face slackening and the contours changing to the drawn shape of illness. The gray shadows round his eyes darkened to a permanent charcoal, and all normal strength seemed to have vanished from his arms and legs.

I fed us both from tins and frozen packets, reading the instructions and doing what they said. Donald thanked me punctiliously and ate what he could, but I doubt if he tasted a thing.

In betweentimes, while he slept, I made progress with both the paintings. The sad landscape was no longer sad but merely Octoberish, with three horses standing around in a field, one of them eating grass. Pictures of this sort, easy to live with and passably expert, were my bread and butter. They sold quite well, and I normally churned one off the production line every ten days or so, knowing that they were all technique and no soul.

The portrait of Regina, though, was the best work I'd done for months. She laughed out of the canvas, alive and glowing, and—to me, at least—seemed vividly herself. Pictures often changed as one worked on them, and day by day the emphasis in my mind had shifted, so that the kitchen background was growing darker and less distinct and Regina herself more luminous. One could still see she was cooking, but it was the girl who was important, not the act. In the end I had painted the kitchen, which was still there, as an impression, and the girl, who was not, as the reality.

I hid that picture in my suitcase whenever I wasn't working on it. I didn't want Donald to come face-to-face with it unaware.

Early Wednesday evening, he came shakily down to the kitchen in his dressing gown, trying to smile and pick up the pieces. He sat at the table, drinking the Scotch I had that day imported, and watching while I cleaned my brushes and tidied the palette.

"You're always so neat," he said.

"Paint's expensive."

He waved a limp hand at the horse picture, which stood drying on the easel. "How much does it cost to paint that?"

"In raw materials, about ten quid. In heat, light, rates, rent, food, Scotch, and general wear and tear on the nervous system, about the amount I'd earn in a week if I chucked it in and went back to selling houses."

"Quite a lot, then," he said seriously.

I grinned. "I don't regret it."

"No. I see that."

I finished the brushes by washing them in soap and water under the tap, pinching them into shape, and standing them upright in a jar to dry. Good brushes were at least as costly as paint.

"After the digging into the company accounts," Donald said abruptly, "they took me along to the police station and tried to prove that I had actually killed her myself."

"I don't believe it!"

"They'd worked out that I could have got home at lunchtime and done it. They said there was time."

I picked up the Scotch from the table and poured a decent-sized shot into a tumbler. Added ice.

"They must be crazy," I said.

"There was another man, besides Frost. A Superintendent. I think his name was Wall. A thin man, with fierce eyes. He never seemed to blink. Just stared and said over and over that I'd killed her because she'd come back and found me supervising the burglary."

"For God's sake!" I said disgustedly. "And anyway, she didn't leave the flower shop until half past two."

"The girl in the flower shop now says she doesn't know to the minute when Regina left. Only that it was soon after lunch. And I didn't get back from the pub until nearly three. I went to lunch late. I was hung up with a client all morning. . . ." He stopped, gripping his tumbler as if it were a support to hold on to. "I can't tell you . . . how awful it was."

The mild understatement seemed somehow to make things worse.

"They said," he added, "that eighty percent of murdered married women are killed by their husbands."

That statement had Frost stamped all over it.

"They let me come home, in the end, but I don't think . . ." His voice shook. He swallowed, visibly trying to keep tight control on his hard-won calm. "I don't think they've finished."

It was five days since he'd walked in and found Regina dead. When I thought of the mental hammerings he'd taken on top, the punishing assault on his emotional reserves, where common humanity would have suggested kindness and consoling help, it seemed marvelous that he had remained as sane as he had.

"Have they got anywhere with catching the thieves?" I said.

He smiled wanly. "I don't even know if they're trying."

"They must be."

"I suppose so. They haven't said." He drank some whisky slowly. "It's ironic, you know. I've always had a great regard for the police. I didn't know they could be . . . the way they are."

A quandary, I thought. Either they leaned on a suspect in the hope of breaking him down or they asked a few polite questions and got nowhere; and under the only effective system the innocent suffered more than the guilty.

"I see no end to it," Donald said. "No end at all."

By midday Friday, the police had called twice more at the house, but for my cousin the escalation of agony seemed to have slowed. He was still exhausted, apathetic, and as gray as smoke, but it was as if he were saturated with suffering and could absorb little more. Whatever Frost and his companion said to him, it rolled off without destroying him further.

"You're supposed to be painting someone's horse, aren't you?" Donald said suddenly as we shaped up to lunch.

"I told them I'd come later."

He shook his head. "I remember you saying, when I asked you to stay, that it would fit in fine before your next commission." He thought a bit. "Tuesday. You should have gone to Yorkshire on Tuesday."

"I telephoned and explained."

"All the same, you'd better go."

He said he would be all right alone now, and thanks for everything. He insisted I look up the times of trains, order a taxi, and alert the people at the other end. I could see in the end that the time had indeed come for him to be by himself, so I packed up my things to depart.

"I suppose," he said diffidently, as we waited for the taxi to fetch me, "that you never paint portraits? People, that is, not horses."

"Sometimes," I said.

"I just wondered. . . . Could you, one day . . . I mean, I've got quite a good photograph of Regina. . . ."

I looked searchingly at his face. As far as I could see, it could do no harm. I unclipped the suitcase and took out the picture with its back toward him.

"It's still wet," I warned. "And not framed, and I can't varnish it for at least six months. But you can have it, if you like."

"Let me see."

I turned the canvas round. He stared and stared, but said nothing at all. The taxi drove up to the front door.

"See you," I said, propping Regina against a wall.

He nodded and punched my arm, opened the door for me, and sketched a farewell wave. Speechlessly, because his eyes were full of tears.

I spent nearly a week in Yorkshire doing my best to immortalize a patient old steeplechaser, and then went home to my noisy flat near Heathrow Airport, taking the picture with me to finish.

Saturday I downed tools and went to the races, fed up with too much nose-to-the-grindstone.

Jump racing at Plumpton, and the familiar swelling of excitement at the liquid movement of race horses. Paintings could never do justice to them: never. The moment caught on canvas was always second best.

I would love to have ridden in races, but hadn't had enough practice or skill; nor, I dare say, nerve. Like Donald, my childhood background was of middle-sized private enterprise, with my father an auctioneer in business on his own account in Sussex. I had spent countless hours in my growing years watching the horses train on the Downs round Findon, and had drawn and painted them from about the age of six. Riding itself had been mostly a matter of begging the wherewithal for an hour's joy from indulgent aunts, since I never had a pony of my own. Art school later had been fine, but at twenty-two, alone in the world with both parents newly dead, I'd had to face the need to eat. It had been a short meant-to-be-temporary step to the estate agents across the street, but I'd liked it well enough to stay.

Half the horse painters in England seemed to have turned up at Plumpton, which was not surprising, as the latest Grand National winner was due to make his first appearance of the new season. It was a commercial fact that a picture called, for instance, "Nijinsky on Newmarket Heath" stood a much better chance of being sold than one labeled "A Horse on Newmarket Heath," and "The Grand National Winner at the Start" won hands down over "A Runner at Plumpton Before the Off." The economic facts of life had brought many a would-be Rembrandt down to market research.

"Todd!" said a voice in my ear. "You owe me fifteen smackers."

"I bloody don't," I said.

"You said Seesaw was a certainty for Ascot."

"Never take sweets from a stranger."

Billy Pyle laughed extravagantly and patted me heavily on the shoulder. Billy Pyle was one of those people you met on racecourses who greeted you as a bosom pal, plied you with drinks and bonhomie, and bored you to death.

On and off, I'd met Billy Pyle at the races for umpteen years, and had never yet worked out how to duck him without positive rudeness. Ordinary evasions rolled off his thick skin like mercury off glass, and I found it less wearing on the whole to get the drink over quickly than dodge him all afternoon.

I waited for him to say "How about a beverage," as he always did.

"How about a beverage?" he said.

"Er . . . sure," I agreed resignedly.

"Your father would never forgive me if I neglected you." He always said that, too. They had been business acquaintances, I knew, but I suspected the reported friendship was posthumous.

"Come along, laddie."

I knew the irritating routine by heart. He would meet his Auntie Sal in the bar, as if by accident, and in my turn I would buy them both a drink. A double brandy and ginger for Auntie Sal.

"Why, there's Auntie Sal," Billy said, pushing through the door. Surprise, surprise.

Auntie Sal was a compulsive racegoer in her seventies, with a perpetual cigarette dangling from the corner of her mouth and one finger permanently inserted in her form book, keeping her place.

"Know anything for the two-thirty?" she demanded.

"Hello," I said.

"What? Oh, I see. Hello. How are you? Know anything for the two-thirty?"

" 'Fraid not."

"Huh."

She peered into the form book. "Treetops is well in at the weights, but can you trust his leg?" She looked up suddenly and with her free hand prodded her nephew, who was trying to attract service from the bar. "Billy, get a drink for Mrs. Matthews."

"Mrs. who?"

"Matthews. What do you want, Maisie?"

She turned to a large middle-aged woman who had been standing in the shadows behind her.

"Oh . . . gin and tonic, thanks."

"Got that, Billy? Double brandy and ginger for me, gin and tonic for Mrs. Matthews."

Maisie Matthews's clothes were noticeably new and expensive, and from lacquered hair via crocodile handbag to gold-trimmed shoes she shouted money without saying a word. The hand that accepted the drink carried the weight of a huge opal set in diamonds. The expression on her expertly painted face showed no joy at all.

"How do you do?" I said politely.

"Eh?" said Auntie Sal. "Oh, yes, Maisie, this is Charles Todd. What do you think of Treetops?"

"Moderate," I said.

Auntie Sal peered worriedly into the form book, and Billy handed round the drinks.

"Cheers," Maisie Matthews said, looking cheerless.

"Down the hatch," said Billy, raising his glass.

"Maisie's had a bit of bad luck," Auntie Sal said.

Billy grinned. "Backed a loser, then, Mrs. Matthews?"

"Her house burned down."

As a light-conversation stopper, it was a daisy.

"Oh . . . I say . . ." said Billy uncomfortably. "Hard luck."

"Lost everything, didn't you, Maisie?"

"All but what I stand up in," she agreed gloomily.

"Have another gin," I suggested.

"Thanks, dear."

When I returned with the refills, she was in full descriptive flood.

". . . I wasn't there, of course. I was staying with my sister Betty up in Birmingham, and there was this policeman on the doorstep telling me what a job they'd had finding me. But by that time it was all over, of course. When I got back to Worthing, there was just a heap of cinders with the chimney breast sticking up in the middle. Well, I had a real job finding out what happened, but anyway they finally said it was a flash fire, whatever that is, but they didn't know what started it, because there'd been no one in the house, of course, for two days."

She accepted the gin, gave me a brief unseeing smile, and returned to her story.

"Well, I was spitting mad, I'll tell you, over losing everything like that, and I said why hadn't they used sea water, what with the sea being only the other side of the tamarisk and down the shingle, because of course they said they hadn't been able to save a thing because they hadn't enough water, and this fireman, the one I was complaining to, he said they couldn't use sea water because for one thing it corroded everything and for an-

41

other the pumps sucked up seaweed and shells and things, and in any case the tide was out."

I smothered an unseemly desire to laugh. She sensed it, however.

"Well, dear, it may seem funny to you, of course, but then you haven't lost all your treasures that you'd been collecting since heaven knows when."

"I'm really sorry, Mrs. Matthews. I don't think it's funny. It was just . . ."

"Yes, well, dear. I suppose you can see the funny side of it, all that water and not a drop to put a fire out with, but I was that mad, I can tell you."

"I think I'll have a bit on Treetops," Auntie Sal said thoughtfully.

Maisie Matthews looked at her uncertainly, and Billy Pyle, who had heard enough of disaster, broke gratefully into geniality, clapped me again on the shoulder, and said yes, it was time to see the next contest.

Duty done, I thought with a sigh, and took myself off to watch the race from the top of the stands, out of sight and earshot.

Treetops broke down and finished last, limping. Too bad for its owner, trainer, and Auntie Sal. I wandered down to the parade ring to see the Grand National winner walk around before his race, but without any thought of drawing him. I reckoned he was just about played out as a subject, and there would shortly be a glut.

The afternoon went quickly, as usual. I won a little, lost a little, and filled my eyes with something better than money. On the stands for the last race, I found myself approached by Maisie Matthews. No mistaking the bright red coat, the air of gloss, and the big kind-looking worldly face. She drew to a halt on the step below me, looking up. Entirely self-confident, though registering doubt.

"Aren't you the young man I had a drink with, with Sal and Billy?" she said.

"Yes, that's right."

"I wasn't sure," she said, the doubt disappearing. "You look older out here."

"Different light," I said, agreeing. She, too, looked older, by about ten years. Fifty-something, I thought. Bar-light always flattered.

"They said you were an artist." Their mild disapproval colored the way she spoke.

"Mmm," I said, watching the runners canter past on the way to the post.

"Not very well paid, is it, dear?"

I grinned at her, liking her directness. "It depends who you are. Picasso didn't grumble."

"How much would you charge to paint a picture for me?"

"What sort of picture?"

"Well, dear, you may say it sounds morbid and I dare say it is, but I was just thinking this morning when I went over there—and really it makes me that mad every time I see it—well, I was thinking actually that it makes a crazy picture, that burnt ruin with the chimney sticking up, and the burnt hedge behind and all that sea, and I was thinking of getting the local photographer who does all the weddings and things to come along and take a color picture, because when its all cleared away and rebuilt, no one will believe how awful it was, and I want to hang it in the new house, just to show them."

"But . . ."

"So how much would you charge? Because I dare say you can see I am not short of the next quid, but if it would be hundreds I might as well get the photographer of course."

"Of course," I agreed gravely. "How about if I came to see the house, or what's left of it, and gave you an estimate?"

She saw nothing odd in that. "All right, dear. That sounds very businesslike. Of course, it will have to be soon, though, because once the insurance people have been, I am having the rubble cleared up."

"How soon?"

"Well, dear, as you're halfway there, could you come today?"

We discussed it. She said she would drive me in her Jaguar, as I hadn't a car, and I could go home by train just as easily from Worthing as from Plumpton.

So I agreed.

One takes the most momentous steps unaware.

The ruin was definitely paintagenic, if there is such a word. On the way there, more or less nonstop, she had talked about her late husband, Archie, who had looked after her very well, dear.

"Well, that's to say, I looked after him, too, dear, because of course I was a nurse. Private, of course. I nursed his first wife all through her illness—cancer it was, dear, of course—and then I stayed on for a bit to look after him, and, well, he asked me to stay on for life, dear, and I did. Of course he was much older, he's been gone more than ten years now. He looked after me very well, Archie did."

She glanced fondly at the huge opal. Many a man would have liked to have been remembered as kindly.

"Since he went, and left me so well off, dear, it seemed a shame not to get some fun out of it, so I carried on with what we were doing when we were together those few years, which was going round to auction sales in big houses, dear, because you pick up such nice things there —quite cheap sometimes—and of course it's ever so much more interesting when the things have belonged to someone well known or famous." She changed gear with a jerk and aggressively passed an inoffensive little van. "And now all those things are burnt to cinders, of course, and all the memories of Archie and the places we went together, and I'll tell you, dear, it makes me mad."

"It's really horrid for you."

"Yes, dear, it is."

I reflected that it was the second time in a fortnight that I'd been cast in the role of comforter; and I felt as inadequate for her as I had for Donald.

She stamped on the brakes outside the remains of her house and rocked us to a standstill. From the opulence of the minor mansions on either side, it appeared that her property had been far from a slum; but all that was left was an extensive sprawling black heap, with jagged pieces of outside wall defining its former shape, and the thick brick chimney, as she'd said, pointing sturdily skyward from the center. Ironic, I thought fleetingly, that the fireplace alone had survived the flames.

"There you are, dear," Maisie said. "What do you think?"

"A very hot fire."

She raised her penciled eyebrows. "But yes, dear, all fires are hot, aren't they? And of course there was a lot of wood. So many of these old seaside houses were built with a lot of wood."

Even before we climbed out of her big pale blue car, I could smell the ash.

"How long ago?" I asked.

"Last weekend, dear. Sunday."

While we surveyed the mess for a moment in silence, a man walked slowly into view from behind the chimney. He was looking down, concentrating, taking a step at a time, and then bending to poke into the rubble.

Maisie, for all her scarlet-coated bulk, was nimble on her feet.

"Hey," she called, hopping out of the car and advancing purposefully. "What do you think you're doing?"

The man straightened up, looking startled. About forty, I judged, with a raincoat, a crisp-looking trilby, and a down-turning mustache.

He raised his hat politely. "Insurance, Madam."

"I thought you were coming on Monday."

"I happened to be in the district. No time like the present, don't you think?"

"Well, I suppose not," Maisie said. "And I hope there isn't going to be any shilly-shallying over you paying up, though of course nothing is going to get my treasures back and I'd rather have them than any amount of money, as I've got plenty of that in any case."

The man was unused to Maisie's brand of chat.

"Er . . ." he said. "Oh, yes. I see."

"Have you found out what started it?" Maisie demanded.

"No, Madam."

"Found anything at all?"

"No, Madam."

"Well, how soon can I get all this cleared away?"

"Anytime you like, Madam."

He stepped carefully toward us, picking his way round clumps of blackened debris. He had steady grayish eyes, a strong chin, and an overall air of intelligence.

"What's your name?" Maisie asked.

"Greene, Madam." He paused slightly, and added, "With an 'e.' "

"Well, Mr. Greene with an 'e,' " Maisie said good-humoredly, "I'll be glad to have all that in writing."

He inclined his head. "As soon as I report back."

Maisie said, "Good," and Greene, lifting his hat again, wished her good afternoon and walked along to a white Ford parked a short way along the road.

"That's all right, then," Maisie said with satisfaction, watching him go. "Now, how much for that picture?"

"Two hundred, plus two nights' expenses in a local hotel."

"That's a bit steep, dear. *One* hundred, and two nights, and I've got to like the results or I don't pay."

"No foal, no fee?"

The generous red mouth smiled widely. "That's it, dear."

We settled on one-fifty if she liked the picture, and fifty if she didn't, and I was to start on Monday unless it was raining.

CHAPTER 4

Monday came up with a bright breezy day and an echo of summer's warmth. I went to Worthing by train and to the house by taxi, and to the interest of the neighbors set up my easel at about the place where the front gates would have been, had they not been unhinged and transplanted by the firemen. The gates themselves lay flat on the lawn, one of them still pathetically bearing a neat painted nameboard: "Treasure Holme."

Poor Archie. Poor Maisie.

I worked over the whole canvas with an unobtrusive coffee-colored underpainting of raw umber much thinned with turpentine and linseed oil, and while it was still wet I drew in, with a paintbrushful of a darker shade of the same color, the shape of the ruined house against the horizontals of hedges, shingle, sea, and sky. It was easy with a tissue to wipe out mistakes of composition at that stage and try again: to get the proportions right, and the perspective, and the balance of the main masses.

That done and drying, I strolled right round the whole garden, looking at the house from different angles, and staring out over the blackened stumps of the tamarisk hedge that had marked the end of the grass and the beginning of the shingle. The sea sparkled in the morning sunshine, with the small hurrying cumulus clouds scattering patches of dark slate-gray shadow. All the waves had white frills: distant because the tide again had receded to the far side of a deserted stretch of wet-looking, wave-rippled sand.

The sea wind chilled my ears. I turned to get back to my task and saw two men in overcoats emerge from a large station wagon and show definite signs of interest in what was left of Treasure Holme.

I walked back toward them, reaching them where they stood by the easel appraising my handiwork.

One heavy and fiftyish. One lean, in the twenties. Both with firm self-confident faces and an air of purpose.

The elder raised his eyes as I approached.

"Do you have permission to be here?" he asked. An inquiry; no belligerence in sight.

"The owner wants her house painted," I said obligingly.

"I see." His lips twitched a fraction.

"And you?" I inquired.

He raised his eyebrows slightly. "Insurance," he said, as if surprised that anyone should ask.

"Same company as Mr. Greene?" I said.

"Mr. who?"

"Greene. With an 'e.' "

"I don't know who you mean," he said. "We are here by arrangement with Mrs. Matthews to inspect the damage to her house, which is insured with us." He looked with some depression at the extent of the so-called damage, glancing about as if expecting Maisie to materialize Phoenixlike from the ashes.

"No Greene?" I repeated.

"Neither with nor without an 'e.' "

I warmed to him. Half an ounce of a sense of humor, as far as I was concerned, achieved results where thumbscrews wouldn't.

"Well . . . Mrs. Matthews is no longer expecting you, because the aforesaid Mr. Greene, who said he was in insurance, told her she could roll in the demolition squad as soon as she liked."

His attention sharpened like a tightened violin string.

"Are you serious?"

"I was here, with her. I saw him and heard him, and that's what he said."

"Did he show you a card?"

48

"No, he didn't." I paused. "And . . . er . . . nor have you."

He reached into an inner pocket and did so, with the speed of a conjurer. Producing cards from pockets was a reflex action, no doubt.

"Isn't it illegal to insure the same property with two companies?" I asked idly, reading the card.

Foundation Life & Surety

D. J. Lagland   Area Manager

"Fraud." He nodded.

"Unless of course Mr. Greene with an 'e' had nothing to do with insurance."

"Much more likely."

I put the card in my trouser pocket, Arran sweaters not having been designed noticeably for business transactions. He looked at me thoughtfully, his eyes observant but judgment suspended. He was the same sort of man my father had been, middle-aged, middle-of-the-road, expert at his chosen job, but unlikely to set the world on fire.

Or Treasure Holme, for that matter.

"Gary," he said to his younger sidekick, "go and find a telephone and ring the Beach Hotel. Tell Mrs. Matthews we're here."

"Will do," Gary said. He was that sort of man.

While he was away on the errand, D. J. Lagland turned his attention to the ruin, and I, as he seemed not to object, tagged along at his side.

"What do you look for?" I asked.

He shot me a sideways look. "Evidence of arson. Evidence of the presence of the goods reported destroyed."

"I didn't expect you to be so frank."

"I indulge myself, occasionally."

I grinned. "Mrs. Matthews seems pretty genuine."

"I've never met the lady."

Treat in store, I thought. "Don't the firemen look for signs of arson?" I asked.

"Yes, and also the police, and we ask them for guidance."

"And what did they say?"

"None of your business, I shouldn't think."

"Even for a wooden house," I said, "it is pretty thoroughly burnt."

49

"Expert, are you?" he said with irony.

"I've built a lot of Guy Fawkes bonfires, in my time."

He turned his head.

"They burn a lot better," I said, "if you soak them in paraffin. Especially round the edges."

"I've been looking at fires since before you were born," he said. "Why don't you go over there and paint?"

"What I've done is still wet."

"Then if you stay with me, shut up."

I stayed with him, silent, and without offense. He was making what appeared to be a preliminary reconnaissance, lifting small solid pieces of debris, inspecting them closely, and carefully returning them to their former positions. None of the things he chose in that way were identifiable to me from a distance of six feet, and as far as I could see none of them gave him much of a thrill.

"Permission to speak?" I asked.

"Well?"

"Mr. Greene was doing much what you are, though in the area behind the chimney breast."

He straightened from replacing yet another black lump. "Did he take anything?" he said.

"Not while we were watching, which was a very short time. No telling how long he'd been there."

"No." He considered. "Wouldn't you think he was a casual sightseer, poking around out of curiosity?"

"He hadn't the air."

D. J. frowned. "Then what did he want?"

A rhetorical question. Gary rolled back, and soon after him Maisie. In her Jaguar. In her scarlet coat. In a temper.

"What do you mean," she said, advancing upon D. J. with eyes flashing fortissimo, "the question of arson isn't yet settled? Don't tell me you're trying to wriggle out of paying my check, now. Your man said on Saturday that everything was all right and I could start clearing away and rebuilding, and anyway even if it had been arson you would still have to pay up, because the insurance covered arson of course."

D. J. opened and shut his mouth several times and finally found his voice.

"Didn't our Mr. Robinson tell you that the man you saw here on Saturday wasn't from us?"

Our Mr. Robinson, in the shape of Gary, nodded vigorously.

"He—Mr. Greene—distinctly said he *was*," Maisie insisted.

"Well . . . what did he look like?"

"Smarmy," said Maisie without hesitation. "Not as young as Charles"—she gestured toward me—"or as old as you." She thought, then shrugged. "He looked like an insurance man, that's all."

D. J. swallowed the implied insult manfully.

"About five feet ten," I said. "Suntanned skin with a sallow tinge, gray eyes with deep upper eyelids, widish nose, mouth straight under heavy drooping dark mustache, straight brown hair brushed back and retreating from the two top corners of his forehead, ordinary eyebrows, greeny-brown trilby of smooth felt, shirt, tie, fawn unbuttoned raincoat, gold signet ring on little finger of right hand, suntanned hands."

I could see him in memory as clearly as if he still stood there in the ashes before me, taking off his hat and calling Maisie "Madam."

"Good God," D. J. said.

"An artist's eye, dear," said Maisie admiringly. "Well, I never."

D. J. said he was certain they had no one like that in their poking-into-claims department, and Gary agreed.

"Well," said Maisie, with a resurgence of crossness, "I suppose that still means you are looking for arson, though why you think that anyone in his right senses would want to burn down my lovely home and all my treasures is something I'll never understand."

Surely Maisie, worldly Maisie, could not be so naïve. I caught a deep glimmer of intelligence in the glance she gave me, and knew that she certainly wasn't. D. J., however, who didn't know, made frustrated little motions with his hands and voted against explaining. I smothered a few more laughs, and Maisie noticed.

"Do you want your picture," I asked, "to be sunny like today, or cloudy and sad?"

She looked up at the bright sky.

"A bit more dramatic, dear," she said.

D. J. and Gary inch-by-inched over the ruin all afternoon, and I tried to infuse it with a little Gothic romance. At five o'clock, on the dot, we all knocked off.

"Union hours?" said D. J. sarcastically, watching me pack my suitcase.

"The light gets too yellow in the evenings."

"Will you be here tomorrow?"

I nodded. "And you?"

"Perhaps."

I went by foot and bus along to the Beach Hotel, cleaned my brushes, thought a bit, and at seven met Maisie downstairs in the bar, as arranged.

"Well, dear," she said, as her first gin and tonic gravitated comfortably. "Did they find anything?"

"Nothing at all, as far as I could see.'"

"Well, that's good, dear."

I tackled my pint of draught. Put the glass down carefully.

"Not altogether, Maisie."

"Why not?"

"What exactly were your treasures, which were burned?"

"I dare say you wouldn't think so much of them, of course, but we had ever such fun buying them, and so have I since Archie's gone, and well, dear, things like an antique spear collection that used to belong to old Lord Stequers, whose niece I nursed once, and a whole wall of beautiful butterflies, which professors and such came to look at, and a wrought-iron gate from Lady Tythe's old home, which divided the hall from the sitting room, and six warming pans from a castle in Ireland, and two tall vases with eagles on the lids signed by Angelica Kauffmann, which once belonged to a cousin of Mata Hari— they really did, dear—and a copper fire screen with silver bosses which was a devil to polish, and a marble table from Greece, and a silver tea urn which was once used by Queen Victoria, and really, dear, that's just the beginning; if I tell you them all, I'll go on all night."

"Did the Foundation insurance company have a full list?"

"Yes, they did, dear, and why do you want to know?"

"Because," I said regretfully, "I don't think many of those things were inside the house when it burned down."

"What?" Maisie, as far as I could tell, was genuinely astounded. "But they must have been."

"D. J. as good as told me they were looking for traces of them, and I don't think they found any."

"D. J.?"

"Mr. Lagland. The elder one."

Alternate disbelief and anger kept Maisie going through two more double gins. Disbelief, eventually, won.

"You got it wrong, dear," she said finally.

"I hope so."

"Inexperience of youth, of course."

"Maybe."

"Because of course everything was in its place, dear, when I went off last Friday week to stay with Betty, and I only went to Betty's with not having seen her for so long while I'd been away, which is ironic when you think of it, but of course you can't stay at home forever on the off chance your house is going to catch fire and you can save it, can you, dear, as you'd never go anywhere and I would have missed my trip to Australia."

She paused for breath. Coincidence, I thought.

"All I can say, dear, is that it's a mircle I took most of my jewelry with me to Betty's, because I don't always, except that Archie always said it was safer, and of course he was always so sensible and thoughtful and sweet."

"Australia?" I said.

"Well, yes, dear, wasn't that nice? I went out there for a visit to Archie's sister, who's lived there since heaven knows when and was feeling lonely since she'd been widowed, poor dear, and I went out for a bit of fun, dear, because of course I'd never really met her, only ex-changed postcards of course, and I was out there for six weeks with her. She wanted me to stay, and of course we got on together like a house on fire. . . . Oh, dear, I didn't mean that exactly. . . . Well, anyway, I said I wanted to come back to my little house by the sea and think it over, and of course I took my jewelry with me on that trip, too, dear."

I said idly, "I don't suppose you bought a Munnings while you were there."

I didn't know why I'd said it, apart from thinking of Donald in Australia. I was totally unprepared for her reaction.

Astounded she had been before: this time, poleaxed. Before, she had been incredulous and angry. This time, incredulous and frightened.

She knocked over her gin, slid off her barstool, and covered her open mouth with four trembling red-nailed fingers.

"You didn't!" I said disbelievingly.

"How do you know?"

"I don't. . . ."

"Are you from Customs and Excise?"

"Of course not."

"Oh, dear. Oh, dear . . ." She was shaking, almost as shattered as Donald.

I took her arm and led her over to an armchair beside a small bar table.

"Sit down," I said coaxingly, "and tell me."

It took ten minutes and a refill double gin.

"Well, dear, I'm not an art expert, as you can probably guess, but there was this picture by Sir Alfred Munnings, signed and everything, dear, and it was such a bargain really, and I thought how tickled Archie would have been to have a real Munnings on the wall, what with us both liking the races, of course, and, well, Archie's sister egged me on a bit, and I felt quite . . . I suppose you might call it *high,* dear, so I bought it."

She stopped.

"Go on," I said.

"Well, dear, I suppose you've guessed from what I said just now."

"You brought it into this country without declaring it?"

She sighed. "Yes, dear, I did. Of course it was silly of me but I never gave customs duty a thought when I bought the painting, not until just before I came home—a week later, that was—and Archie's sister asked if I was going to declare it, and well, dear, I really *resent* having to pay duty on things, don't you? So anyway I thought I'd better find out just how much the duty would be, and I found it wasn't duty at all in the ordinary way, dear—there isn't duty on secondhand pictures being brought in from Australia—but would you believe it they said I would have to pay value-added tax, sort of tax on buying things, you know, dear, and I would have to pay eight percent on whatever I had bought the picture for. Well, I ask you! I was that mad, dear, I can tell you. So Archie's sister said why didn't I leave the painting with her, because then if I went back to Australia I would have paid the tax for nothing, but I wasn't sure I'd go back and anyway I did want to see Sir Alfred Munnings on the wall where Archie would have loved it, so, well, dear, it was all done up nicely in boards and brown paper so I just camouflaged it a bit with my best nightie and popped it in my suitcase, and pushed it through the 'Nothing to Declare' lane at Heathrow when I got back, and nobody stopped me."

"How much would you have had to pay?" I said.

"Well, dear, to be precise, just over seven hundred pounds. And I know that's not a fortune, dear, but it made me so mad to have to pay tax here because I'd bought something nice in Australia."

I did some mental arithmetic. "So the painting cost about nine thousand?"

"That's right, dear. Nine thousand." She looked anxious. "I wasn't done, was I? I've asked one or two people since I got back and they say lots of Munnings cost fifteen or more."

"So they do," I said absently. And some could be got for fifteen hundred, and others, I dared say, for less.

"Well, anyway, dear, it was only when I began to think about insurance that I wondered if I would be found out—if, say, the insurance people wanted a *receipt* or anything, which they probably would, of course—so I didn't do anything about it, because of course if I *did* go back to Australia I could just take the picture with me and no harm done."

"Awkward," I agreed.

"So now it's burnt, and I dare say you'll think it serves me right, because the nine thousand's gone up in smoke and I won't see a penny of it back."

She finished the gin and I bought her another.

"I know it's not my business, Maisie, but how did you happen to have nine thousand handy in Australia? Aren't there rules about exporting that much cash?"

She giggled. "You don't know much about the world, do you, dear? But anyway, this time it was all hunky-dory. I just toddled along with Archie's sister to a jeweler's and sold him a brooch I had, a nasty sort of *toad,* dear, with a socking big diamond in the middle of its forehead, something to do with Shakespeare, I think, thought I never got it clear; anyway, I never wore it, it was so ugly, but of course I'd taken it with me because of it being worth so much, and I sold it for nine thousand five, though in Australian dollars of course, so there was no problem, was there?"

Maisie took it for granted I would be eating with her, so we drifted in to dinner. Her appetite seemed healthy, but her spirits were damp.

"You won't *tell* anyone, will you, dear, about the picture?"

"Of course not, Maisie."

"I could get into such trouble, dear."

"I know."

"A fine, of course," she said. "And I suppose that might be the least of it. People can be so beastly about a perfectly innocent little bit of smuggling."

"No one will find out, if you keep quiet." A thought struck me. "Unless, that is, you've told anyone already that you'd bought it?"

"No, dear, I didn't, because of thinking I'd better pretend I'd had it for years, and of course I hadn't even hung it on the wall yet, because one of the rings was loose in the frame and I thought it might fall down and be damaged, and I couldn't decide who to ask to fix it." She paused for a mouthful of prawn cocktail. "I expect you'll think me silly, dear, but I suppose I was feeling a bit scared of being found out—not guilty exactly because I really don't see why we *should* pay that irritating tax, but anyway I didn't not only not hang it up, I hid it."

"You hid it? Still wrapped up?"

"Well, yes, dear, more or less wrapped up. Of course I'd opened it when I got home, and that's when I found the ring coming loose with the cord through it, so I wrapped it up again until I'd decided what to do."

I was fascinated. "Where did you hide it?"

She laughed. "Nowhere very much, dear. I mean, I was only keeping it out of sight to stop people asking about it, of course, so I slipped it behind one of the radiators in the lounge, and don't look so horrified, dear, the central heating was turned off."

I painted at the house all the next day, but neither D.J. nor anyone else turned up.

In between stints at the easel, I poked around a good deal on my own account, searching for Maisie's treasures. I found a good many recognizable remains, durables like bed frames, kitchen machines, and radiators, all of them twisted and buckled not merely by heat but by the weight of the whole edifice from roof down having collapsed inward. Occasional remains of heavy rafters lay black in the thick ash, but apart from these, everything combustible had totally, as one might say, combusted.

Of all the treasures Maisie had described, and of all the dozens she hadn't, I found only the wrought-iron gate from Lady Tythe's old home, which had divided the hall from the sitting room. Lady Tythe would never have recognized it.

No copper warming pans, which after all had been designed to withstand red-hot coals. No metal fire screen. No marble table. No antique spears.

Naturally, no Munnings.

When I took my paint-stained fingers back to the Beach at five o'clock, I found Maisie waiting for me in the hall. Not the kindly, basically cheerful Maisie I had come to know, but a belligerent woman in a full-blown state of rage.

"I've been waiting for you," she said, fixing me with a furious eye.

I could't think how I could have offended her.

"What's the matter?" I said.

"The bar's shut," she said. "So come upstairs to my room. Bring all your stuff with you." She gestured to the suitcase. "I'm so *mad* I think I'll absolutely *burst.*"

She did indeed, in the lift, look in danger of it. Her cheeks were bright red, with hard outlines of color against the pale surrounding skin. Her blond-rinsed hair, normally lacquered into sophistication, stuck out in wispy spikes, and for the first time since I'd met her, her mouth was not glistening with lipstick.

She threw open the door of her room and stalked in. I followed, closing it after me.

"You'll never believe it," she said forcefully, turning to face me and letting go with all guns blazing. "I've had the police here half the day, and those insurance men here the other half, and *do you know what they're saying?*"

"Oh, Maisie." I sighed inwardly. It had been inevitable.

"What do you think I am, I asked them," she said. "I was so *mad.* There they were, having the nerve to suggest I'd sold all my treasures and overinsured my house, and was trying to take the insurance people for a ride. I told them, I told them over and over, that everything was in its place when I went to Betty's and if it was overinsured it was to allow for inflation, and anyway the brokers had advised me to put up the amount pretty high, and I'm glad I took their advice, but that Mr. Lagland says they won't be paying out until they have investigated further and he was proper sniffy about it, and no sympathy at all for me having lost everything. They were absolutely *beastly,* and I *hate* them all."

57

She paused to regather momentum, vibrating visibly with the strength of her feelings. "They made me feel so *dirty,* and maybe I *was* screaming at them a bit, I was so mad, but they'd no call to be so *rude,* and making out I was some sort of criminal, and just what *right* have they to tell me to pull myself together when it is because of *them* and their bullying that I am yelling at them at the top of my voice?"

It must, I reflected, have been quite an encounter. I wondered in what state the police and D. J. had retired from the field.

"They say it was definitely arson, and I said why did they think so now when they hadn't thought so at first, and it turns out that it was because that Lagland couldn't find any of my treasures in the ashes or any trace of them at all, and they said even if I hadn't sold the things first, I had arranged for them to be stolen and the house burnt to cinders while I was away at Betty's, and they kept on and on asking me who I'd paid to do it, and I got more and more furious, and if I'd had anything handy I would have *hit* them, I really would."

"What you need is a stiff gin, "I said.

"I told them they ought to be out looking for whoever had done it instead of hounding helpless women like me, and the more I thought of someone walking into *my* house and stealing *my* treasures and then callously setting fire to everything, the madder I got, and somehow that made me even *madder* with those stupid men who couldn't see any further than their stupid noses."

It struck me after a good deal more of similar diatribe that genuine though Maisie's anger undoubtedly was, she was stoking herself up again every time her temper looked in danger of relapsing to normal. For some reason, she seemed to need to be in the position of the righteous wronged.

I wondered why; and in a breath-catching gap in the flow of hot lava, I said, "I don't suppose you told them about the Munnings."

The red spots on her cheeks burned suddenly brighter.

"I'm not *crazy,*" she said bitingly. "If they found out about that, there would have been a fat chance of convincing them I'm telling the truth about the rest."

"I've heard," I said tentatively, "that nothing infuriates a crook more than being had up for the one job he didn't do."

58

It looked for a moment as if I'd just elected myself as the new target for hatred, but suddenly, as she glared at me in rage, her sense of humor reared its battered head and nudged her in the ribs. The stiffness round her mouth relaxed, her eyes softened and glimmered, and after a second or two she ruefully smiled.

"I dare say you're right, dear, when I come to think of it." The smile slowly grew into a giggle. "How about that gin?"

Little eruptions continued all evening through drinks and dinner, but the red-centered volcano had subsided to manageable heat.

"You didn't seem surprised, dear, when I told you what the police thought I'd done." She looked sideways at me over her coffee cup, eyes sharp and inquring.

"No." I paused. "You see, something very much the same has just happened to my cousin. Too much the same, in too many ways. I think, if you will come, and he agrees, that I'd like to take you to meet him."

"But why, dear?"

I told her why. The anger she felt for herself burned up again fiercely for Donald.

"How *dreadful*. How *selfish* you must think *me,* after all that that poor man has suffered."

"I don't think you're selfish at all. In fact, Maisie, I think you're a proper trouper."

She looked pleased and almost kittenish, and I had a vivid impression of what she had been like with Archie.

"There's one thing, though, dear," she said awkwardly. "After today, and all that's been said, I don't think I want that picture you're doing. I don't any more want to remember the house as it is now, only like it used to be. So if I give you just the fifty pounds, do you mind?"

CHAPTER 5

We went to Shropshire in Maisie's Jaguar, sharing the driving.

Donald on the telephone had sounded unenthusiastic at my suggested return, but also too lethargic to raise objections. When he opened his front door to us, I was shocked.

It was two weeks since I'd left him to go to Yorkshire. In that time he had shed at least fourteen pounds and aged ten years. His skin was tinged with blueish shadows, the bones in his face showed starkly, and his hair seemed speckled with gray.

The ghost of the old Donald put an obvious effort into receiving us with good manners.

"Come in," he said. "I'm in the dining room now. I expect you'd like a drink."

"That would be very nice, dear," Maisie said.

He looked at her with dull eyes, seeing, as I saw, a large good-natured lady with glossy hair and expensive clothes, her smart appearance walking a tightrope between vulgarity and elegance and just making it to the safer side.

He waved to me to pour the drinks, as if it would be too much for him, and invited Maisie to sit down. The dining room had been roughly refurnished, now containing a large rug, all the sunroom armchairs, and a couple of small tables from the bedrooms. We sat in a fairly close group round one of the tables, because I had come to ask questions and I wanted to write down the answers. My cousin watched the production of notebook and ballpoint with no show of interest.

"Don," I said, "I want you to listen to a story."

"All right."

Maisie for once, kept it short. When she came to the bit about buying a Munnings in Australia, Donald's head lifted a couple of inches and he looked from her to me with the first stirring of attention. When she stopped, there was a small silence.

"So," I said finally, "you both went to Australia, you both bought a Munnings, and soon after your return you both had your houses burgled."

"Extraordinary coincidence," Donald said; but he meant simply that, nothing more. "Did you come all this way just to tell me that?"

"I wanted to see how you were."

"Oh. I'm all right. Kind of you, Charles, but I'm all right."

Even Maisie, who hadn't known him before, could see that he wasn't.

"Where did you buy your picture, Don? Where exactly, I mean."

"I suppose . . . Melbourne. In the Hilton Hotel. Opposite the cricket ground."

I looked doubtful. Although hotels quite often sold pictures by local artists, they seldom sold Munnings.

"Fellow met us there," Don added. "Brought it up to our room. From the gallery where we saw it first."

"Which gallery?"

He made a slight attempt to remember. "Might have been something like Fine Arts."

"Would you have it on a check stub, or anything?"

He shook his head. "The wine firm I was dealing with paid for it for me, and I sent a check to their British office when I got back."

"Which wine firm?"

"Monga Vineyards Proprietory, Limited, of Adelaide and Melbourne."

I wrote it all down.

"And what was the picture like? I mean, could you describe it?"

Donald looked tired. "One of those 'Going Down to the Start' things. Typical Munnings."

"So was mine," said Maisie, surprised. "A nice long row of jockeys in their colors against a darker sort of sky."

"Mine had only three horses," Donald said.

"The biggest—I suppose you might say the *nearest*—jockey in my picture had a purple shirt and green cap," Maisie said, "and I expect you'll think I was silly, but that was one of the reasons I bought it, because when Archie and I were thinking what fun it would be to buy a horse and go to the races as owners, we decided we'd like purple with a green cap for our colors, if no one else already had that, of course."

"Don?" I said.

"Mmm? Oh . . . three bay horses cantering . . . in profile . . . one in front, two slightly overlapping behind. Bright colors on the jockeys. I don't remember exactly. White race-track rails and a lot of sunny sky."

"What size?"

He frowned slightly. "Not very big. About twenty-four inches by eighteen, inside the frame."

"And yours, Maisie?"

"A bit smaller, dear, I should think."

"Look," Donald said. "What are you getting at?"

"Trying to make sure that there are no more coincidences."

He stared, but without any particular feeling.

"On the way up here," I said, "Maisie told me everything"—but *everything*—"of the way she came to buy her picture. So could you possibly tell us how you came to buy yours? Did you, for example, deliberately go looking for a Munnings?"

Donald passed a weary hand over his face, obviously not wanting the bother of answering.

"Please, Don," I said.

"Oh . . ." A long sigh. "No. I wasn't especially wanting to buy anything at all. We just went into the Melbourne Art Gallery for a stroll round. We came to the Munnings they have there . . . and while we were looking at it we just drifted into conversation with a woman near us, as one does in art galleries. She said there was another Munnings, not far away, for sale in a small commercial gallery, and it was worth seeing even if one didn't intend to buy it. We had time to spare, so we went."

Maisie's mouth had fallen open. "But, dear," she said, recovering, "that was *just* the same as us, my sister-in-law and me, though it was Sydney Art Gallery, not Melbourne. They have this marvelous picture there, 'The Coming Storm,' and we were admiring it when this man sort of drifted up to us and joined in. . . ."

Donald suddenly looked a great deal more exhausted, like a sick person overdone by healthy visitors.

"Look . . . Charles . . . you aren't going to the police with all this? Because I . . . I don't think . . . I could stand . . . a whole new lot . . . of questions."

"No, I'm not," I said.

"Then what . . . does it matter?"

Maisie finished her gin and tonic and smiled a little too brightly.

"Which way to the little girls' room, dear?" she asked, and disappeared to the cloakroom.

Donald said faintly, "I can't concentrate. . . . I'm sorry, Charles, but I can't seem to do anything . . . while they still have Regina . . . unburied . . . just *stored.*"

Time, far from dulling the agony, seemed to have preserved it, as if the keeping of Regina in a refrigerated drawer had stopped dead the natural progression of mourning. I had been told that the bodies of murdered people could be held in that way for six months or more in unsolved cases. I doubted whether Donald would last that long.

He stood up suddenly and walked away out the door to the hall. I followed. He crossed the hall, opened the door of the sitting room, and went in.

Hesitantly, I went after him.

The sitting room still contained only the chintz-covered sofas and chairs, now ranged overtidily round the walls. The floor where Regina had lain was clean and polished. The air was cold.

Donald stood in front of the empty fireplace looking at my picture of Regina, which was propped on the mantelpiece.

"'I stay in here with her, most of the time," he said. "It's the only place I can bear to be."

He walked to one of the armchairs and sat down, directly facing the portrait.

"You wouldn't mind seeing yourselves out, would you, Charles?" he said. "I'm really awfully tired."

"Take care of yourself." Useless advice. One could see he wouldn't.

"I'm all right," he said. "Quite all right. Don't you worry."

I looked back from the door. He was sitting immobile, looking at Regina. I didn't know whether it would have been better or worse if I hadn't painted her.

Maisie was quiet for the whole of the first hour of the return journey, a record in itself.

From Donald's house we had driven first to one of the neighbors who had originally offered refuge, because he clearly needed help more now than ever.

Mrs. Neighbor had listened with sympathy, but had shaken her head.

"Yes, I know he should have company and get away from the house, but he won't. I've tried several times. Called. So have lots of people round here. He just tells us he's all right. He won't let anyone help him."

Maisie drove soberly, mile after mile. Eventually she said, "We shouldn't have bothered him. Not so soon after . . ."

Three weeks, I thought. Only three weeks. To Donald it must have seemed like three months, stretched out in slow motion. You could live a lifetime in three weeks' pain.

"I'm going to Australia," I said.

"You're very fond of him, dear, aren't you?" Maisie said.

Fond? I wouldn't have used that word, I thought; but perhaps after all it was accurate.

"He's eight years older than me, but we've always got on well together." I looked back, remembering. "We were both only children. His mother and mine were sisters. They used to visit each other, with me and Donald in tow. He was always pretty patient about having a young kid under his feet."

"He looks very ill, dear."

"Yes."

She drove another ten miles in silence. Then she said, "Are you sure it wouldn't be better to tell the police? About the paintings, I mean? Because you do think they had something to do with the burglaries, don't you, dear, and the police might find out things more easily than you."

I agreed. "I'm sure they would, Maisie. But how can I tell them? You heard what Donald said, that he couldn't stand a new lot of questions. Seeing him today, do you think he could? And as for you, it wouldn't just be confessing to a bit of smuggling and paying a fine, but having a conviction against your name for always, and having the customs search your baggage every time you traveled, and all sorts of other complications and humiliations. Once you get on any blacklist nowadays, it is just about impossible to get off."

"I didn't know you cared, dear." She tried a giggle, but it didn't sound right.

We stopped after a while to exchange places. I liked driving her car, particularly as for the last three years, since I'd given up a steady income, I'd owned no wheels myself. The power purred elegantly under the pale blue bonnet and ate up the southward miles.

"Can you afford the fare, dear?" Maisie said. "And hotels, and things?"

"I've a friend out there. Another painter. I'll stay with him."

She looked at me doubtfully. "You can't get there by hitch-hiking, though."

I smiled. "I'll manage."

"Yes, well, dear, I dare say you can, but all the same —and I don't want any silly arguments—I've got a great deal of this world's goods, thanks to Archie, and you haven't, and as because it's partly because of me having gone in for smuggling that you're going yourself at all, I am insisting that you let me buy your ticket."

"No, Maisie."

"Yes, dear. Now be a good boy, dear, and do as I say."

You could see, I thought, why she'd been a good nurse. Swallow the medicine, dear, there's a good boy. I didn't like accepting her offer, but the truth was that I would have had to borrow anyway.

"Shall I paint your picture, Maisie, when I get back?"

"That will do very nicely, dear."

I pulled up outside the house near Heathrow whose attic was my home, and from where Maisie had picked me up that morning.

"How do you stand all this noise, dear?" she said, wincing as a huge jet climbed steeply overhead.

"I concentrate on the cheap rent."

She smiled, opening the crocodile handbag and producing her checkbook. She wrote out and gave me the slip of paper that was far more than enough for my fare.

"If you're so fussed, dear," she said across my protests, "you can give me back what you don't spend." She gazed at me earnestly with her gray-blue eyes. "You will be careful, dear, won't you?"

"Yes, Maisie."

"Because of course, dear, you might turn out to be a nuisance to some really *nasty* people."

I landed at Mascot Airport at noon five days later, wheeling in over Sydney and seeing the harbor bridge and the opera house down below, looking like postcards.

Jik met me on the other side of customs with a huge grin and a waving bottle of champagne.

"Todd the sod," he said. "Who'd have thought it?" His voice soared easily over the din. "Come to paint Australia red."

He slapped me on the back with an enthusiastic horny hand, not knowing his own strength. Jik Cassavetes, longtime friend, my opposite in almost everything.

Bearded, which I was not. Exuberant, noisy, extravagant, unpredictable; qualities I envied. Blue eyes and sun-blond hair. Muscles that left mine gasping. An outrageous way with girls. An abrasive tongue; and a wholehearted contempt for the things I painted.

We had met at art school, drawn together by mutual truancy on race trains. Jik compulsively went racing, but strictly to gamble, never to admire the contestants, and certainly not to paint them. Horse painters, to him, were the lower orders. No *serious* artist, he frequently said, would be seen dead painting horses.

Jik's paintings, mostly abstract, were the dark reverse of the bright mind: fruits of depression, full of despair at the hatred and pollution destroying the fair world.

Living with Jik was like a toboggan run, downhill, dangerous, and exhilarating. We'd spent the last two years at art school sharing a studio flat and kicking each other out for passing girls. They would have chucked him out of school except for his prodigious talent, because he'd missed weeks in the summer for his other love, which was sailing.

I'd been out with him, deep sea, several times in the

years afterward. I reckoned he'd taken us, on several occasions, a bit nearer death than was strictly necessary, but it had been a nice change from the office. He was a great sailor, efficient, neat, quick, and strong, with an instinctive feeling for wind and waves. I had been sorry when one day he had said he was setting off single-handed round the world. We'd had a paralytic farewell party on his last night ashore; and the next day, when he'd gone, I'd given the estate agent my notice.

Jik had brought a car to fetch me: his car, it turned out. A British M.G. sports, dark blue. Both sides of him right there, extrovert and introvert, the flamboyant statement in a somber color.

"Are there many of these here?" I asked, surprised, loading suitcase and satchel into the back. "It's a long way from the birth pangs."

He grinned. "A few. They're not popular now, because petrol passes through them like salts." The engine roared to life, agreeing with him, and he switched on the windscreen wiper against a starting shower. "Welcome to sunny Australia. It rains all the time here. Puts Manchester in the sun."

"But you like it?"

"Love it, mate. Sydney's like rugger, all guts and go and a bit of grace in the line-out."

"And how's business?"

"There are thousands of painters in Australia. It's a flourishing cottage industry." He glanced at me sideways. "A hell of a lot of competition."

"I haven't come to seek fame and fortune."

"But I scent a purpose," he said.

"How would you feel about harnessing your brawn?"

"To your brain? As in the old days?"

"Those were pastimes."

His eyebrows rose. "What are the risks?"

"Arson and murder, to date."

"Jesus."

The blue car swept gracefully into the center of the city. Skyscrapers grew like beanstalks.

"I live right out on the other side," Jik said. "God, that sounds banal. Suburban. What has become of me?"

"Contentment oozing from every pore," I said, smiling.

"Yes. So O.K., for the first time in my life I've been actually happy. I dare say you'll soon put that right."

The car nosed onto the expressway, pointing toward the bridge.

"If you look over your right shoulder," Jik said, "you'll see the triumph of imagination over economics. Like the Concorde. Long live madness, it's the only thing that gets us anywhere."

I looked. It was the opera house, glimpsed, gray with rain.

"Dead in the day," Jik said. "It's a night bird. Fantastic."

The great arch of the bridge rose above us, intricate as steel lace. "This is the only flat bit of road in Sydney," Jik said. We climbed again on the other side.

To our left—half seen at first behind other familiar-looking high-rise blocks, but then revealed in its full glory —stood a huge shiny red-orange building, all its sides set with regular rows of large curve-cornered square windows of bronze-colored glass.

Jik grinned. "The shape of the twenty-first century. Imagination and courage. I love this country."

"Where's your natural pessimism?"

"When the sun sets, those windows glow like gold." We left the gleaming monster behind. "It's the water-board offices," Jik said sardonically. "The guy at the top moors his boat near mine."

The road went up and down out of the city through close-packed rows of one-story houses, whose roofs, from the air, had looked like a great red-squared carpet.

"There's one snag," Jik said. "Three weeks ago, I got married."

The snag was living with him aboard his boat, which was moored among a colony of others near a headland he called The Spit: and you could see why—temporarily, at least—the glooms of the world could take care of themselves.

She was not plain, but not beautiful. Oval-shaped face, mid-brown hair, so-so figure, and a practical line in clothes. None of the style or instant vital butterfly quality of Regina. I found myself the critically inspected target of bright brown eyes that looked out with impact-making intelligence.

"Sarah," Jik said. "Todd. Todd, Sarah."

We said hi and did I have a good flight and yes I did. I gathered she would have preferred me to have stayed at home.

Jik's thirty-foot ketch, which had set out from England as a cross between a studio and a chandler's warehouse, now sported curtains, cushions, and a flowering plant. When Jik opened the champagne, he poured it into shining tulip glasses, not plastic mugs.

"By God," he said. "It's good to see you."

Sarah toasted my advent politely, not sure that she agreed. I apologized for gate-crashing the honeymoon.

"Nuts to that," Jik said, obviously meaning it. "Too much domestic bliss is bad for the soul."

"It depends," said Sarah neutrally, "on whether you need love or loneliness to get you going."

For Jik before, it had always been loneliness. I wondered what he had painted recently; but there was no sign in the now comfortable cabin of so much as a brush.

"I walk on air," Jik said. "I could bound up Everest and do a handspring on the summit."

"As far as the galley will do," Sarah said, "if you remembered to buy the crayfish."

Jik, in our shared days, had been the cook; and times, it seemed, had not changed. It was he, not Sarah, who with speed and efficiency chopped open the crayfish, covered them with cheese and mustard, and set them under the grill. He who washed the crisp lettuce and assembled crusty bread and butter. We ate the feast round the cabin table with rain pattering on portholes and roof and the sea water slapping against the sides in the freshening wind. Over coffee, at Jik's insistence, I told them why I had come to Australia.

They heard me out in concentrated silence. Then Jik, whose politics had not changed much since student pink, muttered darkly about "pigs," and Sarah looked nakedly apprehensive.

"Don't worry," I told her. "I'm not asking for Jik's help, now that I know he's married."

"You have it. You have it," he said explosively.

I shook my head. "No."

Sarah said, "What precisely do you plan to do first?"

"Find out where the two Munningses came from."

"And after?"

"If I knew what I was looking for, I wouldn't need to look."

"That doesn't follow," she said absently.

"Melbourne," Jik said suddenly. "You said one of the pictures came from Melbourne. Well, that settles it. Of course we'll help. We'll go there at once. It couldn't be better. Do you know what next Tuesday is?"

"No," I said. "What is it?"

"The day of the Melbourne Cup!"

His voice was triumphant. Sarah stared at me darkly across the table.

"I wish you hadn't come," she said.

CHAPTER 6

I slept that night in the converted boathouse which con-
stituted Jik's postal address. Apart from a bed alcove,
new-looking bathroom, and rudimentary kitchen, he was
using the whole space as studio.

A huge old easel stood in the center, with a table to
each side holding neat arrays of paints, brushes, knives,
pots of linseed and turpentine, and cleaning fluid: all the
usual paraphernalia.

No work in progress. Everything shut and tidy. Like its
counterpart in England, the large rush mat in front of the
easel was black with oily dirt, owing to Jik's habit of
rubbing his roughly rinsed brushes on it between colors.
The tubes of paint were characteristically squeezed flat in
the middle, impatience forbidding an orderly progress
from the bottom. The palette was a small oblong, not
needed any larger because he used most colors straight
from the tube and got his effects by overpainting. A huge
box of rags stood under one table, ready to wipe clean
everything used to apply paint to picture, not just brushes
and knives, but fingers, palms, nails, wrists, anything that
took his fancy. I smiled to myself. Jik's studio was as
identifiable as his pictures.

Along one wall, a two-tiered rack held rows of can-

71

vases, which I pulled out one by one. Dark, strong, dramatic colors, leaping to the eye. Still the troubled vision, the perception of doom. Decay and crucifixions, obscurely horrific landscapes, flowers wilting, fish dying, everything to be guessed, nothing explicit.

Jik hated to sell his paintings, and seldom did, which I thought was just as well, as they made uncomfortable roommates, enough to cause depression in a skylark. They had a vigor, though, that couldn't be denied. All those who saw his assembled work remembered it, and had their thoughts modified, and perhaps even their basic attitudes changed. He was a major artist in a way I would never be, and he would have looked upon easy popular acclaim as personal failure.

In the morning, I walked down to the boat and found Sarah there alone.

"Jik's gone for milk and newspapers," she said. "I'll get you some breakfast."

"I came to say goodbye."

She looked at me levelly. "The damage is done."

"Not if I go."

"Back to England?"

I shook my head.

"I thought not." A dim smile appeared briefly in her eyes. "Jik told me last night that you were the only person he knew who had a head cool enough to calculate a ship's position for a Mayday call by dead reckoning at night, after tossing around violently for four hours in a force-ten gale with a hole in the hull and the pumps packed up, and get it right."

I grinned. "But he patched the hull and mended the pump, and we canceled the Mayday when it got light."

"You were both stupid."

"Better to stay safely at home?" I said.

She turned away. *"Men,"* she said. "Never happy unless they're risking their necks."

She was right, to some extent. A little healthy danger wasn't a bad feeling, especially in retrospect. It was only the nerve-breakers that gave you the shakes and put you off repetition.

"Some women, too," I said.

"Not me."

"I won't take Jik with me."

Her back was still turned. "You'll get him killed," she said.

Nothing looked less dangerous than the small suburban gallery from which Maisie had bought her picture. It was shut for good. The bare premises could be seen nakedly through the shop-front window, and a succinct and unnecessary card hanging inside the glass door said "Closed."

The little shops on each side shrugged their shoulders.

"They were only open for a month or so. Never seemed to do much business. No surprise they folded."

Did they, I asked, know which estate agent was handling the letting? No, they didn't.

"End of inquiry," Jik said.

I shook my head. "Let's try the local agents."

We split up and spent a fruitless hour. None of the firms on any of the "For Sale" boards in the district admitted to having the gallery on its books.

We met again outside the uninformative door.

"Where now?"

"Gallery of Art?"

"In the Domain," Jik said, which turned out to be a chunk of park in the city center. The Gallery of Art had a suitable façade of six pillars outside and the Munnings, when we ran it to earth, inside.

No one else was looking at it. No one approached to fall into chat and advise us we could buy another one cheap in a little gallery in an outer suburb.

We stood there for a while, with me admiring the absolute mastery that set the two gray ponies in the shaft of pre-storm light at the head of the darker herd, and Jik grudgingly admitting that at least the man knew how to handle paint.

Absolutely nothing else happened. We drove back to the boat in the M.G., and lunch was an anticlimax.

"What now?" Jik said.

"A spot of work with the telephone, if I could borrow the one in the boathouse."

It took nearly all afternoon, but alphabetically systematic calls to every estate agent as far as Holloway & Son in the classified directory produced the goods in the end. The premises in question, said Holloway & Son, had been let to North Sydney Fine Arts on a short lease.

How short?

Three months, dating from September 1st.

No, Holloway & Son did not know the premises were now empty. They could not relet them until December 1st, because North Sydney Fine Arts had paid all the rent in advance; and they did not feel able to part with the name of any individual concerned. I blarneyed a bit, giving a delicate impression of being in the trade myself, with a client for the empty shop. Holloway & Son mentioned a Mr. John Grey, with a post-office box number for an address. I thanked them. Mr. Grey, they said, warming up a little, had said he wanted the gallery for a short private exhibition, and they were not really surprised he had already gone.

How could I recognize Mr. Grey if I met him? They really couldn't say: all the negotiations had been done by telephone and post. I could write to him myself, if my client wanted the gallery before December 1st.

Ta ever so, I thought.

All the same, it couldn't do much harm. I unearthed a suitable sheet of paper, and in twee and twirly lettering in black ink told Mr. Grey I had been given his name and box number by Holloway & Son, and asked him if he would sell me the last two weeks of his lease, so that I could mount an exhibition of a young friend's *utterly meaningful* watercolors. Name his own price, I said, within reason. Yours sincerely, I said: Peregrine Smith.

I walked down to the boat to ask if Jik or Sarah would mind me putting their own box number as a return address.

"He won't answer," Sarah said, reading the letter. "If he's a crook. I wouldn't."

"The first principle of fishing," Jik said, "is to dangle a bait."

"This wouldn't attract a starving piranha."

I posted it anyway, with Sarah's grudging consent. None of us expected it to bring forth any result.

Jik's own session on the telephone proved more rewarding. Melbourne, it seemed, was crammed to the rooftops for the richest race meeting of the year, but he had been offered last-minute cancellations. Very lucky indeed, he insisted, looking amused.

"Where?" I asked suspiciously.

"In the Hilton," he said.

I couldn't afford it, but we went anyway. Jik in his student days had lived on cautious handouts from a family trust, and it appeared that the source of bread was still flowing. The boat, the boathouse, the M.G., and the wife were none of them supported by paint.

We flew south to Melbourne the following morning, looking down on the Snowy mountains en route and thinking our own chilly thoughts. Sarah's disapproval from the seat behind froze the back of my head, but she had refused to stay in Sydney. Jik's natural bent and enthusiasm for dicey adventure looked like being curbed by love, and his reaction to danger might not henceforth be uncomplicatedly practical. That was, if I could find any dangers for him to react to. The Sydney trail was dead and cold, and maybe Melbourne, too, would yield an unlooked-at public Munnings and a gone-away private gallery. And if it did, what then? For Donald the outlook would be bleaker than the strange puckered ranges sliding away underneath.

If I could take home enough to show beyond doubt that the plundering of his house had its roots in the sale of a painting in Australia, it should get the police off his neck, the life back to his spirit, and Regina into a decent grave.

If.

And I would have to be quick, or it would be too late to matter. Donald, staring hour after hour at a portrait in an empty house . . . Donald, on the brink.

Melbourne was cold and wet and blowing a gale. We checked gratefully into the warm plushy bosom of the Hilton, souls cosseted from the door onward by rich reds and purples and blues, velvety fabrics, copper and gilt and glass. The staff smiled. The lifts worked. There was polite shock when I carried my own suitcase. A long way from the bare boards of home.

I unpacked, which is to say, hung up my one suit, slightly crumpled from the squashy satchel, and then went to work again on the telephone.

The Melbourne office of the Monga Vineyards Proprietory, Ltd., cheerfully told me that the person who dealt with Mr. Donald Stuart from England was the managing director, Mr. Hudson Taylor, and he could be found at present in his office at the vineyard itself, which was north of Adelaide. Would I like the number?

Thanks very much.

"No sweat," they said, which I gathered was Australian shorthand for "It's no trouble, and you're welcome."

I pulled out the map of Australia I'd acquired on the flight from England. Melbourne, capital of the state of

Victoria, lay right down in the southeast corner. Adelaide, capital of South Australia, lay about four hundred and fifty miles northwest. Correction, seven hundred and twenty-five kilometers: the Australians had already gone metric, to the confusion of my mental arithmetic.

Hudson Taylor was not in his vineyard office. An equally cheerful voice there told me he'd left for Melbourne to go to the races. He had a runner in the Cup. Reverence, the voice implied, was due.

Could I reach him anywhere, then?

Sure, if it was important. He would be staying with friends. Number supplied. Ring at nine o'clock.

Sighing a little, I went two floors down and found Jik and Sarah bouncing around their room with gleeful satisfaction.

"We've got tickets for the races tomorrow and Tuesday," he said, "and a car pass, and a car. And the West Indies play Victoria at cricket on Sunday opposite the hotel and we've tickets for that, too."

"Miracles courtesy of the Hilton," Sarah said, looking much happier at this program. "The whole package was on offer with the canceled rooms."

"So what do you want us to do this afternoon?" finished Jik expansively.

"Could you bear the Arts Centre?"

It appeared they could. Even Sarah came without forecasting universal doom, my lack of success so far having cheered her. We went in a taxi to keep her curled hair dry.

The Victoria Arts Centre was huge, modern, inventive, and endowed with the largest stained-glass roof in the world. Jik took deep breaths as if drawing the living spirit of the place into his lungs, and declaimed at the top of his voice that Australia was the greatest, the greatest, the only adventurous country left in the corrupt, stagnating, militant, greedy, freedom-hating, mean-minded, strait-jacketed, rotting, polluted world. Passersby stared in amazement and Sarah showed no surprise at all.

We ran the Munnings to earth, eventually, deep in the labyrinth of galleries. It glowed in the remarkable light that suffused the whole building: the "Departure of the Hop Pickers," with its great wide sky and the dignified gypsies with their ponies, caravans, and children.

A young man was sitting at an easel slightly to one side, painstakingly working on a copy. On a table beside him stood large pots of linseed oil and turps, and a jar with brushes in cleaning fluid. A comprehensive box of paints lay open to hand. Two or three people stood about, watching him and pretending not to, in the manner of gallery-goers the world over.

Jik and I went round behind him to take a look. The young man glanced at Jik's face, but saw nothing there except raised eyebrows and blandness. We watched him squeeze flake white and cadmium yellow from tubes onto his palette and mix them together into a nice pale color with a hog's-hair brush.

On the easel stood his study, barely started. The outlines were there, as precise as tracings, and a small amount of blue had been laid on the sky.

Jik and I watched in interest while he applied the pale yellow to the shirt of the nearest figure.

"Hey," Jik said loudly, suddenly slapping him on the shoulder and shattering the reverent gallery hush into kaleidoscopic fragments. "You're a fraud. If you're an artist, I'm a gas-fitter's mate."

Hardly polite, but not a hanging matter. The faces of the scattered onlookers registered embarrassment, not affront.

On the young man, though, the effect was galvanic. He leaped to his feet, overturning the easel and staring at Jik with wild eyes; and Jik, with huge enjoyment, put in the clincher.

"What you're doing is *criminal*," he said.

The young man reacted to that with ruthless reptilian speed, snatching up the pots of linseed and turps and flinging the liquids at Jik's eyes.

I grabbed his left arm. He scooped up the paint-laden palette in his right hand and swung round fiercely, aiming at my face. I ducked instinctively. The palette missed me and struck Jik, who had his hands to his eyes and was yelling very loudly.

Sarah rushed toward him, knocking into me hard in her anxiety and loosening my grip on the young man. He tore his arm free, ran precipitously for the exit, dodged round behind two open-mouthed middle-aged spectators who were on their way in, and pushed them violently into my chasing path. By the time I'd disentangled myself, he had vanished from sight. I ran through several halls and passages, but couldn't find him. He knew his way, and I did not: and it took me long enough, when I finally gave up the hunt, to work out the route back to Jik.

A fair-sized crowd had surrounded him, and Sarah was in a roaring fury based on fear, which she unleashed on me as soon as she saw me return.

"Do something!" she screamed. "Do something, he's going blind. . . . He's going *blind*. I knew we should never have listened to you!"

I caught her wrists as she advanced in near hysteria to do at least some damage to my face in payment for Jik's. Her strength was no joke.

"Sarah," I said fiercely. "Jik is *not* going blind."

"He is. He is," she insisted, kicking my shins.

"Do you *want* him to?" I shouted.

She gasped sharply in outrage. What I'd said was at least as good as a slap in the face. Sense reasserted itself suddenly like a drench of cold water, and the manic power receded back to normal angry-girl proportions.

"Linseed oil will do no harm at all," I said positively. "The turps is painful, but that's all. It absolutely will not affect his eyesight."

She glared at me, pulled her wrists out of my grasp, and turned back to Jik, who was rocking around in agony and cupping his fingers over his eyes with rigid knuckles. Also, being Jik, he was exercising his tongue.

"The slimy little bugger . . . wait till I catch him. . . . Jesus Christ Almighty, I can't bloody see. Sarah, where's that bloody Todd? . . . I'll strangle him. . . . Get an ambulance . . . my eyes are burning out . . . bloody buggering hell . . ."

I spoke loudly in his ear. "Your eyes are O.K."

"They're my bloody eyes, and if I say they're not O.K. they're bloody not."

"You know damn well you're not going blind, so stop hamming it up."

"They're not your eyes, you sod."

"And you're frightening Sarah," I said.

That message got through. He took his hands away and stopped rolling about.

At the sight of his face, the riveted audience let out a murmur of pleasant horror. Blobs of bright paint from the young man's palette had streaked one side of his jaw yellow and blue; his eyes were red with inflammation and pouring with tears, and looked very sore indeed.

"Jesus, Sarah," he said, blinking painfully. "Sorry, love. The bastard's right. Turps never blinded anybody."

78

"Not permanently," I said, because to do him justice he obviously couldn't see anything but tears at the moment.

Sarah's animosity was unabated. "Get him an ambulance, then."

I shook my head. "All he needs is water and time."

"You're a stupid, heartless *pig*. He obviously needs a doctor, and hospital care."

Jik, having abandoned histrionics, produced a handkerchief and gently mopped his streaming eyes.

"He's right, love. Lots of water, as the man said. Washes the sting away. Lead me to the nearest gents."

With Sarah unconvinced but holding one arm, and a sympathetic male spectator the other, he was solicitously helped away like an amateur production of Samson. The chorus in the shape of the audience bent reproachful looks on me, and cheerfully awaited the next act.

I looked at the overturned mess of paints and easel that the young man had left. The onlookers looked at them, too.

"I suppose," I said slowly, "that no one here was talking to the young artist before any of this happened?"

"We were," said one woman, surprised at the question.

"So were we," said another.

"What about?"

"Munnings," said one, and, "Munnings," said the other, both looking immediately at the painting on the wall.

"Not about his own work?" I said, bending down to pick it up. A slash of yellow lay wildly across the careful outlines, result of Jik's slap on the back.

Both of the ladies, and also their accompanying husbands, shook their heads and said they had talked with him about the pleasure of hanging a Munnings on their own walls, back home.

I smiled slowly.

"I suppose," I said, "that he didn't happen to know where you could get one?"

"Well, yeah," they said. "As a matter of fact, he sure did."

"Where?"

"Well, look here, young fellow . . ." The elder of the husbands, a seventyish American with the unmistakable stamp of wealth, began shushing the others to silence with a practiced damping movement of his right hand. Don't give information away, it said, you may lose by it. "You're asking a lot of questions."

"I'll explain," I said. "Would you like some coffee?"

They all looked at their watches and said doubtfully they possibly would.

"There's a coffee shop just down the hall," I said. "I saw it when I was trying to catch that young man . . . to make him tell why he flung turps in my friend's eyes."

Curiosity sharpened in their faces. They were hooked.

The rest of the spectators drifted away, and I, asking the others to wait a moment, started moving the jumbled painting stuff off the center of the floor to a tidier wall-side heap.

None of it was marked with its owner's name. All regulation kit, obtainable from art shops. Artists' quality, not students' cheaper equivalents. None of it new, but not old, either. The picture itself was on a standard-sized piece of commercially prepared hardboard, not on stretched canvas. I stacked everything together, added the empty jars that had held linseed and turps, and wiped my hands on a piece of rag.

"Right," I said. "Shall we go?"

They were all Americans, all rich, retired, and fond of racing. Mr. and Mrs. Howard K. Petrovitch, of Ridgeville, New Jersey, and Mr. and Mrs. Wyatt L. Minchless from Carter, Illinois.

Wyatt Minchless, the one who shushed the others, called the meeting to order over four richly creamed iced coffees and one plain black. The black was for himself. Heart condition, he murmured, patting the revelvant area of suiting. A white-haired man, black-framed specs, pale indoor complexion, pompous manner.

"Now, young fellow, let's hear it from the top."

"Um," I said. Where exactly was the top? "The artist boy attacked my friend Jik because Jik called him a criminal."

"Yuh." Mrs. Petrovitch nodded. "I heard him. Just as we were leaving the gallery. Now why would he do that?"

"It isn't criminal to copy good painting," Mrs. Minchless said knowledgeably. "In the Louvre in Paris, France, you can't get near the 'Mona Lisa' for those irritating students."

She had blue-rinsed puffed-up hair, uncreasable navy and green clothes, and enough diamonds to attract a top-rank thief. Deep lines of automatic disapproval ran downward from the corners of her mouth. Thin body. Thick mind.

"It depends what you are copying *for*," I said. "If you're going to try to pass your copy off as an original, then that definitely is a fraud."

Mrs. Petrovitch began, "Do you think the young man was *forging*—" but was interrupted by Wyatt Minchless, who smothered her question by both the damping hand and his louder voice.

"Are you saying that this young artist boy was painting a Munnings he later intended to sell as the real thing?"

"Er . . ." I said.

Wyatt Minchless swept on. "Are you saying that the Munnings picture he told us we might be able to buy is itself a forgery?"

The others looked both horrified at the possibility and admiring of Wyatt L. for his perspicacity.

"I don't know," I said. "I just thought I'd like to see it."

"You don't want to buy a Munnings yourself? You are not acting as an agent for anyone else?" Wyatt's questions sounded severe and inquisitorial.

"Absolutely not," I said.

"Well, then." Wyatt looked round the other three, collected silent assents. "He told Ruthie and me there was a good Munnings racing picture at a very reasonable price in a little gallery not far away. . . ." He fished with forefinger and thumb into his outer breast pocket. "Yes, here we are. Yarra River Fine Arts. Third turning off Swanston Street about twenty yards along."

Mr. and Mrs. Petrovitch looked resigned. "He told us exactly the same."

"He seemed such a nice young man," Mrs. Petrovitch added sadly. "So interested in our trip. Asked us what we'd be betting on in the Cup."

"He asked where we would be going after Melbourne," Mr. Petrovitch said, nodding. "We told him Adelaide and Alice Springs, and he said Alice Springs was a mecca for artists and to be sure to visit the Yarra River gallery there. The same firm, he said. Always had good pictures."

Mr. Petrovitch would have misunderstood if I had leaned across and hugged him. I concentrated on my fancy coffee and kept my excitement to myself.

"We're going on to Sydney," pronounced Wyatt L. "He didn't offer any suggestions for Sydney."

The tall glasses were nearly empty. Wyatt looked at his watch and swallowed the last of his plain black.

"You didn't tell us," Mrs. Petrovitch said, looking puzzled, "why your friend called the young man a criminal. I mean . . . I can see why the young man attacked your friend and ran away if he *was* a criminal, but why did your friend *think* he was?"

"Just what I was about to ask," said Wyatt, nodding away heavily. Pompous liar, I thought.

"My friend Jik," I said, "is an artist himself. He didn't think much of the young man's effort. He called it criminal. He might just as well have said lousy."

"Is that all?" said Mrs. Petrovitch, looking disappointed.

"Well . . . the young man was painting with paints which won't really mix. Jik's a perfectionist. He can't stand seeing paint misused."

"What do you mean, won't mix?"

"Paints are chemicals," I said apologetically. "Most of them don't have any effect on each other, but you have to be careful."

"What happens if you aren't?" demanded Ruthie Minchless.

"Um . . . nothing explodes," I said, smiling. "It's just that—well, if you mix flake white, which is lead, with cadmium yellow, which contains sulfur, like the young man was doing, you get a nice pale color to start with, but the two minerals react against each other and in time darken and alter the picture."

"And your friend called this criminal?" Wyatt said in disbelief. "It couldn't possibly make that much difference."

"Er . . ." I said. "Well, Van Gogh used a light bright new yellow made of chrome when he painted a picture of sunflowers. Cadmium yellow hadn't been developed then. But chrome yellow has shown that over a couple of hundred years it decomposes and in the end turns greenish black, and the sunflowers are already an odd color, and I don't think anyone has found a way of stopping it."

"But the young man wasn't painting for posterity," said Ruthie with irritation. "Unless he's another Van Gogh, surely it doesn't matter."

I didn't think they'd want to hear that Jik hoped for recognition in the twenty-third century. The permanence of colors had always been an obsession with him, and he'd dragged me along once to a course on their chemistry.

The Americans got up to go.

"All very interesting," Wyatt said with a dismissive smile. "I guess I'll keep my money in regular stocks."

CHAPTER 7

Jik had gone from the gents, gone from the whole Arts
Centre. I found him back with Sarah in their hotel room,
being attended by the Hilton's attractive resident nurse.
The door to the corridor stood open, ready for her to
leave.

"Try not to rub them, Mr. Cassavetes," she was saying.
"If you have any trouble, call the reception desk, and I'll
come back."

She gave me a professional half-smile in the open doorway and walked briskly away, leaving me to go in.

"How are the eyes?" I said, advancing tentatively.

"Ruddy awful." They were bright pink, but dry. Getting better.

Sarah said, with tight lips, "This has all gone far
enough. I know that this time Jik will be all right again in
a day or two, but we are not taking any more risks."

Jik said nothing and didn't look at me.

It wasn't exactly unexpected. I said, "O.K. . . . Well,
have a nice weekend, and thanks anyway."

"Todd . . ." Jik said.

Sarah leaped in fast. "No, Jik. It's not our responsibility. Todd can think what he likes, but his cousin's trou-
bles are nothing to do with us. We are not getting involved

any further. I've been against all this silly poking around all along, and this is where it stops."

"Todd will go on with it," Jik said.

"Then he's a fool." She was angry, scornful, biting.

"Sure," I said. "Anyone who tries to right a wrong these days is a fool. Much better not to meddle, not to get involved, not to think it's your responsibility. I really ought to be painting away safely in my attic at Heathrow, minding my own business and letting Donald rot. Much more sensible, I agree. The trouble is that I simply can't do it. I see the hell he's in. How can I just turn my back? Not when there's a chance of getting him out. True enough, I may not manage it, but what I can't face is not having tried."

I came to a halt.

A blank pause.

"Well," I said, raising a smile. "Here endeth the lesson according to the world's foremost nit. Have fun at the races. I might go, too, you never know."

I sketched a farewell and eased myself out. Neither of them said a word. I shut the door quietly and took the lift up to my own room.

A pity about Sarah, I thought. She would have Jik in cotton wool and slippers if he didn't look out; and he'd never paint those magnificent brooding pictures any more, because they sprang from a torment he would no longer be allowed. Security, to him, would be a sort of abdication; a sort of death.

I looked at my watch and decided the Yarra River Fine Arts setup might still have its doors open. Worth trying.

I wondered, as I walked along Wellington Parade and up Swanston Street, whether the young turps-flinger would be there, and if he was, whether he would know me. I'd seen only glimpses of his face, as I'd mostly been standing behind him. All one could swear to was light brown hair, acne on the chin, a round jawline, and a full-lipped mouth. Under twenty. Perhaps not more than seventeen. Dressed in blue jeans, white T-shirt, and tennis shoes. About five feet eight, a hundred and thirty pounds. Quick on his feet, and liable to panic. And no artist.

The gallery was open, brightly lit, with a horse painting on a gilt display easel in the center of the window. Not a Munnings. A portrait picture of an Australian horse and jockey, every detail sharp-edged, emphatic, and, to my taste, overpainted. Beside it a notice, gold embossed on black, announced a special display of distinguished equine art; and beside that, less well produced but with larger letters, stood a display card saying, "Welcome to the Melbourne Cup."

The gallery looked typical of hundreds of others round the world; narrow frontage, with premises stretching back a good way from the street. Two or three people were wandering about inside, looking at the merchandise on the well-lit neutral gray walls.

I had gone there intending to go in. To go in was still what I intended, but I hesitated outside in the street feeling as if I were at the top of a ski jump. Stupid, I thought. Nothing ventured, nothing gained, and all that. If you don't look, you won't see.

I took a ruefully deep breath and stepped over the welcoming threshold.

Greeny-gray carpet within, and an antique desk strategically placed near the door, with a youngish woman handing out small catalogues and large smiles.

"Feel free to look around," she said. "More pictures downstairs."

She handed me a catalogue, a folded glazed white card with several typed sheets clipped into it. I flipped them over. One hundred and sixty-three items, numbered consecutively, with titles, artists' names, and asking price. A painting already sold, it said, would have a red spot on the frame.

I thanked her. "Just passing by," I said.

She nodded and smiled professionally, eyes sliding in a rapid summing-up over my denim clothes and general air of not belonging to the jet set. She herself wore the latest trendy fashion with careless ease and radiated tycoon-catching sincerity. Australian, assured, too big a personality to be simply a receptionist.

"You're welcome anyway," she said.

I walked slowly down the long room, checking the pictures against their notes. Most were by Australian artists, and I could see what Jik had meant about the hot competition. The field was just as crowded as at home, if not more so, and the standard in some respects better. As usual when faced with other people's flourishing talents, I began to have doubts of my own.

At the far end of the ground-floor display there was a

staircase leading downward, adorned with a large arrow and a notice repeating "More Pictures Downstairs."

I went down. Same carpet, same lighting, but no scattered customers looking from pictures to catalogues and back again.

Belowstairs, the gallery was not one straight room but a series of small rooms off a long corridor, apparently the result of not being able to knock down all the dividing and load-bearing walls. A room to the rear of the stairs was an office, furnished with another distinguished desk, two or three comfortable chairs for prospective clients, and a civilized row of teak-faced filing cabinets. Heavily framed pictures adorned the walls, and an equally substantial man was writing in a ledger at the desk.

He raised his head, conscious of my presence outside his door.

"Can I help you?" he said.

"Just looking."

He gave me an uninterested nod and went back to his work. He, like the whole place, had an air of permanence and respectability quite unlike the fly-by-night suburban affair in Sydney. This respectable business, I thought, could not be what I was looking for. I had got the whole thing wrong. I would have to wait until Hudson Taylor could look up Donald's check and point me in a new direction.

Sighing, I continued down the line of rooms, thinking I might as well finish taking stock of the opposition. A few of the frames were adorned with red spots, but the prices on everything good were a mile from a bargain and a deterrent to all but the rich.

In the end room, which was larger than the others, I came across the Munningses. Three of them. All with horses: one racing scene, one hunting, one of gypsies.

They were not in the catalogue.

They hung without ballyhoo in a row of similar subjects, and to my eyes stuck out like thoroughbreds among hacks.

Prickles began up my spine. It wasn't just the workmanship, but one of the pictures itself: Horses going down to the start. A long line of jockeys, bright against a dark sky. The silks of the nearest rider, purple with a green cap.

Maisie's chatty voice reverberated in my inner ear, describing what I saw. ". . . I expect you'll think I was silly, but that was one of the reasons I bought it . . . because Archie and I decided we'd like purple with a green cap for our colors, if no one already had that. . . ."

Munnings had always used a good deal of purple and green in shadows and distances. All the same . . . This picture, size, subject, and coloring, was exactly like Maisie's, which had been hidden behind a radiator, and, presumably, burned.

The picture in front of me looked authentic. The right sort of patina for the time since Munnings's death, the right excellence of draftsmanship, the right indefinable something that separated the great from the good. I put out a gentle finger to feel the surface of canvas and paint. Nothing there that shouldn't be.

An English voice from behind me said, "Can I help you?"

"Isn't that a Munnings?" I said casually, turning round.

A man was standing in the doorway looking in, his expression full of the guarded helpfulness of one whose best piece of stock is being appraised by someone apparently too poor to buy it.

I knew him instantly. Brown receding hair combed back, gray eyes, drooping mustache, suntanned skin: all last on view thirteen days ago beside the sea in Sussex, England, prodding around in a smoky ruin.

Mr. Greene. With an "e."

It took him only a fraction longer. Puzzlement as he glanced from me to the picture and back, then the shocking realization of where he'd seen me. He took a sharp step backward and raised his hand to the wall outside.

I was on my way to the door, but I wasn't quick enough. A steel-mesh gate slid down very fast in the doorway and clicked into some sort of bolt in the floor. Mr. Greene stood on the outside, disbelief still stamped on every feature and his mouth hanging open. I revised all my early theories about danger being good for the soul and felt as frightened as I'd ever been in my life.

"What's the matter?" called a deeper voice from up the corridor.

Mr. Greene's tongue was stuck. The man from the office appeared at his shoulder and looked at me through the imprisoning steel.

"A thief?" he asked with irritation.

Mr. Greene shook his head. A third person arrived

outside, his young face bright with curiosity, and his acne showing like measles.

"Hey," he said, in loud Australian surprise. "He was the one at the Art Centre. The one who chased me. I swear he didn't follow me. I swear it."

"Shut up," said the man from the office briefly. He stared at me steadily. I stared back.

I was standing in the center of a brightly lit room of about fifteen feet square. No windows. No way out except through the guarded door. Nowhere to hide, no weapons to hand. A long way down the ski jump and no promise of a soft landing.

"I say," I said plaintively. "Just what is all this about?" I walked up to the steel gate and tapped on it. "Open this up, I want to get out."

"What are you doing here?" the office man asked. He was bigger than Greene and obviously more senior in the gallery. Heavy dark spectacle frames over unfriendly eyes, and a blue bow tie with polka dots under a double chin. Small mouth with a full lower lip. Thinning hair.

"Looking," I said, trying to sound bewildered. "Just looking at pictures." An innocent at large, I thought, and a bit dim.

"He chased me in the Art Centre," the boy repeated.

"You threw some stuff in that man's eyes," I said indignantly. "You might have blinded him."

"Friend of yours, was he?" the office man said.

"No," I said. "I was just there, that was all. Same as I'm here. Just looking at pictures. Nothing wrong in that, is there? I go to lots of galleries, all the time."

Mr. Greene got his voice back. "I saw him in England," he said to the office man. His eyes returned to the Munnings; then he put his hand on the office man's arm and pulled him up the corridor out of my sight.

"Open the door," I said to the boy, who still gazed in.

"I don't know how," he said. "And I don't reckon I'd be popular, somehow."

The two other men returned. All three gazed in. I began to feel sympathy for creatures in cages.

"Who *are* you?" said the office man.

"Nobody. I mean, I'm just here for the racing, of course, and the cricket."

"Name?"

"Charles Neil." Charles Neil Todd.

"What were you doing in England?"

89

"I live there!" I said. "Look," I went on, as if trying to be reasonable under great provocation. "I saw this man here," I nodded to Greene, "at the home of a woman I know slightly in Sussex. She was giving me a lift home from the races, see, as I'd missed my train to Worthing, and was thumbing along the road from the Members' car park. Well, she stopped and picked me up, and then said she wanted to make a detour to see her house which had lately been burnt, and when we got there, this man was there. He said his name was Greene and that he was from an insurance company, and that's all I know about him. So what's going on?"

"It is a coincidence that you should meet here again, so soon."

"It certainly is," I agreed fervently. "But that's no bloody reason to lock me up."

I read indecision on all their faces. I hoped the sweat wasn't running visibly down my own.

I shrugged exasperatedly. "Fetch the police or something, then," I said, "if you think I've done anything wrong."

The man from the office put his hand to the switch on the outside wall and carefully fiddled with it, and the steel gate slid up out of sight, a good deal more slowly than it had come down.

"Sorry," he said perfunctorily. "But we have to be careful, with so many valuable paintings on the premises."

"Well, I see that," I said, stepping forward and resisting a strong impulse to make a dash for it. "But all the same . . ." I managed an aggrieved tone. "Still, no harm done, I suppose." Magnanimous, as well.

They all walked behind me along the corridor and up the stairs and through the upper gallery, doing my nerves no slightest good. All the other visitors seemed to have left. The receptionist was locking the front door.

My throat was dry beyond swallowing.

"I thought everyone had gone," she said in surprise.

"Slight delay," I said, with a feeble laugh.

She gave me the professional smile and reversed the locks. Opened the door. Held it, waiting for me.

Six steps.

Out in the fresh air.

God Almighty, it smelled good. I half turned. All four stood in the gallery watching me go. I shrugged and nodded and trudged away into the drizzle, feeling as weak as a field mouse dropped by a hawk.

I caught a passing tram and traveled a good way into unknown regions of the huge city, conscious only of an urgent desire to put a lot of distance between myself and that basement prison.

They would have second thoughts. They were bound to. They would wish they had found out more about me before letting me go. They couldn't be certain it wasn't a coincidence that I'd turned up at their gallery, because far more amazing coincidences did exist, like Lincoln at the time of his assassination having a secretary called Kennedy, and Kennedy having a secretary called Lincoln; but the more they thought about it, the less they would believe it.

If they wanted to find me, where would they look? Not at the Hilton, I thought in amusement. At the races: I had told them I would be there. On the whole, I wished I hadn't.

At the end of the tramline I got off and found myself opposite a small interesting-looking restaurant with "B.Y.O." in large letters on the door. Since hunger was as usual rearing its healthy head, I went in and ordered a steak, and asked for a look at the wine list.

The waitress looked surprised. "It's B.Y.O.," she said.

"What's B.Y.O.?"

Her eyebrows went still higher. "You a stranger? Bring Your Own. We don't sell drinks here, only food."

"Oh."

"If you want something to drink, there's a drive-in bottle shop a hundred yards down the road that'll still be open. I could hold the steak until you get back."

I shook my head and settled for a teetotal dinner, grinning all through coffee at a notice on the wall saying, "We have an arrangement with our bank. They don't fry steaks and we don't cash cheques."

When I set off back to the city center on the tram, I passed the bottle shop, which at first sight looked so like a garage that if I hadn't known I would have thought the line of cars was queuing for petrol. I could see why Jik liked the Australian imagination: both sense and fun.

The rain had stopped. I left the tram and walked the last couple of miles through the bright streets and dark parks, asking the way. Thinking of Donald and Maisie

91

and Greene with an "e," and of paintings and burglaries and violent minds.

The overall plan had all along seemed fairly simple: to sell pictures in Australia and steal them back in England, together with everything else lying handy. As I had come across two instances within three weeks, I had been sure there had to be more, because it was impossible that I could have stumbled on the *only* two, even given the double link of racing and painting. Since I'd met the Petrovitches and the Minchlesses, it seemed I'd been wrong to think of all the robberies taking place in England. Why not in America? Why not anywhere that was worth the risk?

Why not a mobile force of thieves shuttling container-fuls of antiques from continent to continent, selling briskly to a ravenous market? As Inspector Frost had said, few antiques were ever recovered. The demand was insatiable and the supply, by definition, limited.

Suppose I were a villain, I thought, and I didn't want to waste weeks in foreign countries finding out exactly which houses were worth robbing. I could just stay quietly at home in Melbourne selling paintings to rich visitors who could afford an impulse buy of ten thousand pounds or so. I could chat away with them about their picture collections back home, and I could shift the conversation easily to their silver and china and objects d'art.

I wouldn't want the sort of customers who had Rembrandts or Fabergés or anything well known and unsalable like that. Just the middling wealthy with Georgian silver and lesser Gauguins and Chippendale chairs.

When they bought my paintings, they would give me their addresses. Nice and easy. Just like that.

I would be a supermarket type of villain, with a large turnover of small goods. I would reckon that if I kept the victims reasonably well scattered, the fact that they had been to Australia within the past year or so would mean nothing to each regional police force. I would reckon that among the thousands of burglary claims they had to settle, Australia visits would bear no significance to insurance companies.

I would not, though, reckon on a crossed wire like Charles Neil Todd.

If I were a villain, I thought, with a well-established business and a good reputation, I wouldn't put myself at risk by selling fakes. Forged oil paintings were almost always detectable under a microscope, even if one discounted that the majority of experienced dealers could tell them at a glance. A painter left his signature all over a painting, not just in the corner, because the way he held his brush was as individual as handwriting. Brush strokes could be matched as conclusively as grooves on bullets.

If I were a villain, I'd wait in my spider's web with a real Munnings, or maybe a real Picasso drawing, or a genuine work by a recently dead good artist whose output had been voluminous, and along would come the rich little flies, carefully steered my way by talkative accomplices who stood around in the states' capitals' art galleries for the purpose. Both Donald and Maisie had been hooked that way.

Supposing when I'd sold a picture to a man from England and robbed him, and got my picture back again, I then sold it to someone from America. And then robbed him, and got it back, and so on round and round.

Suppose I sold a picture to Maisie in Sydney, and got it back, and started to sell it again in Melbourne. . . . My supposing stopped right there, because it didn't fit.

If Maisie had left her picture in full view, it would have been stolen like her other things. Maybe it even had been, and was right now glowing in the Yarra River Fine Arts, but if so, why had the house been burned, and why had Mr. Greene turned up to search the ruins?

It only made sense if Maisie's picture had been a copy, and if the thieves hadn't been able to find it. Rather than leave it around, they'd burned the house. But I'd just decided that I wouldn't risk fakes. Except that . . . would Maisie know an expert copy if she saw one? No, she wouldn't.

I sighed. To fool even Maisie, you'd have to find an accomplished artist willing to copy instead of pressing on with his own work, and they weren't that thick on the ground. All the same, she'd bought her picture in the short-lived Sydney gallery, not in Melbourne, so maybe in other places besides Melbourne they would take a risk with fakes.

The huge bulk of the hotel rose ahead of me across the last stretch of park. The night air blew cool on my head. I had a vivid feeling of being disconnected, a stranger in a vast continent, a speck under the stars. The noise and warmth of the Hilton brought the expanding universe down to imaginable size.

Upstairs, I telephoned to Hudson Taylor at the number his secretary had given me. Nine o'clock on the dot. He sounded mellow and full of good dinner, his voice strong, courteous, and vibrantly Australian.

"Donald Stuart's cousin? Is it true about little Regina being killed?"

"I'm afraid so."

"It's a real tragedy. A real nice lass, that Regina."

"Yes."

"Lookee here, then, what can I do for you? Is it tickets for the races?"

"Er, no," I said. It was just that since the receipt and provenance letter of the Munnings had been stolen along with the picture, Donald would like to get in touch with the people who had sold it to him, for insurance purposes, but he had forgotten their name. And as I was coming to Melbourne for the Cup . . .

"That's easy enough," Husdon Taylor said pleasantly. "I remember the place well. I went with Donald to see the picture there, and the guy in charge brought it along to the Hilton afterwards, when we arranged the finance. Now, let's see . . ." There was a pause for thought. "I can't remember the name of the place just now. Or the manager. It was some months ago, do you see? But I've got him on record here in the Melbourne office, and I'm calling in there anyway in the morning, so I'll look them up. You'll be at the races tomorrow?"

"Yes," I said.

"How about meeting for a drink, then? You can tell me about poor Donald and Regina, and I'll have the information he wants."

I said that would be fine, and he gave me detailed instructions as to where I would find him, and when. "There will be a huge crowd," he said, "but if you stand on that exact spot I shouldn't miss you."

The spot he had described sounded public and exposed. I hoped that it would only be he who found me on it.

"I'll be there," I said.

CHAPTER 8

Jik called through on the telephone at eight next morning.

"Come down to the coffee shop and have breakfast."

"O.K."

I went down in the lift and along the foyer to the hotel's informal restaurant. He was sitting at a table alone, wearing dark glasses and making inroads into a mountain of scrambled eggs.

"They bring you coffee," he said, "but you have to fetch everything else from that buffet." He nodded toward a large well-laden table in the center of the breezy blue and sharp green décor. "How's things?"

"Not what they used to be."

He made a face. "Bastard."

"How are the eyes?"

He whipped off the glasses with a theatrical flourish and leaned forward to give me a good look. Pink, they were, and still inflamed, but on the definite mend.

"Has Sarah relented?" I asked.

"She's feeling sick."

"Oh?"

"God knows," he said. "I hope not. I don't want a kid yet. She isn't overdue or anything."

"She's a nice girl," I said.

95

He slid me a glance. "She says she's got nothing against you personally."

"But," I said.

He nodded. "The mother-hen syndrome."

"Wouldn't have cast you as a chick."

He put down his knife and fork. "Nor would I, by God. I told her to cheer up and get this little enterprise over as soon as possible and face the fact she hadn't married a marshmallow."

"And she said?"

He gave a twisted grin. "From my performance in bed last night, that she had."

I wondered idly about the success or otherwise of their sex life. From the testimony of one or two past girls who had let their hair down to me while waiting hours in the flat for Jik's unpredictable return, he was a moody lover, quick to arousal and easily put off. "It only takes a dog barking, and he's gone." Not much, I dared say, had changed.

"Anyway," he said. "There's this car we've got. Damned silly if you didn't come with us to the races."

"Would Sarah," I asked carefully, ". . . scowl?"

"She says not."

I accepted this offer and inwardly sighed. It looked as if he wouldn't take the smallest step henceforth without the nod from Sarah. When the wildest ones got married, was it always like that? Wedded bliss putting nets over the eagles.

"Where did you get to last night?" he said.

"Aladdin's cave," I said. "Treasures galore and damned lucky to escape the boiling oil."

I told him about the gallery, the Munnings, and my brief moment of captivity. I told him what I thought of the burglaries. It pleased him. His eyes gleamed with humor and familiar excitement rose.

"How are we going to prove it?" he said.

He heard the "we" as soon as he said it. He laughed ruefully, the fizz dying away. "Well, how?"

"Don't know yet."

"I'd like to help," he said apologetically.

I thought of a dozen sarcastic replies and stifled the lot. It was I who was the one out of step, not they. The voice of the past had no right to break up the future.

"You'll do what pleases Sarah," I said with finality, and as an order, not a prodding satire.

"Don't sound so bloody bossy."

We finished breakfast amicably trying to build a suitable new relationship on the ruins of the old, and both knowing well what we were about.

When I met them later in the hall at setting-off time, it was clear that Sarah, too, had made a reassessment and put her mind to work on her emotions. She greeted me with an attempted smile and an outstretched hand. I shook the hand lightly and also gave her a token kiss on the cheek. She took it as it was meant.

Truce made, terms agreed, pact signed. Jik the mediator stood around looking smug.

"Take a look at him," he said, flapping a hand in my direction. "The complete stockbroker. Suit, tie, leather shoes. If he isn't careful, they'll have him in the Royal Academy."

Sarah looked bewildered. "I thought that was an honor."

"It depends," said Jik, sneering happily. "Passable artists with polished social graces get elected in their thirties. Masters with average social graces in their forties; masters with no social graces in their fifties. Geniuses who don't give a damn about being elected are ignored as long as possible."

"Putting Todd in the first category and yourself in the last?" Sarah said.

"Of course."

"Stands to reason," I said. "You never hear about Young Masters. Masters are always Old."

"For God's sake," Sarah said. "Let's go to the races."

We went slowly, on account of a continuous stream of traffic going the same way. The car park at Flemington Racecourse, when we arrived, looked like a giant picnic ground, with hundreds of full-scale lunch parties going on between the cars. Tables, chairs, cloths, china, silver, glass. Sun umbrellas optimistically raised in defiance of the rain clouds threatening above. A lot of gaiety and booze and a giant overall statement that "This Was the Life."

To my mild astonishment, Jik and Sarah had come prepared. They whipped out table, chairs, drinks, and food from the rented car's boot and said it was easy when you knew how, you just ordered the whole works.

"I have an uncle," Sarah said, "who holds the title of

Fastest Bar in the West. It takes him roughly ten seconds from putting the brakes on to pouring the first drink."

She was really trying, I thought. Not just putting up with an arrangement for Jik's sake, but actually trying to make it work. If it was an effort, it didn't show. She was wearing an interesting olive-green linen coat, with a broad-brimmed hat of the same color, which she held on from time to time against little gusts of wind. Overall, a new Sarah, prettier, more relaxed, less afraid.

"Champagne?" Jik offered, popping the cork. "Steak and oyster pie?"

"How will I go back to cocoa and chips?"

"Fatter."

We demolished the goodies, repacked the boot, and, with a sense of taking part in some vast semireligious ritual, squeezed along with the crowd through the gate to the Holy of Holies.

"It'll be much worse than this on Tuesday," observed Sarah, who had been to these junkets several times in the past. "Melbourne Cup Day is a public holiday. The city has three million inhabitants and half of them will try to get here." She was shouting above the crowd noises and holding grimly on to her hat against the careless buffeting all around.

"If they've got any sense, they'll stay home and watch it on the box," I said breathlessly, receiving a hefty kidney punch from the elbow of a man fighting his way into a can of beer.

"It won't be on the television in Melbourne, only on the radio."

"Good grief. Whyever not?"

"Because they want everyone to come. It's televised all over the rest of Australia, but not on its own doorstep."

"Same with the golf and the cricket," Jik said with a touch of gloom. "And you can't even have a decent bet on those."

We went through the bottleneck and, by virtue of the inherited badges, through a second gate and round into the calmer waters of the green oblong of Members' lawn. Much like on many a Derby Day at home, I thought. Same triumph of will over weather. Bright faces under gray skies. Warm coats over the pretty silks, umbrellas at the ready for the occasional top hat. When I painted pictures of racegoers in the rain, which I sometimes did, most people laughed. I never minded. I reckoned it meant they understood that the inner warmth of a pleasure couldn't be externally damped: that they, too, might play a trumpet in a thunderstorm.

Come to think of it, I thought, why didn't I paint a racegoer playing a trumpet in a thunderstorm? It might be symbolic enough even for Jik.

My friends were deep in a cross-talking assessment of the form of the first race. Sarah, it appeared, had a betting pedigree as long as her husband's, and didn't agree with him.

"I know it was soft going at Randwick last week. But it's pretty soft here, too, after all this rain, and he likes it on top."

"He was only beaten by Boyblue at Randwick, and Boyblue was out of sight in the Caulfield Cup."

"Please your silly self," Sarah said loftily. "But it's still too soft for Grapevine."

"Want to bet?" Jik asked me.

"Don't know the horses."

"As if that mattered."

"Right." I consulted the race card. "Two dollars on Generator."

They both looked him up, and they both said, "Why?"

"If in doubt, back number eleven. I once went nearly through the card on number eleven."

They made clucking and pooh-poohing noises and told me I could make a gift of my two dollars to the bookies or the T.A.B.

"The what?"

"Totalisator Agency Board."

The bookmakers, it seemed, were strictly on-course only, with no big firms as in England. All off-course betting shops were run by the T.A.B., which returned a good share of the lolly to racing. Racing was rich, rock-solid, and flourishing. Bully for Australia, Jik said.

We took our choice and paid our money, and Generator won at twenty-fives.

"Beginners' luck," Sarah said.

Jik laughed. "He's no beginner. He got kicked out of play school for running a book."

They tore up their tickets, set their minds to race two, and made expeditions to place their bets. I settled for four dollars on number one.

"Why?"

"Double my stake on half of eleven."

99

"Oh, God," said Sarah. "You're something else."

One of the more aggressive clouds started scattering rain, and the less hardy began to make for shelter.

"Come on," I said, "let's go and sit up there in the dry."

"You two go," Sarah said. "I can't."

"Why not?"

"Because those seats are only for men."

I laughed. I thought she was joking, but it appeared it was no joke. Very unfunny, in fact. About two-thirds of the best seats in the Members' stands were reserved for males.

"What about their wives and girl friends?" I said incredulously.

"They can go up on the roof."

Sarah, being Australian, saw nothing very odd in it. To me, and surely to Jik, it was ludicrous.

He said, with a carefully straight face, "On a lot of the bigger courses, the men who run Australian racing give themselves leather armchairs behind glass to watch from, and thick-carpeted restaurants and bars to eat and drink like kings in, and let their women eat in the cafeterias and sit on hard plastic chairs on the open stands among the rest of the crowd. They consider this behavior quite normal. All anthropological groups consider their most bizarre tribal customs quite normal."

"I thought you were in love with all things Australian."

Jik sighed heavily. "Nowhere's perfect."

"I'm getting wet," Sarah said.

We escalated to the roof, which had a proportion of two women to one man and was windy and damp, with bench seating.

"Don't worry about it," Sarah said amused at my aghastness on behalf of womankind. "I'm used to it."

"I thought this country made a big thing about equality for all."

"For all except half the population," Jik said.

We could see the whole race superbly from our eyrie. Sarah and Jik screamed encouragement to their fancies, but number one finished in front by two lengths, at eight to one.

"It's disgusting," said Sarah, tearing up more tickets. "What number do you fancy for the third?"

"I won't be with you for the third. I've got an appointment to have a drink with someone who knows Donald."

She took it in, and the lightness went out of her manner.

"More . . . investigating?"

"I have to."

"Yes." She swallowed and made a visible effort. "Well . . . good luck."

"You're a great girl."

She looked surprised that I should think so and suspicious that I was intending sarcasm, and also partly pleased. I returned earthward with her multiple expressions amusing my mind.

The Members' lawn was bounded on one long side by the stands and on the opposite side by the path taken by the horses on their way from the saddling boxes to the parade ring. One short side of the lawn lay alongside part of the parade ring itself; and it was at the corner of lawn where the horses' path reached the parade ring that I was to meet Hudson Taylor.

The rain had almost stopped, which was good news for my suit. I reached the appointed spot and stood there waiting, admiring the brilliant scarlet of the long bedful of flowers that lined the railing between horsewalk and lawn. Cadmium-red mixtures with highlights of orange and white and maybe a streak or two of expensive vermilion . . .

"Charles Todd?"

"Yes . . . Mr. Taylor?"

"Hudson. Glad to know you." He shook hands, his grip dry and firm. Late forties, medium height, comfortable build, with affable, slightly sad eyes sloping downward at the outer corners. He was one of the minority of men in morning suits, and he wore it as comfortably as a sweater.

"Let's find somewhere dry," he said. "Come this way."

He led me steadily up the bank of steps, in through an entrance door, down a wide interior corridor running the whole length of the stands, past a uniformed guard and a notice saying "Committee Only," and into a large square comfortable room fitted out as a small-scale bar. The journey had been one long polite push through expensively dressed cohorts, but the bar was comparatively quiet and empty. A group of four—two men, two women —stood chatting with half-filled glasses held close to their chests, and two women in furs were complaining loudly of the cold.

"They love to bring out the sables," Hudson Taylor said, chuckling, as he fetched two glasses of Scotch and gestured to me to sit by a small table. "Spoils their fun, the years it's hot for this meeting."

"Is it usually hot?"

"Melbourne's weather can change twenty degrees in an hour." He sounded proud of it. "Now, then, this business of yours." He delved into an inner breast pocket and surfaced with a folded paper. "Here you are, typed out for Donald. The gallery was called Yarra River Fine Arts."

I would have been astounded if it hadn't been.

"And the man we dealt with was someone called Ivor Wexford."

"What did he look like?" I asked.

"I don't remember very clearly. It was back in April, do you see?"

I thought briefly and pulled a small slim sketchbook out of my pocket.

"If I draw him, might you know him?"

He looked amused. "You never know."

I drew quickly in soft pencil a reasonable likeness of Greene, but without the mustache.

"Was it him?"

Hudson Taylor looked doubtful. I drew in the mustache. He shook his head decisively. "No, that wasn't him."

"How about this?"

I flipped over the page and started again. Hudson Taylor looked pensive as I did my best with the man from the basement office.

"Maybe," he said.

I made the lower lip fuller, added heavy-framed spectacles, and a bow tie with spots.

"That's him," said Hudson in surprise. "I remember the bow tie, anyway. You don't see many of those these days. How did you know? You must have met him."

"I walked round a couple of galleries yesterday afternoon."

"That's quite a gift you have there," he said with interest, watching me put the notebook away.

"Practice, that's all." Years of seeing people's faces as matters of shapes and proportions and planes, and remembering which way the lines slanted. I could already have drawn Hudson's eyes from memory. It was a knack I'd had from childhood.

"Sketching is your hobby?" Hudson asked.

"And my work. I mostly paint horses."

"Really?" He glanced at the equine portraits decorating the wall. "Like these?"

I nodded, and we talked a little about painting for a living.

"Maybe I can give you a commission, if my horse runs well in the Cup." He smiled, the outer edges of his eyes crinkling finely. "If he's down the field, I'll feel more like shooting him."

He stood up and gestured me to follow. "Time for the next race. Care to watch it with me?"

We emerged into daylight in the prime part of the stands, overlooking the big square enclosure that served for both parading the runners before the race and unsaddling the winners after. I was amused to see that the front rows of seats were all for men: two couples walking in front of us split like amoebas, the husbands going down left, the women up right.

"Down here," Hudson said, pointing.

"May we only go up there if accompanied by a lady?" I asked.

He glanced at me sideways, and smiled. "You find our ways odd? We'll go up, by all means."

He led the way and settled comfortably among the predominantly female company, greeting several people and introducing me companionably as his friend Charles from England. Instant first names, instant acceptance, Australian-style.

"Regina hated all this division of the sexes, poor lass," he said. "But it has interesting historical roots." He chuckled. "Australia was governed nearly all last century with the help of the British Army. The officers and gentlemen left their wives back in England, but such is nature, they all set up liaisons here with women of low repute. They didn't want their fellow officers to see the vulgarity of their choice, so they invented a rule that the officers' enclosures were for men only, which effectively silenced their popsies' pleas to be taken."

I laughed. "Very neat."

"It's easier to establish a tradition," Hudson said, "than to get rid of it."

"You're establishing a great tradition for fine wines, Donald says."

The sad-looking eyes twinkled with civilized pleasure.

"He was most enthusiastic. He traveled round all the big vineyards, of course, besides visiting us."

The horses for the third race cantered away to the start, led by a fractious chestnut colt with too much white about his head.

"Ugly brute," Hudson said. "But he'll win."

"Are you backing it?"

He smiled. "I've a little bit on."

The race started and the field sprinted, and Hudson's knuckles whitened so much from his grip as he gazed intently through his binoculars that I wondered just how big the little bit was. The chestnut colt was beaten into fourth place. Hudson put his race glasses down slowly and watched the unsatisfactory finish with a blank expression.

"Oh, well," he said, his sad eyes looking even sadder. "Always another day." He shrugged resignedly, cheered up, shook my hand, told me to remember him to Donald, and asked if I could find my own way out.

"Thank you for your help," I said.

He smiled. "Anytime. Anytime."

With only a couple of wrong turnings, I reached ground level, listening on the way to fascinating snippets of Australian conversation.

". . . They say he's an embarrassment as a Committee man. He only opens his mouth to change feet. . . ."

". . . a beastly stomach wog, so he couldn't come . . ."

". . . told him to stop whingeing like a bloody Pommy, and get on with it . . ."

". . . won twenty dollars? Good on yer, Joanie. . . ."

And everywhere the diphthong vowels that gave the word "No" about five separate sounds, defying my attempts to copy it. I'd been told on the flight over, by an Australian, that all Australians spoke with one single accent. It was about as true as saying all Americans spoke alike, or all British. English was infinitely elastic; and alive, well, and living in Melbourne.

Jik and Sarah, when I rejoined them, were arguing about their fancies for the Victoria Derby, next race on the card.

"Ivory Ball is out of his class and has as much chance as a blind man in a blizzard."

Sarah ignored this. "He won three days ago at Moonee Valley and two of the tipsters pick him."

"Those tipsters must have been drunk."

"Hello, Todd," Sarah said. "Pick a number, for God's sake."

"Ten."

"Why ten?"

"Eleven minus one."

"Jesus," Jik said. "You used to have more sense."

Sarah looked it up. "Royal Road. Compared with Royal Road, Ivory Ball's a certainty."

We bought our tickets and went up to the roof, and none of our bets came up. Sarah disgustedly yelled at Ivory Ball, who at least managed fifth, but Royal Road fell entirely by the wayside. The winner was number twelve.

"You should have *added* eleven and one," Sarah said. "You make such silly mistakes."

"What are you staring at?" Jik said.

I was looking attentively down at the crowd that had watched the race from ground level on the Members' lawn.

"Lend me your race glasses."

Jik handed them over. I raised them, took a long look, and slowly put them down.

"What is it?" Sarah said anxiously. "What's the matter?"

"That," I said, "has not only torn it, but ripped the bloody works apart."

"What has?"

"Do you see those two men . . . about twenty yards along from the parade-ring railing . . . one of them in a gray morning suit?"

"What about them?" Jik said.

"The man in the morning suit is Hudson Taylor, the man I just had a drink with. He's the managing director of a wine-making firm, and he saw a lot of my cousin Donald when he was over here. And the other man is called Ivor Wexford, and he's the manager of the Yarra River Fine Arts gallery."

"So what?" Sarah said.

"So I can just about imagine the conversation that's going on down there," I said. "Something like 'Excuse me, sir, but didn't I sell a picture to you recently?' 'Not to me, Mr. Wexford, but to my friend Donald Stuart.' 'And who was that young man I saw you talking to just now?' 'That was Donald Stuart's cousin, Mr. Wexford.' 'And what do you know about him?' 'That he's a painter by trade and drew a picture of you, Mr. Wexford, and asked me for your name.' "

I stopped. "Go on," Jik said.

I watched Wexford and Hudson Taylor stop talking, nod casually to each other, and walk their separate ways.

"Ivor Wexford now knows he made a horrible mistake in letting me out of his gallery last night."

Sarah looked searchingly at my face. "You really do think that's very serious."

"Yes, I really do." I loosened a few tightened muscles and tried a smile. "At the least, he'll be on his guard."

"And at the most," Jik said, "he'll come looking for you."

"Er . . ." I said thoughtfully. "What do either of you feel about a spot of instant travel?"

"Where to?"

"Alice Springs?" I said.

CHAPTER 9

Jik complained all the way to the airport on various counts. One, that he would be missing the cricket. Two, that I hadn't let him go back to the Hilton for his paints. Three, that his Derby clothes would be too hot in Alice. Four, that he wasn't missing the Melbourne Cup for any little ponce with a bow tie.

None of the colorful gripes touched on the fact that he was paying for all our fares with his credit card, as I had left my traveler's checks in the hotel.

It had been Sarah's idea not to go back there.

"If we're going to vanish, let's get on with it," she said. "It's running back into fires for handbags that gets people burnt."

"You don't have to come," I said tentatively.

"We've been through all that. What do you think the rest of my life would be like if I stopped Jik helping you and you came to grief?"

"You'd never forgive me."

She smiled ruefully. "You're dead right."

As far as I could tell, we had left the race course unobserved, and certainly no one car had followed us to the airport. Neither Greene nor the boy non-artist appeared underfoot to trip us up, and we traveled uneventfully on a half-full aircraft on the first leg to Adelaide, and an even emptier one from there to Alice Springs.

The country beneath us from Adelaide northward turned gradually from fresh green to gray green, and finally to a fierce brick red.

"GABA," said Jik, pointing downward.

"What?"

"GABA," he said. "GABA. Stands for Great Australian Bugger All."

I laughed. The land did indeed look baked, deserted, and older than time, but there were tracklike roads here and there, and incredibly isolated homesteads. I watched in fascination until it grew dark, the purple shadows rushing in like a tide as we swept north into the central wastelands.

The night air at Alice was hot, as if someone had forgotten to switch off the oven. The luck that had presented us with an available flight as soon as we reached Melbourne Airport seemed still to be functioning: a taciturn taxi-driver took us straight to a new-looking motel, which proved to have room for us.

"The season is over," he grunted when we congratulated and thanked him. "It will soon be too hot for tourists."

Our rooms were air-conditioned, however. Jik and Sarah's was down on the ground floor, their door opening directly onto a shady covered walk that bordered a small garden with a pool. Mine, in an adjacent wing across the car park, was two tall floors up, reached by an outside tree-shaded staircase and a long open gallery. The whole place looked greenly peaceful in the scattered spotlights that shone unobtrusively from palms and gums.

The motel restaurant had closed for the night at eight o'clock, so we walked along the main street to another. The road surface itself was tarmacadamed, but some of the side roads were not, nor were the footpaths uniformly paved. Often enough we were walking on bare fine grit, and we could see from the dust haze in the headlights of passing cars that the grit was bright red.

"Bull dust," Sarah said. "I've never seen it before. My aunt swore it got inside her locked trunk once when she and my uncle drove out to Ayers Rock."

"What's Ayers Rock?" I said.

"Ignorant Pommy," Sarah said. "It's a chunk of sandstone two miles long and a third of a mile high left behind by some careless glacier in the ice age."

"Miles out in the desert," Jik added. "A place of ancient magic regularly desecrated by the plastic society."

"Have you been there?" I asked dryly.

He grinned. "Nope."

"What difference does that make?" Sarah asked.

"He means," Jik said, "our pompous friend here means that one shouldn't make judgments from afar."

"You haven't actually got to be swallowed by a shark before you believe it's got sharp teeth," Sarah said. "You can believe what other people see."

"It depends from where they're looking."

"Facts are not judgments, and judgments are not facts," Jik said. "A bit of Todd's Law from way back."

Sarah gave me a glance. "Have you got iced water in that head?"

"Emotion is a rotten base for politics. He used to say that, too," Jik said. "Envy is the root of all evil. What have I left out?"

"The most damaging lies are told by those who believe they're true."

"There you are," Jik said. "A pity you can't paint."

"Thanks very much."

We reached the restaurant and ate a meal of such excellence as to wonder at the organization it took to bring every item of food and clothing and everyday life to an expanding town of thirteen and a half thousand inhabitants surrounded by hundreds of miles of desert in every direction.

"It was started here, a hundred years ago, as a relay station for sending cables across Australia," Sarah said. "And now they're bouncing messages off the stars."

Jik said, "Bet the messages aren't worth the technology. Think of 'See you Friday, Ethel,' chattering round the eternal spheres."

With instructions from the restaurant, we walked back a different way and sought out the Yarra River Fine Arts gallery, Alice Springs variety.

It was located in a paved shopping arcade closed to traffic, one of several prosperous-looking boutiques. There were no lights on in the gallery, nor in the other shops. From what we could see in the single dim streetlight, the merchandise in the gallery window consisted of two bright orange landscapes of desert scenes.

"Crude," said Jik, whose own colors were not noted for pastel subtlety.

"The whole place," he said, "will be full of local copies of Albert Namatjira. Tourists buy them by the ton."

We strolled back to the motel more companionably than at any time since my arrival. Maybe the desert distances all around us invoked their own peace. At any rate, when I kissed Sarah's cheek to say good night, it was no longer as a sort of pact, as in the morning, but with affection.

At breakfast she said, "You'll never guess. The main street here is Todd Street. So is the river. Todd River."

"Such is fame," I said modestly.

"And there are eleven art galleries."

"She's been reading the Alice Springs Tourist Promotion Association Inc.'s handout," Jik explained.

"There's also a Chinese takeaway."

Jik made a face. "Just imagine all this lot dumped down in the middle of the Sahara."

The daytime heat, in fact, was fierce. The radio was cheerfully forecasting a noon temperature of thirty-nine, which was a hundred and two in the old Fahrenheit shade. The single step from a cool room to the sun-roasting balcony was a sensuous pleasure, but the walk to the Yarra River gallery, though less than half a mile, was surprisingly exhausting.

"I suppose one would get used to it if one lived here," Jik said. "Thank God Sarah's got her hat."

We dodged in and out of the shadows of overhanging trees, and the local inhabitants marched around bareheaded as if the branding iron in the sky were pointing another way. The Yarra River gallery was quiet and air-conditioned and provided chairs near the entrance for flaked-out visitors.

As Jik had prophesied, all visible space was knee-deep in the hard clear watercolor paintings typical of the disciples of Namatjira. They were fine if you liked that sort of thing, which on the whole I didn't. I preferred the occasional fuzzy outline, indistinct edge, shadows encroaching, suggestion, impression, and ambiguity. Namatjira, given his due as the first and greatest of the Aboriginal artists, had had a vision as sharp as a diamond. I vaguely remembered reading somewhere that he'd produced more than two thousand paintings himself, and certainly his influence on the town where he'd been born

110

had been extraordinary. Eleven art galleries. Mecca for artists. Tourists buying pictures by the ton. He had died, a plaque on the wall said, in Alice Springs Hospital on August 8, 1959.

We had been wandering around for a good five minutes before anyone came. Then the plastic-strip curtain over a recessed doorway parted, and the gallery-keeper came gently through.

"See anything you fancy?" he said.

His voice managed to convey an utter boredom with tourists and a feeling that we should pay up quickly and go away. He was small, languid, long-haired, and pale, and had large dark eyes with tired-looking lids. About the same age as Jik and myself, though a lot less robust.

"Do you have any other pictures?" I asked.

He glanced at our clothes. Jik and I wore the trousers and shirts in which we'd gone to the races: no ties and no jackets, but more promising to picture-sellers than denims. Without discernible enthusiasm, he held back half of the strip curtain, inviting us to go through.

"In here," he said.

The inner room was bright from skylights, and its walls were almost entirely covered with dozens of pictures that hung closely together. Our eyes opened wide. At first sight we were surrounded by an incredible feast of Dutch interiors, French Impressionists, and Gainsborough portraits. At second blink one could see that although they were original oil paintings, they were basically second rate. The sort sold as "school of" because the artists hadn't bothered to sign them.

"All European, in this room," the gallery-keeper said. He still sounded bored. He wasn't Australian, I thought. Nor British. Maybe American. Difficult to tell.

"Do you have any pictures of horses?" I asked.

He gave me a long steady gaze. "Yes, we do, but this month we are displaying works by native Australians and lesser Europeans." His voice had the faintest of lisps. "If you wish to see horse paintings, they are in racks through there." He pointed to a second plastic-strip curtain directly opposite the first. "Are you looking for anything in particular?"

I murmured the names of some of the Australians whose work I had seen in Melbourne. There was a slight brightening of the lackluster eyes.

"Yes, we do have a few by those artists."

He led us through the second curtain into the third and, from our point of view, most interesting room. Half of it, as promised, was occupied by well-filled double tiers of racks. The other half was the office and packing and framing department. Directly ahead, a glass door led out to a dusty parched-looking garden, but most of the lighting in here, too, came from the roof.

Beside the glass door stood an easel bearing a small canvas with its back toward us. Various unmistakable signs showed work currently in progress and recently interrupted.

"Your own effort?" asked Jik inquisitively, walking over for a look.

The pale gallery-keeper made a fluttering movement with his hand as if he would have stopped Jik if he could, and something in Jik's expression attracted me to his side like a magnet.

A chestnut horse, three-quarters view, its elegant head raised as if listening. In the background, the noble lines of a mansion. The rest, a harmonious composition of trees and meadow. The painting, as far as I could judge, was more or less finished.

"That's great," I said with enthusiasm. "Is that for sale? I'd like to buy that."

After the briefest hesitation he said, "Sorry. That's commissioned."

"What a pity! Couldn't you sell me that one, and paint another?"

He gave me a small regretful smile. "I'm afraid not."

"Do tell me your name," I said earnestly.

He was unwillingly flattered. "Harley Renbo."

"Is there anything else of yours here?"

He gestured toward the racks. "One or two. The horse paintings are all in the bottom row, against the wall."

We all three of us pulled out the paintings one by one, making amateur-type comments.

"That's nice," said Sarah, holding a small picture of a fat gray pony with two old-fashioned country boys. "Do you like that?" She showed it to Jik and me.

We looked at it.

"Very nice," I said kindly.

Jik turned away as if uninterested. Harley Renbo stood motionless.

"Oh, well," Sarah said, shrugging. "I just thought it looked nice." She put it back in the rack and pulled out the next. "How about this mare and foal? I think this is pretty."

Jik could hardly bear it. "Sentimental tosh," he said.

Sarah looked downcast. "It may not be Art, but I like it."

We found one with a flourishing signature: Harley Renbo. Large canvas, varnished, unframed.

"Ah," I said appreciatively. "Yours."

Harley Renbo inclined his head. Jik, Sarah, and I gazed at his acknowledged work.

Derivative Stubbs-type. Elongated horses set in a Capability Brown landscape. Composition fair, anatomy poor, execution good, originality nil.

"Great," I said. "Where did you paint it?"

"Oh . . . here."

"From memory?" Sarah said admiringly. "How clever."

Harley Renbo, at our urging, brought out two more examples of his work. Neither was better than the first, but one was a great deal smaller.

"How much is this?" I asked.

Jik glanced at me sharply, but kept quiet.

Harley Renbo mentioned a sum that had me shaking my head at once.

"Awfully sorry," I said. "I like your work, but . . ."

The haggling continued politely for quite a long time, but we came to the usual conclusion, higher than the buyer wanted, lower than the painter hoped. Jik resignedly lent his credit card, and we bore our trophy away.

"Jesus Christ," Jik exploded when we were safely out of earshot. "You could paint better than that when you were in your cradle. Why the hell did you want to buy that rubbish?"

"Because," I said contendedly, "Harley Renbo is the copier."

"But this"—Jik pointed to the parcel under my arm—"is his own abysmal original work."

"Like fingerprints?" Sarah said. "You can check other things he paints against this?"

"Got brains, my wife," Jik said. "But that picture he wouldn't sell was nothing like any Munnings I've ever seen."

"You never look at horse paintings if you can help it."

"I've seen more of your pathetic daubs than I care to."

"How about Raoul Millais?" I said.

"Jesus."

We walked along the scorching street almost without feeling it.

"I don't know about you two," Sarah said, "but I'm going to buy a bikini and spend the rest of the day in the pool."

We all bought swimming things, changed into them, splashed around for ages, and laid ourselves out on towels to dry. It was peaceful and quiet in the shady little garden. We were the only people there.

"That picture of a pony and two boys that you thought was nice," I said to Sarah.

"Well, it was," she repeated defensively. "I liked it."

"It was a Munnings."

She sat up abruptly on her towel.

"Whyever didn't you say so?"

"I was waiting for our friend Renbo to tell us, but he didn't."

"A real one?" Sarah asked. "Or a copy?"

"Real," Jik said, with his eyes shut against the sun dappling through palm leaves.

I nodded lazily. "I thought so, too," I said. "An old painting. Munnings had that gray pony for years when he was young, and painted it dozens of times. It's the same one you saw in Sydney in 'The Coming Storm.'"

"You two do know a lot," Sarah said, sighing and lying down again.

"Engineers know all about nuts and bolts," Jik said. "Do we get lunch in this place?"

I looked at my watch. Nearly two o'clock. "I'll go and ask," I said.

I put shirt and trousers on over my sun-dried trunks and ambled from the outdoor heat into the refrigerated air of the lobby. No lunch, said the reception desk. We could buy lunch nearby at a takeaway and eat in the garden. Drink? Same thing. Buy your own at a bottle shop. There was an ice-making machine and plastic glasses just outside the door to the pool.

"Thanks," I said.

"You're welcome."

I looked at the ice-making machine on the way out. Beside it swung a neat notice: "We don't swim in your toilet. Please don't pee in our pool." I laughed across to Jik and Sarah, and told them the food situation.

"I'll go and get it," I said. "What do you want?"

Anything, they said.

"And drink?"

"Cinzano," Sarah said, and Jik nodded. "Dry white."

"O.K."

I picked up my room key from the grass and set off to collect some cash for shopping. Walked along to the tree-shaded outside staircase, went up two stories, and turned onto the blazing hot balcony.

There was a man walking along it toward me, about my own height, build, and age; and I heard someone else coming up the stairs at my back.

Thought nothing of it. Motel guests like me. What else?

I was totally unprepared both for the attack itself, and for its ferocity.

CHAPTER 10

They simply walked up to me, one from in front, one from behind.

They reached me together. They sprang into action like cats. They snatched the dangling room key out of my hand.

The struggle, if you could call it that, lasted less than five seconds. Between them, with Jik's type of strength, they simply picked me up by my legs and armpits and threw me over the balcony.

It probably takes a very short time to fall two stories. I found it long enough for thinking that my body, which was still whole, was going to be smashed. That disaster, not yet reached, was inevitable. Very odd, and very nasty.

What I actually hit first was one of the young trees growing round the staircase. Its boughs bent and broke, and I crashed on through them to the hard driveway beneath.

The monstrous impact was like being wiped out. Like fusing electrical circuits. A flash into chaos. I lay in a semiconscious daze, not knowing if I was alive or dead.

I felt warm. Simply a feeling, not a thought.

I wasn't aware of anything else at all. I couldn't move

any muscle. Couldn't remember I had muscles to move. I felt like pulp.

It was ten minutes, Jik told me later, before he came looking for me; and he came only because he wanted to ask me to buy a lemon to go with the Cinzano, if I had not gone already.

"Jesus Christ Almighty," Jik's voice, low and horrified, near my ear.

I heard him clearly. The words made sense.

I'm alive, I thought. I think, therefore I exist.

Eventually I opened my eyes. The light was brilliant. Blinding. There was no one where Jik's voice had been. Perhaps I'd imagined it. No, I hadn't. The world began coming back fast, very sharp and clear.

I knew also that I hadn't imagined the fall. I knew, with increasing insistence, that I hadn't broken my neck and hadn't broken my back. Sensation, which had been crushed out, came flooding back with vigor from every insulted tissue. It wasn't so much a matter of which bits of me hurt as of finding out which didn't. I remembered hitting the tree. Remembered the ripping of its branches. I felt both torn to shreds and pulverized. Frightfully jolly.

After a while I heard Jik's voice returning. "He's alive," he said, "and that's about all."

"It's impossible for anyone to fall off our balcony. It's more than waist high." The voice of the receptionist desk, sharp with anger and anxiety. A bad business for motels, people falling off their balconies.

"Don't . . . panic," I said. It sounded a bit croaky.

"Todd!" Sarah appeared, kneeling on the ground and looking pale.

"If you give me time," I said, ". . . I'll fetch . . . the Cinzano." How much time? A million years should be enough.

"You sod," Jik said, standing at my feet and staring down. "You gave us a shocking fright." He was holding a broken-off branch of tree.

"Sorry."

"Get up, then."

"Yeah . . . in a minute."

"Shall I cancel the ambulance?" said the reception desk hopefully.

"No," I said. "I think I'm bleeding."

Alice Springs Hospital, even on a Sunday, was as efficient as one would expect from a Flying Doctor base. They investigated and X-rayed and stitched, and presented me with a list.

One broken shoulder blade. (Left).
Two broken ribs. (Left side. No lung puncture).
Large contusion, left side of head. (No skull fracture).
Four jagged tears in skin of trunk, thigh, and left leg. (Stitched).
Several other small cuts.
Grazes and contusions on practically all of left side of body.

"Thanks," I said, sighing.
"Thank the tree. You'd've been in a right mess if you'd missed it."
They suggested I stop there for the rest of the day and also all night. Better, they said, a little too meaningfully.
"O.K.," I said resignedly. "Are my friends still here?"
They were. In the waiting room. Arguing over my near-dead body about the favorite for the Melbourne Cup.
"Newshound *stays*—"
"Stays in the same place . . ."
"Jesus," Jik said as I shuffled stiffly in. "He's on his feet."
"Yeah." I perched gingerly on the arm of a chair, feeling a bit like a mummy, wrapped in bandages from neck to waist, with my left arm totally immersed, as it were, and anchored firmly inside.
"Don't damn well laugh," I said.
"No one but a raving lunatic would fall off that balcony," Jik said.
"Mmm," I agreed. "I was pushed."
Their mouths opened like landed fish. I told them exactly what had happened.
"Who were they?" Jik said.
"I don't know. Never seen them before. They didn't introduce themselves."
Sarah said, definitely, "You must tell the police."
"Yes," I said. "But . . . I don't know your procedures here, or what the police are like. I wondered . . . if you would explain to the hospital, and start things rolling in an orderly and unsensational manner."

"Sure," she said, "if anything about being pushed off a balcony could be considered orderly and unsensational."

"They took my room key first," I said. "Would you see if they've pinched my wallet?"

They stared at me in awakening unwelcome awareness.

I nodded. "Or that picture," I said.

Two policemen came, listened, took notes, and departed. Very noncommittal. Nothing like that had happened in The Alice before. The locals wouldn't have done it. The town had a constant stream of visitors, so, by the law of averages, some would be muggers. I gathered that there would have been much more fuss if I'd been dead. Their downbeat attitude suited me fine.

By the time Jik and Sarah came back, I'd been given a bed, climbed into it, and felt absolutely rotten. Shivering. Cold deep inside. Gripped by the system's aggrieved reaction to the injury—or, in other words, shock.

"They did take the painting," Jik said. "And your wallet as well."

"And the gallery's shut," Sarah said. "The girl in the boutique opposite said she saw Harley close early today, but she didn't see him actually leave, as he goes out the back way, because he parks his car there."

"The police've been to the motel," Jik said. "We told them about the picture being missing, but I don't think they'll do much more about it unless you tell them the whole story."

"I'll think about it," I said.

"So what do we do now?" Sarah asked.

"Well . . . there's no point in staying here any more. Tomorrow we'll go back to Melbourne."

"Thank God," she said, smiling widely. "I thought you were going to want us to miss the Cup."

In spite of a battery of pills and various ministering angels, I spent a viciously uncomfortable and wide-awake night. Unable to lie flat. Feverishly hot on the pendulum from shock. Throbbing in fifteen places. Every little movement screechingly sticky, like an engine without oil. No wonder the hospital had told me it would be better to stay.

I counted my blessings until daybreak. It could have been so very much worse.

119

What was most alarming was not the murderous nature of the attackers, but the speed with which they'd found us. I'd known ever since I'd seen Regina's head that the directing mind was ruthlessly violent. The acts of the team always reflected the nature of the boss. A less savage attitude would have left Regina gagged and bound, not brutally dead.

I had to conclude that it was chiefly this pervading callousness which had led to my being thrown over the balcony. As a positive means of murder, it was too chancy. It was quite possible to survive a fall from such a height, even without a cushioning tree. The two men had not, as far as I could remember, bothered to see whether I was alive or dead, and they had not, while I lay half unconscious and immobile, come along to finish the job.

So it had either been simply a shattering way of getting rid of me while they robbed my room, or they'd had the deliberate intention of injuring me so badly that I would have to stop poking my nose into their affairs.

Or both.

And how had they found us?

I puzzled over it for some time but could arrive at no definite answer. It seemed most likely that Wexford or Greene had telephoned from Melbourne and told Harley Renbo to be on his guard in case I turned up. Even the panic that would have followed the realization that I'd seen the Munnings and the fresh Millais copy, and actually carried away a specimen of Renbo's work, could not have transported two toughs from Melbourne to Alice Springs in the time available.

There had only been about four hours between purchase and attack, and some of that would have had to be spent on finding out which motel we were in, and which rooms, and waiting for me to go upstairs from the pool.

Perhaps we had, after all, been followed all the way from Flemington Racecourse, or traced from the airplane passenger lists. But if that was the case, surely Renbo would have been warned we were on our way, and would never have let us see what we had.

I gave it up. I didn't even know if I would recognize my attackers again if I saw them. Certainly not the one who had been behind me, because I hadn't had a single straight look at him.

They could, though, reasonably believe they had done

a good job of putting me out of action; and indeed, if I had any sense, they had.

If they wanted time, what for?

To tighten up their security, and cover their tracks, so that any investigation I might persuade the police to make into a paintings-robbery link would come up against the most respectable of brick walls.

Even if they knew I'd survived, they would not expect any action from me in the immediate future; therefore the immediate future was the best time to act.

Right.

Easy enough to convince my brain. From the neck down, a different story.

Jik and Sarah didn't turn up until eleven, and I was still in bed. Sitting up, but not exactly perky.

"God," Sarah said. "You look much worse than yesterday."

"So kind."

"You're never going to make it to Melbourne." She sounded despondent. "So goodbye, Cup."

"Nothing to stop you going," I said.

She stood beside the bed. "Do you expect us just to leave you here—like this—and go and enjoy ourselves?"

"Why not?"

"Don't be so bloody stupid."

Jik sprawled in a visitor's chair. "It isn't our responsibility if he gets himself thrown from heights," he said.

Sarah whirled on him. "How *can* you say such a thing?"

"We don't want to be involved," Jik said.

I grinned. Sarah heard the sardonic echo of what she'd said so passionately herself only three days ago. She flung out her arms in exasperated realization.

"You absolutely bloody beast," she said.

Jik smiled like a cream-fed cat. "We went round to the gallery," he said. "It's still shut. We also found our way round into the back garden, and looked in through the glass door, and you can guess what we saw."

"Nothing."

"Dead right. No easel with imitation Millais. Everything dodgy carefully hidden out of sight. Everything else respectable and normal."

I shifted a bit to relieve one lot of aches, and set up protests from another. "Even if you'd got in, I doubt if you'd've found anything dodgy. I'll bet everything the

121

least bit incriminating disappeared yesterday afternoon."

Jik nodded. "Sure to."

Sarah said, "We asked the girl in the reception desk at the motel if anyone had been asking for us."

"And they had?"

She nodded. "A man telephoned. She thought it was soon after ten o'clock. He asked if a Mr. Charles Todd was staying there with two friends, and when she said yes, he asked for your room number. He said he had something to deliver to you."

"Christ." Some delivery. Express. Downward.

"She told him the room number but said if he left the package at the desk, she would see you got it."

"He must have laughed."

"He wouldn't have that much sense of humor," Jik said.

"Soon after ten?" I said, considering.

"While we were out," Sarah said, nodding. "It must have been fairly soon after we'd left the gallery . . . and while we were buying the swimming things."

"Why didn't the girl tell us someone had been inquiring for us?"

"She went off for a coffee break, and didn't see us when we came back. And after that, she forgot. She hadn't anyway thought it of any importance."

"There aren't all that many motels in Alice," Jik said. "It wouldn't have taken long to find us, once they knew we were in the town. I suppose the Melbourne lot telephoned Renbo, and that set the bomb ticking."

"I guess."

"They must have been apoplectic when they heard you'd bought that picture."

"I wish I'd hidden it," I said. The words reminded me of Maisie, who had hidden her picture and had her house burned.

Sarah sighed. "Well . . . what are we going to do?"

"Last chance to go home," I said.

"Are you going?" she demanded.

I listened briefly to the fierce plea from my battered shell, and I thought, too, of Donald in his cold house. I didn't actually answer her at all.

She listened to my silence. "Quite," she said. "So what do we do next?"

"Well . . ." I said. "First of all, tell the girl in the reception desk at the motel that I'm in a pretty poor state and likely to be in hospital for at least a week."

"No exaggeration," Jik murmured.

"Tell her it's O.K. to pass on that news, if anyone inquires. Tell her you're leaving for Melbourne, pay all our bills, confirm your bookings on the afternoon flight, and cancel mine, and make a normal exit to the airport on the airport bus."

"But what about you?" Sarah said. "When will you be fit to go?"

"With you," I said. "If between you you can think of some unobtrusive way of getting a bandaged mummy onto an airplane without anyone noticing."

"Jesus," Jik said. He looked delighted. "I'll do that."

"Telephone the airport and book a seat for me under a different name."

"Right."

"Buy me a shirt and some trousers. Mine are in the dustbin."

"It shall be done."

"And reckon all the time that you may be watched."

"Put on sad faces, do you mean?" Sarah said.

I grinned. "I'd be honored."

"And after we get to Melbourne, what then?" Jik said.

I chewed my lip. "I think we'll have to go back to the Hilton. All our clothes are there, not to mention my passport and money. We don't know if Wexford and Greene ever knew we were staying there, so it may well be a hundred percent safe. And anyway, where else in Melbourne are we likely to get beds on the night before the Melbourne Cup?"

"If you get thrown out of the Hilton's windows, you won't be alive to tell the tale," he said cheerfully.

"They don't open far enough," I said. "It's impossible."

"How reassuring."

"And tomorrow," Sarah said. "What about tomorrow?"

Hesitantly, with a pause or two, I outlined what I had in mind for Cup Day. When I had finished, they were both silent.

"So now," I said. "Do you want to go home?"

Sarah stood up. "We'll talk it over," she said soberly. "We'll come back and let you know."

Jik stood also, but I knew from the jut of his beard which way he'd vote. It had been he who'd chosen the bad-weather routes we'd taken into the Atlantic and the North Sea. At heart he was more reckless than I.

They came back at two o'clock lugging a large fruit-shop carrier with a bottle of Scotch and a pineapple sticking out of the top.

"Provisions for hospitalized friend," said Jik, whisking them out and putting them on the end of the bed. "How do you feel?"

"With every nerve ending."

"You don't say. Well, Sarah says we go ahead."

I looked searchingly at her face. Her dark eyes stared steadily back, giving assent without joy. There was no antagonism, but no excitement. She was committed, but from determination, not conviction.

"O.K.," I said.

"Item," said Jik, busy with the carrier, "one pair of medium gray trousers. One light blue cotton shirt."

"Great."

"You won't be wearing those, though, until you get to Melbourne. For leaving Alice Springs, we bought something else."

I saw the amusement in both their faces. I said with misgiving, "What else?"

With rising glee, they laid out what they had brought for my unobtrusive exit from Alice Springs.

Which was how I came to stroll around the little airport, in the time gap between signing in and boarding, with the full attention of everyone in the place. Wearing faded jeans cut off and busily frayed at mid-calf. No socks. Flip-flop rope-soled sandals. A brilliant orange, red, and magenta poncho-type garment, which hung loosely over both arms like a cape from shoulders to crotch. A sloppy white T-shirt underneath. A large pair of sunglasses. Artificial suntan on every visible bit of skin. And, to top it all, a large straw sun hat with a two-inch raffia fringe round the brim, the sort of hat in favor out in the bush for keeping flies away. Flies were the torment of Australia. The brushing-away-of-flies movement of the right hand was known as the Great Australian Salute.

On this hat there was a tourist-type hatband, bright and distinctly legible. It said "I Climbed Ayers Rock."

Accompanying all this jazz, I carried the Trans-Australia Airline bag Sarah had bought on the way up. Inside it, the garments of sanity and discretion.

"No one," Jik had said with satisfaction, laying out my wardrobe, "will guess you're a walking stretcher case, if you're wearing these."

"More like a nut case."

"Not far out," Sarah said dryly.

They were both at the airport, sitting down and looking glum, when I arrived. They gave me a flickering glance and gazed thereafter at the floor, both of them, they told me later, fighting off terrible fits of giggles at seeing all that finery on the march.

I walked composedly down to the postcard stand and waited there on my feet, for truth to tell it was more comfortable than sitting. Most of the postcards seemed to be endless views of the huge crouching orange monolith out in the desert: Ayers Rock at dawn, at sunset, and every five minutes in between.

Alternatively with inspecting the merchandise, I took stock of the room. About fifty prospective passengers, highly assorted. Some airline ground staff, calm and unhurried. A couple of aborigines with shadowed eyes and patient black faces, waiting for the airport bus back to dreamtime. Air conditioning doing fine, but everyone inside still moving with the slow walk of life out in the sun.

No one remotely threatening.

The flight was called. The assorted passengers, including Jik and Sarah, stood up, picked up their hand luggage, and straggled out to the tarmac.

It was then, and then only, that I saw him.

The man who had come toward me on the balcony to throw me over.

I was almost sure at once, and then certain. He had been sitting among the waiting passengers reading a newspaper, which he was now folding up. He stood still, watching Jik and Sarah present their boarding passes at the door and go through to the tarmac. His eyes followed them right across to the aircraft. When they'd filed up the steps and vanished, he peeled off and made a beeline in my direction.

My heart lurched painfully. I absolutely could not run.

He looked just the same. Exactly the same. Young, strong, purposeful, as well-coordinated as a cat. Coming toward me.

As Jik would have said, *Jesus.*

He didn't even give me a glance. Three yards before

125

he reached me, he came to a stop beside a wall telephone and fished in his pocket for coins.

My feet didn't want to move. I was still sure he would see me, look at me carefully, recognize me . . . and do something I would regret. I could feel the sweat prickling under the bandages.

"Last call for flight to Adelaide and Melbourne."

I would have to, I thought. Have to walk past him to get to the door.

I unstuck my feet. Walked. Waiting with every awful step to hear his voice shouting after me. Or even worse, his heavy hand.

I got to the door, presented the boarding pass, made it out onto the tarmac.

Couldn't resist glancing back. I could see him through the glass, earnestly telephoning, and not even looking my way.

The walk to the aircraft was, all the same, quite far enough. God help us all, I thought, if the slightest fright is going to leave me so weak.

CHAPTER 11

I had a window seat near the rear of the aircraft, and spent the first part of the journey in the same sort of fascination as on the way up, watching the empty red miles of the ancient land roll away underneath. A desert with water underneath it in most places; with huge lakes and many rock pools. A desert that could carry dormant seeds for years in its burning dust, and bloom like a garden when it rained. A place of pulverizing heat, harsh and unforgiving and, in scattered places, beautiful.

GABA, I thought. I found it awesome, but it didn't move me in terms of paint.

After a while I took off the exaggerated hat, laid it on the empty seat beside me, and tried to find a comfortable way to sit, my main frustration being that if I leaned back in the ordinary way my broken shoulder blade didn't care for it. You wouldn't think, I thought, that one *could* break a shoulder blade. Mine, it appeared, had suffered from the full thud of my five-eleven frame hitting terra extremely firma.

Oh, well . . . I shut my eyes for a bit and wished I didn't still feel so shaky.

My exit from hospital had been the gift of one of the doctors, who had said he couldn't stop me if I chose to go, but another day's rest would be better.

"I'd miss the Cup," I said, protesting.

"You're crazy."

"Yeah . . . Would it be possible for you to arrange that the hospital said I was 'satisfactory' and 'progressing' if anyone telephoned to ask, and not on any account to say that I'd left?"

"Whatever for?"

"I'd just like those muggers who put me here to think I'm still flat out. For several days, if you don't mind. Until I'm long gone."

"But they won't try again."

"You never know."

He shrugged. "You mean you're nervous?"

"You could say so."

"All right. For a couple of days, anyway. I don't see any harm in it, if it will set your mind at rest."

"It would indeed," I said gratefully.

"Whatever are these?" He gestured to Jik's shopping, still lying on the bed.

"My friend's idea of suitable traveling gear."

"You're having me on?"

"He's an artist," I said, as if that explained any excesses.

He returned an hour later with a paper for me to sign before I left, Jik's credit card having again come up trumps, and at the sight of me he nearly choked. I had struggled slowly into the clothes and was trying on the hat.

"Are you going to the airport dressed like that?" he said incredulously.

"I sure am."

"How?"

"Taxi, I suppose."

"You'd better let me drive you," he said, sighing. "Then if you feel too rotten I can bring you back."

He drove carefully, his lips twitching. "Anyone who has the courage to go around like that shouldn't worry about a couple of thugs." He dropped me solicitously at the airport door and departed laughing.

Sarah's voice interrupted the memory.

"Todd?"

I opened my eyes. She had walked toward the back of the airplane and was standing in the aisle beside my seat.

"Are you all right?"

"Mmm."

128

She gave me a worried look and went on into the toilet compartment. By the time she came out, I'd assembled a few more wits, and stopped her with the flap of the hand.

"Sarah . . . you were followed to the airport. I think you'll very likely be followed from Melbourne. Tell Jik . . . tell Jik to take a taxi, spot the tail, lose him, and take a taxi back to the airport to collect the hired car. O.K.?"

"Is this—this tail—on the airplane?" She looked alarmed at the thought.

"No. He telephoned . . . from Alice."

"All right."

She went away up front to her seat. The airplane landed at Adelaide, people got off, people got on, and we took off again for the hour's flight to Melbourne. Halfway there, Jik himself came back to make use of the facilities.

He, too, paused briefly beside me on the way back.

"Here are the car keys," he said. "Sit in it and wait for us. You can't go into the Hilton like that, and you're not fit enough to change on your own."

"Of course I am."

"Don't argue. I'll lose any tail and come back. You wait."

He went without looking back. I picked up the keys and put them in my jeans pocket, and thought grateful thoughts to pass the time.

I dawdled a long way behind Jik and Sarah at disembarkation. My gear attracted more scandalized attention in this solemn financial city, but I didn't care in the least. Nothing like fatigue and anxiety for killing off embarrassment.

Jik and Sarah, with only hand baggage, walked without ado past the suitcase-unloading areas and straight out toward the waiting queue of taxis. The whole airport was bustling with Cup-eve arrivals, but only one person that I could see was bustling exclusively after my fast-departing friends.

I smiled briefly. Young and eellike, he slithered through the throng, pushing a woman with a baby out of the way to grab the next taxi behind Jik's. They'd sent him, I supposed, because he knew Jik by sight. He'd flung turps in his eyes at the Arts Centre.

Not too bad, I thought. The boy wasn't overintelligent, and Jik should have little trouble in losing him. I wandered around for a bit looking gormless, but as there was no one else who seemed the remotest threat, I eventually eased out to the car park.

The night was chilly after Alice Springs. I unlocked the car, climbed into the back, took off the successful hat, and settled to wait for Jik's return.

They were gone nearly two hours, during which time I grew stiffer and ever more uncomfortable and started swearing.

"Sorry," Sarah said breathlessly, pulling open the car door and tumbling into the front seat.

"We had the devil's own job losing the little bugger," Jik said, getting in beside me in the back. "Are you all right?"

"Cold, hungry, and cross."

"That's all right, then," he said cheerfully. "He stuck like a bloody little leech. That boy from the Arts Centre."

"Yes, I saw him."

"We hopped into the Victoria Royal, meaning to go straight out again by the side door and grab another cab, and there he was following us in through the front. So we peeled off for a drink in the bar and he hovered around in the lobby looking at the bookstall."

"We thought it would be better not to let him know we'd spotted him, if we could," Sarah said. "So we did a rethink, went outside, called another taxi, and set off to the Naughty Ninety, which is about the only noisy big dine, dance, and cabaret place in Melbourne."

"It was absolutely packed," Jik said. "It cost me ten dollars to get a table. Marvelous for us, though. All dark corners and psychedelic colored lights. We ordered and paid for some drinks, and read the menu, and then got up and danced."

"He was still there when we saw him last, standing in the queue for tables just inside the entrance door. We got out through an emergency exit down a passage past some cloakrooms. We'd dumped our bags there when we arrived, and simply collected them again on the way out."

"I don't think he'll know we ducked him on purpose," Jik said. "It's a proper scrum there tonight."

"Great."

With Jik's efficient help, I exchanged Tourist, Alice-style, for Racing Man, Melbourne Cup. He drove us all back to the Hilton, parked in its car park, and we walked into the front hall as if we'd never been away.

No one took any notice of us. The place was alive with

pre-race excitement. People in evening dress flooding downstairs from the ballroom to stand in loud-talking groups before dispersing home. People returning from eating out, and calling for one more nightcap. Everyone discussing the chances of the next day's race.

Jik collected our room keys from the long desk.

"No messages," he said. "And they don't seem to have missed us."

"Fair enough."

"Todd," Sarah said. "Jik and I are going to have some food sent up. You'll come as well?"

I nodded. We went up in the lift and along to their room, and ate a subdued supper out of collective tiredness.

" 'Night," I said eventually, getting up to go. "And thanks for everything."

"Thank us tomorrow," Sarah said.

The night passed. Well, it passed.

In the morning, I did a spot of one-handed shaving and some highly selective washing, and Jik came up, as he'd insisted, to help with my tie. I opened the door to him in underpants and dressing gown, and endured his comments when I took the latter off.

"Jesus God Almighty, is there any bit of you neither blue nor patched?"

"I could have landed face-first."

He stared at the thought. *"Jesus."*

"Help me rearrange these bandages," I said.

"I'm not touching that lot."

"Oh, come on, Jik. Unwrap the swaddling bands. I'm itching like hell underneath and I've forgotten what my left hand looks like."

With a variety of blasphemous oaths, he undid the expert handiwork of the Alice Hospital. The outer bandages proved to be large strong pieces of linen, fastened with clips, and placed so as to support my left elbow and hold my whole arm statically in one position, with my hand across my chest and pointing up toward my right shoulder. Under the top layer there was a system of crêpe bandages tying my arm in that position. Also a sort of tight cummerbund of adhesive strapping, presumably to deal with the broken ribs. Also, just below my shoulder blade, a large padded wound dressing, which Jik kindly told me after a delicate inspection from one corner, covered a mucky-looking bit of darning.

"You damn near tore a whole flap of skin off. There are four lots of stitching. Looks like Clapham Junction."

"Fasten it up again."

"I have, mate, don't you worry."

There were three similar dressings, two on my left thigh and one, a bit smaller, just below my knee—all fastened with both adhesive strips and tapes with clips. We left them all untouched.

"What the eye doesn't see doesn't scare the patient," Jik said. "What else do you want done?"

"Untie my arm."

"You'll fall apart."

"Risk it."

He laughed and undid another series of clips and knots. I tentatively straightened my elbow. Nothing much happened except that the hovering ache and soreness stopped hovering and came down to earth.

"That's not so good," Jik observed.

"It's my muscles as much as anything. Protesting about being stuck in one position all that time."

"What now, then?"

From the bits and pieces, we designed a new and simpler sling that gave my elbow good support but was less of a straight jacket. I could get my hand out easily, and also my whole arm, if I wanted to. When we'd finished, we had a small heap of bandages and clips left over.

"That's fine," I said.

We all met downstairs in the hall at ten-thirty.

Around us, a buzzing atmosphere of anticipation pervaded the chattering throng of would-be winners, who were filling the morning with celebratory drinks. The hotel, I saw, had raised a veritable fountain of champagne at the entrance to the bar-lounge end of the lobby, and Jik, his eyes lighting up, decided it was too good to be missed.

"Free booze," he said reverently, picking up a glass and holding it under the prodigal bubbly that flowed in delicate gold streams from a pressure-fed height. "Not bad, either," he added, tasting. He raised his glass. "Here's to Art. God rest his soul."

"Life's short. Art's long," I said.

"I don't like that," Sarah said, looking at me uneasily.

"It was Alfred Munnings's favorite saying. And don't worry, love, he lived to be eighty plus."

"Let's hope you do."

I drank to it. She was wearing a cream dress with gold buttons; neat, tailored, a touch severe. An impression of the military for a day in the front line.

"Don't forget," I said. "If you think you see Wexford or Greene, make sure they see you."

"Give me another look at their faces," she said.

I pulled the small sketchbook out of my pocket and handed it to her again, though she'd studied it on and off all the previous evening through supper.

"As long as they look like this, maybe I'll know them," she said, sighing. "Can I take it?" She put the sketchbook in her handbag.

Jik laughed. "Give Todd his due, he can catch a likeness. No imagination, of course. He can only paint what he sees." His voice, as usual, was full of disparagement.

Sarah said, "Don't you mind the awful things Jik says of your work, Todd?"

I grinned. "I know exactly what he thinks of it."

"If it makes you feel any better," Jik said to his wife, "he was the star pupil of our year. The art school lacked judgment, of course."

"You're both crazy."

I glanced at the clock. We finished the champagne and put down the glasses.

"Back a winner for me," I said to Sarah, kissing her cheek.

"Your luck might run out."

I grinned. "Back number eleven."

Her eyes were dark with apprehension. Jik's beard was at the bad-weather angle for possible storms ahead.

"Off you go," I said cheerfully. "See you later."

I watched them through the door and wished strongly that we were all three going for a simple day out to the Melbourne Cup. The effort ahead was something I would have been pleased to avoid. I wondered if others ever quaked before the task they'd set themselves and wished they'd never thought of it. The beginning, I supposed, was the worst. Once you were in, you were committed. But before, when there was still time to turn back, to rethink, to cancel, the temptation to retreat was demoralizing.

Why climb Everest if at its foot you could lie in the sun?

Sighing, I went to the cashier's end of the reception desk and changed a good many traveler's checks into cash. Maisie's generosity had been farsighted. There would be little enough left by the time I got home.

Four hours to wait. I spent them upstairs in my room calming my nerves by drawing the view from the window. Black clouds still hung around the sky like cobwebs, especially in the direction of Flemington Racecourse. I hoped it would stay dry for the Cup.

Half an hour before it was due to be run, I left the Hilton on foot, walking unhurriedly along toward Swanston Street and the main area of shops. They were all shut, of course. Melbourne Cup Day was a national public holiday. Everything stopped for the Cup.

I had taken my left arm out of its sling and threaded it gingerly through the sleeves of shirt and jacket. A man with his jacket hunched over one shoulder was too memorable for sense. I found that by hooking my thumb into the waistband of my trousers I got quite good support.

Swanston Street was far from its usual bustling self. People still strode along with the breakneck speed that seemed to characterize all Melbourne pedestrians, but they strode in tens, not thousands. Trams ran up and down the central tracks with more vacant seats than passengers. Cars sped along with the drivers, eyes down, fiddling dangerously with radio dials. Fifteen minutes to the race that annually stopped Australia in its tracks.

Jik arrived exactly on time, driving up Swanston Street in the hired gray car and turning smoothly round the corner where I stood waiting. He stopped outside the Yarra River Fine Arts Gallery, got out, opened the boot, and put on a brown coat-overall, of the sort worn by storemen.

I walked quietly along toward him. He brought out a small radio, switched it on, and stood it on top of the car. The commentator's voice emerged tinnily, giving details of the runners currently walking round the parade ring at Flemington races.

"Hello," he said unemotionally when I reached him. "All set?" I nodded, and walked to the door of the gallery. Pushed it. It was solidly shut. Jik dived again into the boot, which held further fruits of his second shopping expedition in Alice Springs.

"Gloves," he said, handing me some, and putting some on himself. They were of white cotton, with ribbed wristbands, and looked a lot too new and clean. I wiped the backs of mine along the wings of Jik's car, and he gave me a glance and did the same with his.

"Handles and impact adhesive."

He gave me the two handles to hold. They were simple chromium-plated handles, with flattened pieces at each end, pierced by screw holes for fixing. Sturdy handles, big enough for gripping with the whole hand. I held one steady, bottom side up, while Jik covered the screw-plate areas at each end with adhesive. We couldn't screw these handles where we wanted them. They had to be stuck.

"Now the other. Can you hold it in your left hand?"

I nodded. Jik attended to it. One or two people passed, paying no attention. We were not supposed to park there, but no one told us to move.

We walked across the pavement to the gallery. Its frontage was not one unbroken line across its whole width, but was recessed at the right-hand end to form a doorway. Between the front-facing display window and the front-facing glass door, there was a joining window at right angles to the street.

To this sheet of glass we stuck the handles—or, rather, Jik did—at just above waist height. He tested them after a minute, and he couldn't pull them off. We returned to the car.

One or two more people passed, turning their heads to listen to the radio on the car roof, smiling in brotherhood at the universal national interest. The street was noticeably emptying as the crucial time drew near.

"... *Vinery carries the colors of Mr. Hudson Taylor, of Adelaide, and must be in with a good outside chance. Fourth in the Caulfield Cup, and before that second at Randwick against Brain-Teaser, who went on to beat Afternoon Tea ...*"

"Stop listening to the damn race!" Jik said sharply.

"Sorry."

"Ready?"

"Yes."

We walked back to the entrance to the gallery, Jik carrying the sort of glass cutter used by, among others, picture framers. Without casting a glance around for possible onlookers, he applied the diamond cutting edge to the matter in hand, using considerable strength as he pushed the professional tool round the outside of the pane. I stood behind him to block any passing curious glances.

"Hold the right-hand handle," he said as he started on the last of the four sides, the left-hand vertical.

I stepped past him and slotted my hand through the grip. None of the few people left in the street paid the slightest attention.

"When it goes," Jik said, "for God's sake don't drop it."

"No."

"Put your knee against the glass. Gently, for God's sake."

I did what he said. He finished the fourth long cut.

"Press smoothly."

I did that. Jik's knee, too, was firmly against the glass. With his left hand he gripped the chromium handle, and with the palm of his right he began jolting the top perimeter of the heavy pane.

Jik had cut a lot of glass in his time, even if not in exactly these circumstances. The big flat sheet cracked away evenly all round under our pressure and parted with hardly a splinter. The weight fell suddenly onto the handle I held in my right hand, and Jik steadied the now free sheet of glass with hands and knees and blasphemy.

"Jesus, don't let go."

"No."

The heavy vibrations set up in the glass by the breaking process subsided, and Jik took over the right-hand handle from me. Without any seeming inconvenience, he pivoted the sheet of glass so that it opened like a door. He stepped through the hole, lifted the glass up wholesale by the two handles, carried it several feet, and propped it against the wall to the right of the more conventional way in.

He came out, and we went over to the car. From there, barely ten feet away, one could not see that the gallery was not still securely shut. There were by now, in any case, very few to look.

"... Most jockeys have now mounted and the horses will soon be going out onto the course. . . ."

I picked up the radio. Jik exchanged the glass cutter for a metal saw, a hammer, and a chisel, and shut the boot, and we walked through the unorthodox entrance as if it were all in the day's work. Often only the furtive manner gave away the crook. If you behaved as if you had every right to, it took longer for anyone to suspect.

It would really have been best had we next been able

to open the real door, but a quick inspection proved it impossible. There were two useful locks, and no keys.

"The stairs are at the back," I said.

"Lead on."

We walked the length of the plushy green carpet and down the beckoning stairs. There was a bank of electric switches at the top; we pressed those lighting the basement and left the upstairs lot off.

Heart-thumping time, I thought. It would take only a policeman to walk along and start fussing about a car parked in the wrong place to set Cassavetes and Todd on the road to jail.

"... horses are now going out onto the course. Four-square in front, sweating up and fighting jockey Ted Nester for control ..."

We reached the bottom of the stairs. I turned back toward the office, but Jik took off fast down the corridor.

"Come back," I said urgently. "If that steel gate shuts down ..."

"Relax," Jik said. "You told me." He stopped before reaching the threshold of the furthest room. Stood still, and looked. Came back rapidly.

"O.K. The Munningses are all there. Three of them. Also something else which will stun you. Go and look while I get this door open."

"... cantering down to the start, and the excitement is mounting here now ..."

With a feeling of urgency, I trekked down the passage, stopped safely short of any electric gadgets that might trigger the gate and set off alarms, and looked into the Munnings room. The three paintings still hung there, as they had before. But along the row from them was something that, as Jik had said, stunned me. Chestnut horse with head raised, listening. Stately home in the background. The Raoul Millais picture we'd seen in Alice.

I went back to Jik, who with hammer and chisel had bypassed the lock on the office door.

"Which is it?" he said. "Original or copy?"

"Can't tell from that distance. Looks like real."

He nodded. We went into the office and started work.

"... Derriby and Special Bet coming down to the start now, and all the runners circling while the girths are checked ..."

I put the radio on Wexford's desk, where it sat like an hourglass ticking away the minutes as the sands ran out.

Jik turned his practical attention to the desk drawers, but they were all unlocked. One of the waist-high line of filing cabinets, however, proved to be secure. Jik's strength and know-how soon insured that it didn't remain that way.

In his wake I looked through the drawers. Nothing much in them except catalogues and stationery.

In the broken-open filing cabinet, a gold mine.

Not that I realized it at first. The contents looked merely like ordinary files with ordinary headings.

". . . *moved very freely coming down to the start and is prime fit to run for that hundred-and-ten-thousand-dollar prize . . .*"

There were a good many framed pictures in the office, some on the walls but even more standing in a row on the floor. Jik began looking through them at high speed, almost like flicking through a rack of record albums.

". . . *handlers are beginning to load the runners into the starting stalls, and I see Vinery playing up . . .*"

Half of the files in the upper of the two drawers seemed to deal in varying ways with insurance. Letters, policies, revaluations, and security. I didn't really know what I was looking for, which made it all a bit difficult.

"Jesus Almighty," Jik said.

"What is it?"

"Look at this."

". . . *more than a hundred thousand people here today to see the twenty-three runners fight it out over the three thousand two hundred meters . . .*"

Jik had reached the end of the row and was looking at the foremost of three unframed canvases tied loosely together with string. I peered over his shoulder. The picture had Munnings written all over it. It had "Alfred Munnings" written large and clear in the right-hand bottom corner. It was a picture of four horses with jockeys cantering on a racecourse; and the paint wasn't dry.

"What are the others?" I said.

Jik ripped off the string. The two other pictures were exactly the same.

"God Almighty," Jik said in awe.

". . . *Vinery carries only fifty-one kilograms and has a good barrier position, so it's not impossible . . .*"

"Keep looking," I said, and went back to the files.

Names. Dates. Places. I shook my head impatiently.

We needed more than those Munnings copies, and I couldn't find a thing.

"Jesus!" Jik said.

He was looking inside the sort of large flat two-by-three-foot folder that was used in galleries to store prints.

". . . only Derriby now to enter the stalls . . ."

The print folder had stood between the end of the desk and the nearby wall. Jik seemed transfixed.

"OVERSEAS CUSTOMERS." My eyes flicked over the heading and then went back. Overseas customers. I opened the file. Lists of people, sorted into countries. Pages of them. Names and addresses.

England.

A long list. Not alphabetical. Too many to read through in the shortage of time.

A good many of the names had been crossed out.

". . . They're running! This is the moment you've all been waiting for, and Special Bet is out in front . . ."

"Look at this," Jik said.

Donald Stuart. Donald Stuart, crossed out. Wrenstone House, Shropshire, England. Crossed out.

I practically stopped breathing.

". . . as they pass the stands for the first time, it's Special Bet, Foursquare, Newshound, Derriby, Wonderbug, Vinery . . ."

"Look at this," Jik said again, insistently.

"Bring it," I said. "We've got less than three minutes before the race ends and Melbourne comes back to life."

"But."

"Bring it," I said. "And also those three copies."

". . . Special Bet still making it, from Newshound close second, then Wonderbug . . ."

I shoved the filing drawer shut.

"Put this file in the print folder and let's get out."

I picked up the radio and Jik's tools, as he himself had enough trouble managing all three of the untied paintings and the large print folder.

". . . down the backstretch by the Maribyrnong River it's still Special Bet with Vinery second now . . ."

We went up the stairs. Switched off the lights. Eased round into a view of the car.

It stood there, quiet and unattended, just as we'd left it. No policemen. Everyone elsewhere, listening to the race.

Jik was calling on the Deity under his breath.

". . . rounding the turn towards home, Special Bet is

139

dropping back now and its Derriby with Newshound . . ."

We walked steadily down the gallery.

The commentator's voice rose in excitement against a background of shouting crowds.

". . . Vinery in third with Wonderbug, and here comes Ringwood very fast on the stands side . . ."

Nothing stirred out on the street. I went first through our hole in the glass and stood once more, with a great feeling of relief, on the outside of the beehive. Jik carried out the plundered honey and stacked it in the boot. He took the tools from my hands and stored them also.

"Right?"

I nodded, with a dry mouth. We climbed normally into the car. The commentator was yelling to be heard.

". . . Coming to the line, it's Ringwood by a length from Wonderbug, with Newshound third, then Derriby, then Vinery . . ."

The cheers echoed inside the car as Jik started the engine and drove away.

". . . Might be a record time. Just listen to the cheers. The result again. The result of the Melbourne Cup. In the frame . . . first, Ringwood, owned by Mr. Robert Khami . . . second, Wonderbug . . ."

"Phew," Jik said, his beard jaunty and a smile stretching to show an expanse of gum. "That wasn't a bad effort. We might hire ourselves out sometime for stealing politicians' papers." He chuckled fiercely.

"It's an overcrowded field," I said, smiling broadly myself.

We were both feeling the euphoria that follows the safe deliverance from danger. "Take it easy," I said. "We've a long way to go."

He drove to the Hilton, parked, and carried the folder and pictures up to my room. He moved with his sailing speed, economically and fast, losing as little time as possible before returning to Sarah on the racecourse and acting as if he'd never been away.

"We'll be back here as soon as we can," he promised, sketching a farewell.

Two seconds after he'd shut my door there was a knock on it.

I opened it. Jik stood there.

"I'd better know," he said. "What won the Cup?"

CHAPTER 12

When he'd gone, I looked closely at the spoils.

The more I saw, the more certain it became that we had hit the absolute jackpot. I began to wish most insistently that we hadn't wasted time in establishing that Jik and Sarah were at the races. It made me nervous waiting for them in the Hilton with so much dynamite in my hands. Every instinct urged immediate departure.

The list of overseas customers would to any other eyes have seemed the most harmless of documents. Wexford would not have needed to keep it in better security than a locked filing cabinet, for the chances of anyone seeing its significance in ordinary circumstances were millions to one against.

Donald Stuart, Wrenstone House, Shropshire, England. Crossed out.

Each page had three columns, a narrow one at each side with a broad one in the center. The narrow left-hand column was for dates and the center for names and addresses. In the narrow right-hand column, against each name, was a short line of letters and numbers. Those against Donald's entry, for instance, were MM3109T; and these figures had not been crossed out with his name. Maybe a sort of stock list, I thought, identifying the picture he'd bought.

141

I searched rapidly down all the other crossed-out names in the England sector. Maisie Matthews's name was not among them.

Damn, I thought. Why wasn't it?

I turned all the papers over rapidly. As far as I could see, all the overseas customers came from basically English-speaking countries, and the proportion of crossed-out names was about one in three. If every crossing-out represented a robbery, there had been literally hundreds since the scheme began.

At the back of the file I found there was a second and separate section, again divided into pages for each country. The lists in this section were much shorter.

England.

Halfway down. My eyes positively leaped at it.

Mrs. M. Matthews, Treasure Holme, Worthing, Sussex.

Crossed out.

I almost trembled. The date in the left-hand column looked like the date on which Maisie had bought her picture. The uncrossed-out numbers in the right-hand column were SMC29R.

I put down the file and sat for five minutes staring unseeingly at the wall, thinking.

My first and last conclusions were that I had a great deal to do before Jik and Sarah came back from the races, and that instincts were not always right.

The large print folder, which had so excited Jik, lay on my bed. I opened it flat and inspected the contents.

I dare say I looked completely loony standing there with my mouth open. The folder contained a number of simplified line drawings like the one the boy artist had been coloring in the Arts Centre. Full-sized outline drawings, on flat white canvas, as neat and accurate as tracings.

There were seven of them, all basically of horses. As they were only black-and-white line drawings, I couldn't be sure, but I guessed that three were Munningses, two Raoul Millaises, and the other two . . . I stared at the old-fashioned shapes of the horses . . . They couldn't be Stubbs; he was too well documented. . . . How about Herring? Herring, I thought, nodding. The last two had a look of Herring.

Attached to one of these two canvases by an ordinary paper clip was a small handwritten memo on a piece of scrap paper: "Don't forget to send the original. Also find out what palette he used, if different from usual."

I looked again at the three identical finished paintings that we had also brought away. These canvases, tacked onto wooden stretchers, looked very much as if they might have started out themselves as the same sort of outlines. The canvas used was of the same weave and finish.

The technical standard of the work couldn't be faulted. The paintings did look very much like Munnings's own, and would do much more so after they had dried and been varnished. Different colored paints dried at different speeds, and also the drying time of paints depended very much on the amount of oil or turps used to thin them, but at a rough guess all three pictures had been completed between three and six days earlier. The paint was at the same stage on all of them. They must, I thought, have all been painted at once, in a row, like a production line. Red hat, red hat, red hat . . . It would have saved time and paint.

The brushwork throughout was painstaking and controlled. Nothing slapdash. No time skimped. The quality of care was the same as in the Millais copy at Alice.

I was looking, I knew, at the true worth of Harley Renbo.

All three paintings were perfectly legal. It was never illegal to copy: only to attempt to sell the copy as real.

I thought it all over for a bit longer, and then set rapidly to work.

The Hilton people, when I went downstairs an hour later, were most amiable and helpful.

Certainly they could do what I asked. Certainly I could use the photocopying machine; come this way. Certainly I could pay my bill now and leave later.

I thanked them for their many excellent services.

"Our pleasure," they said; and, incredibly, they meant it.

Upstairs again, waiting for Jik and Sarah, I packed all my things. That done, I took off my jacket and shirt and did my best at rigging the spare bandages and clips back into something like the Alice shape, with my hand inside across my chest. No use pretending that it wasn't a good deal more comfortable that way than the dragging soreness of letting it all swing free. I buttoned my shirt over the top and calculated that if the traffic was bad Jik might still be struggling out of the racecourse.

A little anxiously, and still faintly feeling unwell, I settled to wait.

I waited precisely five minutes. Then the telephone by the bed rang, and I picked up the receiver.

Jik's voice, sounding hard and dictatorial.

"Charles, will you please come down to our room at once?"

"Well . . ." I said hesitantly. "Is it important?"

"Bloody chromic oxide!" he said explosively. "Can't you do anything without arguing?"

Christ, I thought.

I took a breath. "Give me ten minutes," I said. "I need ten minutes. I'm . . . er . . . I've just had a shower. I'm in my underpants."

"Thank you, Charles," he said. The telephone clicked as he disconnected.

A lot of Jik's great oaths galloped across my mind, wasting precious time. If ever we needed divine help, it was now.

Stifling a gut-twisting lurch of plain fear, I picked up the telephone and made a series of internal calls.

"Please could you send a porter up right away to room seventeen eighteen to collect Mr. Cassavetes's bags?"

"Housekeeper? Please will you send someone along urgently to seventeen eighteen to clean the room, as Mr. Cassavetes has been sick?"

"Please will you send the nurse along to seventeen eighteen at once, as Mr. Cassavetes has a severe pain?"

"Please will you send four bottles of your best champagne and ten glasses up to seventeen eighteen immediately?"

"Please bring coffee for three to seventeen eighteen at once."

"Electrician? All the electrics have fused in room seventeen eighteen; please come at once."

". . . the water is overflowing in the bathroom; please send the plumber urgently."

Who else was there? I ran my eye down the list of possible services. One wouldn't be able to summon chiropodists, masseuses, secretaries, barbers, or clothes pressers in a hurry . . . but television, why not?

". . . Please would you see to the television in room

144

seventeen eighteen? There is smoke coming from the back and it smells like burning."

That should do it, I thought. I made one final call for myself, asking for a porter to collect my bags. Right on, they said. Ten-dollar tip, I said, if the bags could be down in the hall within five minutes. No sweat, an Australian voice assured me happily. Coming right that second.

I left my door ajar for the porter and rode down two stories in the lift to floor seventeen. The corridor outside Jik and Sarah's room was still a broad empty expanse of no one doing anything in a hurry.

The ten minutes had gone.

I fretted.

The first to arrive was the waiter with the champagne, and he came not with a tray but a trolley, complete with ice buckets and spotless white cloths. It couldn't possibly have been better.

As he slowed to a stop outside Jik's door, three other figures turned in to the corridor, hurrying, and behind them, distantly, came a cleaner slowly pushing another trolley of linen and buckets and brooms.

I said to the waiter, "Thank you so much for coming so quickly." I gave him a ten-dollar note, which surprised him. "Please go and serve the champagne straight away."

He grinned, and knocked on Jik's door.

After a pause, Jik opeened it. He looked tense and strained.

"Your champagne, sir," said the waiter.

"But I didn't . . ." Jik began. He caught sight of me suddenly, where I stood a little back from his door. I made waving-in motions with my hand, and a faint grin appeared to lighten the anxiety.

Jik retreated into the room, followed by trolley and waiter.

At a rush, after that, came the electrician, the plumber, and the television man. I gave them each ten dollars and thanked them for coming so promptly. "I had a winner," I said. They took the money with more grins, and Jik opened the door to their knock.

"Electrics . . . plumbing . . . television . . ." His eyebrows rose. He looked across to me in rising comprehension. He flung wide his door and invited them in with all his heart.

"Give them some champagne," I said.

"God Almighty."

After that, in quick succession, came the porter, the man with the coffee, and the nurse. I gave them all ten dollars from my mythical winnings and invited them to join the party. Finally came the cleaner, pushing her top-heavy-looking load. She took the ten dollars, congratulated me on my good fortune, and entered the crowded and noisy fray.

It was up to Jik, I thought. I couldn't do any more.

He and Sarah suddenly popped out like the corks from the gold-topped bottles, and stood undecided in the corridor. I gripped Sarah's wrist and tugged her toward me.

"Push the cleaning trolley through the door, and turn it over," I said to Jik.

He wasted no time deliberating. The brooms crashed to the carpet inside the room, and Jik pulled the door shut after him.

Sarah and I were already running on our way to the lifts. She looked extremely pale and wild-eyed, and I knew that whatever had happened in their room had been almost too much for her.

Jik sprinted along after us. There were six lifts from the seventeenth floor, and one never had to wait more than a few seconds for a lift to arrive. The seconds this time seemed like hours but were actually very few indeed. The welcoming doors slid open, and we leaped inside and pushed the "Doors Closed" button like maniacs.

The doors closed.

The lift descended, smooth and fast.

"Where's the car?" I said.

"Car park."

"Get it and come round to the side door."

"Right."

"Sarah . . ."

She stared at me in fright.

"My satchel will be in the hall. Will you carry it for me?"

She looked vaguely at my one-armed state, my jacket swinging loosely over my left shoulder.

"Sarah!"

"Yes . . . all right."

We erupted into the hall, which had filled with people returning from the Cup. Talkative groups mixed and mingled, and it was impossible to see easily from one side to the other. All to the good, I thought.

My suitcase and satchel stood waiting near the front entrance, guarded by a young man in porter's uniform.

I parted with the ten dollars. "Thank you very much," I said.

"No sweat," he said cheerfully. "Can I get you a taxi?"

I shook my head. I picked up the suitcase and Sarah the satchel, and we headed out the door.

Turned right. Hurried. Turned right again, round to the side where I'd told Jik we'd meet him.

"He's not here," Sarah said with rising panic.

"He'll come," I said encouragingly. "We'll just go on walking to meet him."

We walked. I kept looking back nervously for signs of pursuit, but there were none. Jik came round the corner on two wheels and tore millimeters off the tires stopping beside us. Sarah scrambled into the front and I and my suitcase filled the back. Jik made a hair-raising U-turn and took us away from the Hilton at an illegal speed.

"Wowee," he said, laughing with released tension. "Whatever gave you that idea?"

"The Marx Brothers."

He nodded. "Pure crazy comedy."

"Where are we going?" Sarah said.

"Have you noticed," Jik said, "how my wife always brings us back to basics?"

The city of Melbourne covered a great deal of land.

We drove randomly north and east through seemingly endless suburban developments of houses, shops, garages, and light industry, all looking prosperous, haphazard, and, to my eyes, American.

"Where are we?" Jik said.

"Somewhere called Box Hill," I said, reading it on shop fronts.

"As good as anywhere."

We drove a few miles further and stopped at a modern middle-rank motel, which had bright-colored strings of triangular flags fluttering across the forecourt. A far cry from the Hilton, though the rooms we presently took were cleaner than nature intended.

There were plain divans, a square of thin carpet nailed at the edges, and a table lamp screwed to an immovable table. The looking glass was stuck flat to the wall and the swiveling armchair was bolted to the floor. Apart

147

from that, the curtains were bright and the hot tap ran hot in the shower.

"They don't mean you to pinch much," Jik said. "Let's paint them a mural."

"No!" Sarah said, horror-struck.

"There's a great Australian saying," Jik said. "If it moves, shoot it, and if it grows, chop it down."

"What's that got to do with it?" Sarah said.

"Nothing. I just thought Todd might like to hear it."

"Give me strength," she said.

We were trying to, in our inconsequential way.

Jik sat in the armchair in my room, swiveling. Sarah sat on one of the divans, I on the other. My suitcase and satchel stood side by side on the floor.

"You do realize we skipped out of the Hilton without paying," Sarah said.

"No, we didn't," Jik said. "According to our clothes, we are still resident. I'll ring them up later."

"But, Todd . . ."

"I did pay," I said. "Before you go back."

She looked slightly happier.

"How did Greene find you?" I said.

"God knows," Jik said gloomily.

Sarah was astonished. "How did you know about Greene? How did you know there was anyone in our room besides Jik and me? How did you know we were in such awful trouble?"

"Jik told me."

"But he couldn't! He couldn't risk warning you. He just had to tell you to come. He really did . . ." Her voice quivered. The tears weren't far from the surface. "They made him . . ."

"Jik told me," I said matter-of-factly. "First, he called me Charles, which he never does, so I knew something was wrong. Second, he was rude to me, and I know you think he is most of the time, but he isn't, not like that. And third, he told me the name of the man who I was to guess was in your room putting pressure on you both to get me to come down and walk into a nasty little hole. He told me it was chromic oxide, which is the pigment in green paint."

"Green paint!" The tearful moment passed. "You really are both extraordinary," she said.

"Long practice," Jik said cheerfully.

"Tell me what happened," I said.

"We left before the last race, to avoid the traffic, and we just came back normally to the Hilton. I parked the car, and we went up to our room. We'd only been there about a minute when there was this knock on the door, and when I opened it they just pushed in."

"They?"

"Three of them. One was Greene. We both knew him straight away, from your drawing. Another was the boy from the Arts Centre. The third was all biceps and beetle-brows, with his brains in his fists."

He absentmindedly rubbed an area south of his heart.

"He punched you?" I said.

"It was all so quick," he said apologetically. "They just crammed in . . . and biff bang . . . The next thing I knew, they'd got hold of Sarah and were twisting her arm and saying that she wouldn't just get turps in her eyes if I didn't get you to come at once."

"Did they have a gun?" I asked.

"No . . . a cigarette lighter. Look, I'm sorry, mate. I guess it sounds pretty feeble, but beetle-brows had her in a pretty rough grasp, and the boy had this ruddy great cigarette lighter with a flame like a blowtorch just a couple of inches from her cheek, and I was a bit groggy, and Greene said they'd burn her if I didn't get you . . . and I couldn't fight them all at once."

"Stop apologizing," I said.

"Yeah. Well, so I rang you. I told Greene you'd be ten minutes because you were in your underpants, but I think he heard you anyway, because he was standing right beside me, very wary and sharp. I didn't know really whether you'd cottoned on, but I hoped to God . . . and you should have seen their faces when the waiter pushed the trolley in. Beetle-brows let go of Sarah and the boy just stood there with his mouth open and the cigarette lighter flaring up like an oil refinery."

"Greene said we didn't want the champagne and to take it away," Sarah said. "But Jik and I said yes, we did, and Jik asked the waiter to open it at once."

"Before he got the first cork out, the others all began coming, and then they were all picking up glasses and the room was filling up, and Greene and the boy and beetle-brows were all on the window side of the room, sort of pinned in by the trolley and all those people, and I just grabbed Sarah and we ducked round the edge. The last I saw, Greene and the others were trying to push through, but our guests were pretty thick on the ground by then and keen to get their champagne . . . and I should think the cleaning trolley was just about enough to give us that start to the lift."

"I wonder how long the party lasted," I said.

"Until the bubbles ran out."

"They must all have thought you mad," Sarah said.

"Anything goes on Cup Day," I said, "and the staff of the Hilton would be used to eccentric guests."

"What if Greene had had a gun?" Sarah said.

I smiled at her twistedly. "He would have had to wave it around in front of a hell of a lot of witnesses."

"But he might have done."

"He might, but he was a long way from the front door." I bit my thumbnail. "Er . . . how did he know I was in the Hilton?"

There was a tangible silence.

"I told him," Sarah said finally, in a small mixed outburst of shame and defiance. "Jik didn't tell you it all, just now. At first they said—Greene said—they'd burn my face if Jik didn't tell them where you were. He didn't want to . . . but he had to . . . so I told them, so that it wouldn't be him. . . . I suppose that sounds stupid."

I thought it sounded extraordinarily moving. Love of an exceptional order, and a depth of understanding.

I smiled at her. "So they didn't know I was there, to begin with?"

Jik shook his head. "I don't think they knew you were even in Melbourne. They seemed surprised when Sarah said you were upstairs. I think all they knew was that you weren't still in hospital in Alice Springs."

"Did they know about our robbery?"

"I'm sure they didn't."

I grinned. "They'll be schizophrenic when they find out."

Jik and I both carefully shied away from what would have happened if I'd gone straight down to their room, though I saw from his eyes that he knew. With Sarah held as a hostage, I would have had to leave the Hilton with Greene and take my chance. The uncomfortably slim chance that they would have let me off again with my life.

"I'm hungry," I said.

Sarah smiled. "Whenever are you not?"

We ate in a small Bring Your Own restaurant nearby,

with people at tables all around us talking about what they'd backed in the Cup.

"Good heavens," Sarah exclaimed. "I'd forgotten about that."

"About what?"

"Your winnings," she said. "On Ringwood."

"But . . ." I began.

"It was number eleven!"

"I don't believe it."

She opened her handbag and produced a fat wad of notes. Somehow, in all the melee in the Hilton, she had managed to emerge from fiery danger with her cream leather pouch swinging from her arm. The strength of the instinct that kept women attached to their handbags had often astounded me, but never more than that day.

"It was forty to one," she said. "I put twenty dollars on for you, so you've got eight hundred dollars, and I think it's disgusting."

"Share it," I said, laughing.

She shook her head. "Not a cent . . . To be honest, I thought it had no chance at all, and I thought I'd teach you not to bet that way by losing you twenty dollars; otherwise I'd only have staked you ten."

"I owe most of it to Jik, anyway," I said.

"Keep it," he said. "We'll add and subtract later. Do you want me to cut your steak?"

"Please."

He sliced away neatly at my plate, and pushed it back with the fork placed ready.

"What else happened at the races?" I said, spearing the first succulent piece. "Who did you see?" The steak tasted as good as it looked, and I realized that in spite of all the sore patches, I had at last lost the overall feeling of unsettled shaky sickness. Things were on the mend, it seemed.

"We didn't see Greene," Jik said. "Or the boy, or beetle-brows."

"I'd guess they saw you."

"Do you think so?" Sarah said worriedly.

"I'd guess," I said, "that they saw you at the races and simply followed you back to the Hilton."

"Jesus," Jik groaned. "We never spotted them. There was a whole mass of traffic."

I nodded. "And all moving very slowly. If Greene was perhaps three cars behind you, you'd never have seen him, but he could have kept you in sight easily."

"I'm bloody sorry, Todd."

"Don't be silly. And no harm done."

"Except for the fact," Sarah said, "that I've still got no clothes."

"You look fine," I said absently.

"We saw a girl I know in Sydney," Sarah said. "We watched the first two races together and talked to her aunt. And Jik and I were talking to a photographer we both knew just after he got back . . . so it would be pretty easy to prove Jik was at the races all afternoon, as you wanted."

"No sign of Wexford?"

"Not if he looked like your drawing," Sarah said. "Though of course he might have been there. It's awfully difficult to recognize a complete stranger just from a drawing, in a huge crowd like that."

"We talked to a lot of people," Jik said. "To everyone Sarah knew even slightly. She used the excuse of introducing me as her newly bagged husband."

"We even talked to that man you met on Saturday," Sarah agreed, nodding. "Or, rather, he came over and talked to us."

"Hudson Taylor?" I asked.

"The one you saw talking to Wexford," Jik said.

"He asked if you were at the Cup," Sarah said. "He said he'd been going to ask you along for another drink. We said we'd tell you he'd asked."

"His horse ran quite well, didn't it?" I said.

"We saw him earlier than that. We wished him luck and he said he'd need it."

"He bets a bit," I said, remembering.

"Who doesn't?"

"Another commission down the drain," I said. "He would have had Vinery painted if he'd won."

"You hire yourself out like a prostitute," Jik said. "It's obscene."

"And anyway," added Sarah cheerfully, "you won more on Ringwood than you'd've got for the painting."

I looked pained, and Jik laughed.

We drank coffee, went back to the motel, and divided to our separate rooms. Five minutes later, Jik knocked on my door.

"Come in," I said, opening it.

He grinned. "You were expecting me."

"Thought you might come."

He sat in the armchair and swiveled. His gaze fell on my suitcase, which lay flat on one of the divans.

"What did you do with all the stuff we took from the gallery?"

I told him.

He stopped swiveling and sat still.

"You don't mess about, do you?" he said eventually.

"A few days from now," I said, "I'm going home."

"And until then?"

"Um . . . Until then, I aim to stay one jump ahead of Wexford, Greene, Beetle-brows, the Arts Centre boy, and the tough who met me on the balcony at Alice."

"Not to mention our copy artist, Harley Renbo."

I considered it. "Him, too," I said.

"Do you think we can?"

"No. Not from here on. This is where you take Sarah home."

He slowly shook his head. "I don't reckon it would be any safer than staying with you. We're too easy to find. For one thing, we're in the Sydney phone book. What's to stop Wexford from marching onto the boat with a bigger threat than a cigarette lighter?"

"You could tell him what I've just told you."

"And waste all your efforts."

"Retreat is sometimes necessary."

He shook his head. "If we stay with you, retreat may never be necessary. It's the better of two risks. And anyway"—the old fire gleamed in his eye—"it will be a great game. Cat and mouse. With cats who don't know they are mice chasing a mouse who knows he's a cat."

More like a bullfight, I thought, with myself waving the cape to invite the charge. Or a conjurer, attracting attention to one hand while he did the trick with the other. On the whole, I preferred the notion of the conjurer. There seemed less likelihood of being gored.

CHAPTER 13

I spent a good deal of the night studying the list of over-seas customers, mostly because I still found it difficult to lie comfortably to sleep, and partly because I had nothing else to read.

It became more and more obvious that I hadn't really pinched *enough*. The list I'd taken was fine in its way, but would have been doubly useful with a stock list to match the letters and numbers in the right-hand column.

On the other hand, all stock numbers were a form of code, and if I looked at them long enough, maybe some sort of recognizable pattern might emerge.

By far the majority began with the letter M, particularly in the first and much larger section. In the smaller section, which I had found at the back of the file, the M prefixes were few, and S, A, W, and B were much commoner.

Donald's number began with M. Maisie's began with S.

Suppose, I thought, that the M simply stood for Melbourne, and the S for Sydney, the cities where each had bought their pictures.

Then A, W, and B were where? Adelaide, Wagga Wagga, and Brisbane?

Alice?

In the first section, the letters and numbers following

the initial M seemed to have no clear pattern. In the second section, though, the third letter was always C, the last letter always R, and the numbers, divided though they were between several different countries, progressed more or less consecutively. The highest number of all was 54, which had been sold to a Mr. Norman Updike, living in Auckland, New Zealand. The stock number against his name was WHC54R. The date in the left-hand column was only a week old, and Mr. Updike had not been crossed out.

All the pictures in the shorter section had been sold within the past three years. The first dates in the long first section were five and a half years old.

I wondered which had come first five and a half years ago, the gallery or the idea. Had Wexford originally been a full-time crook deliberately setting up an imposing front, or a formerly honest art dealer struck by criminal possibilities? Judging from the respectable air of the gallery and what little I'd seen of Wexford himself, I would have guessed the latter. But the violence lying just below the surface didn't match.

I sighed, put down the lists, and switched off the light. Lay in the dark, thinking of the telephone call I'd made after Jik had gone back to Sarah.

It had been harder to arrange from the motel than it would have been from the Hilton, but the line had been loud and clear.

"You got my cable?" I said.

"I've been waiting for your call for half an hour."

"Sorry."

"What do you want?"

"I've sent you a letter," I said. "I want to tell you what's in it."

"But . . ."

"Just listen," I said. "And talk after." I spoke for quite a long time to a response of grunts from the far end.

"Are you sure of all this?"

"Positive about most," I said. "Some of it's a guess."

"Repeat it."

"Very well." I did so, at much the same length.

"I have recorded all that."

"Good."

"Hmm . . . What do you intend doing now?"

"I'm going home soon. Before that, I think I'll keep looking into things that aren't my business."

"I don't approve of that."

I grinned at the telephone. "I don't suppose you do, but if I'd stayed in England we wouldn't have got this far. There's one other thing. . . . Can I reach you by telex if I want to get a message to you in a hurry?"

"Telex? Wait a minute."

I waited.

"Yes, here you are." A number followed. I wrote it down. "Address any message to me personally and head it urgent."

"Right," I said. "And could you get an answer to some questions for me?" He listened, and said he could. "Thank you very much," I said. "And good night."

Sarah and Jik both looked heavy-eyed and languorous in the morning. A successful night, I judged.

We checked out of the motel, packed my suitcase into the boot of the car, and sat in the passenger seats to plan the day.

"Can't we please get our clothes from the Hilton?" Sarah said, sounding depressed.

Jik and I said "No" together.

"I'll ring them now," Jik said. "I'll get them to pack all our things and keep them safe for us, and I'll tell them I'll send a check for the bill." He levered himself out of the car again and went off on the errand.

"Buy what you need out of my winnings," I said to Sarah.

She shook her head. "I've got some money. It's not that. It's just . . . I wish all this was over."

"It will be soon," I said neutrally. She sighed heavily. "What's your idea of a perfect life?" I asked.

"Oh . . ." She seemed surprised. "I suppose right now I just want to be with Jik on the boat and have fun, like before you came."

"And forever?"

She looked at me broodingly. "You may think, Todd, that I don't know Jik is a complicated character, but you've only got to look at his paintings. . . . They make me shudder. They're a side of Jik I don't know, because he hasn't painted anything since we met. You may think that this world will be worse off if Jik is happy for a bit, but I'm no fool; I know that in the end whatever it is that drives him to paint like that will come back again. . . . I think these first few months together are frantically precious . . . and it isn't just the physical dangers you've dragged us into that I hate, but the feeling that I've lost the rest of that golden time . . . that you remind him of his painting, and that after you've gone he'll go straight back to it . . . weeks and weeks before he might have done."

"Get him to go sailing," I said. "He's always happy at sea."

"You don't care, do you?"

I looked straight into her clouded brown eyes. "I care for you both, very much."

"Then God help the people you hate."

And God help me, I thought, if I became any fonder of my oldest friend's wife. I looked away from her, out the window. Affection wouldn't matter. Anything else would be a mess.

Jik came back with a satisfied air. "That's all fixed. They said there's a letter for you, Todd, delivered by hand a few minutes ago. They asked me for a forwarding address."

"What did you say?"

"I said you'd call them yourself."

"Right . . . Well, let's get going."

"Where to?"

"New Zealand, don't you think?"

"That should be far enough," Jik said dryly.

He drove us to the airport, which was packed with people going home from the Cup.

"If Wexford and Greene are looking for us," Sarah said, "they will surely be watching at the airport."

If they weren't, I thought, we'd have to lay a trail; but Jik, who knew that, didn't tell her.

"They can't do much in public," he said comfortingly.

We bought tickets and found we could either fly to Auckland direct at lunchtime or via Sydney leaving within half an hour.

"Sydney," said Sarah positively, clearly drawing strength from the chance of putting her feet down on her own safe doorstep.

I shook my head. "Auckland direct. Let's see if the restaurant's still open for breakfast."

We squeezed in under the waitresses' pointed consultation of clocks and watches and ordered bacon and eggs lavishly.

"Why are we going to New Zealand?" Sarah said.

"To see a man about a painting and advise him to take out extra insurance."

"Are you actually making sense?"

"Actually," I said, "yes."

"I don't see why we have to go so far when Jik said you found enough in the gallery to blow the whole thing wide open."

"Um . . ." I said. "Because we don't want to blow it wide open. Because we want to hand it to the police in full working order."

She studied my face. "You are very devious."

"Not on canvas," Jik said.

After we'd eaten, we wandered around the airport shops, buying yet more toothbrushes and so on for Jik and Sarah, and another airline bag. There was no sign of Wexford or Greene or the boy or Beetle-brows or Renbo, or the tough who'd been on watch at Alice Springs. If they'd seen us without us seeing them, we couldn't tell.

"I think I'll ring the Hilton," I said.

Jik nodded. I put the call through, with him and Sarah sitting near, within sound and sight.

"I called about a forwarding address," I told the reception desk. "I can't really give you one. I'll be in New Zealand. I'm flying to Auckland in an hour or two."

They asked for instructions about the hand-delivered letter.

"Er . . . would you mind opening it and reading it to me?"

Certainly, they said. Their pleasure. The letter was from Hudson Taylor saying he was sorry to have missed me at the races, and that if while I was in Australia I would like to see round a vineyard, he would be pleased to show me his.

Thanks, I said. Our pleasure, sir, they said. If anyone asked for me, I said, would they please mention where I'd gone. They would. Certainly. Their pleasure.

During the next hour, Jik called the car-hire firm about settling their account and leaving the car in the airport car park, and I checked my suitcase through with Air New Zealand. Passports were no problem: I had mine with me in any case, but for Jik and Sarah they were unnecessary, as passage between New Zealand and Australia was as unrestricted as between England and Ireland.

158

Still no sign of Wexford or Greene. We sat in the departure bay thinking private thoughts.

It was again only when our flight was called that I spotted a spotter. The prickles rose again on my skin. I'd been blind, I thought. Dumb and blind.

Not Wexford, or Greene, or the boy, or Renbo, or any rough set of muscles. A neat day dress, neat hair, unremarkable handbag and shoes. A calm concentrated face. I saw her because she was staring at Sarah. She was standing outside the departure bay, looking in. The woman who had welcomed me into the Yarra River Fine Arts, and given me a catalogue, and let me out again afterward.

As if she felt my eyes upon her, she switched her gaze abruptly to my face. I looked away instantly, blankly, hoping she wouldn't know I'd seen her, or at least wouldn't know that I'd recognized her.

Jik, Sarah, and I stood up and drifted with everyone else toward the departure doors. In their glass I could see the woman's reflection: standing still, watching us go. I walked out toward the aircraft and didn't look back.

Mrs. Norman Updike stood in her doorway, shook her head, and said that her husband would not be home until six.

She was thin and sharp-featured and talked with tight New Zealand vowels. If we wanted to speak to her husband, we would have to come back.

She looked us over: Jik with his rakish blond beard, Sarah in her slightly crumpled but still military cream dress, I with my arm in its sling under my shirt, and jacket loose over my shoulder. Hardly a trio one would easily forget. She watched us retreat down her front path with a sharply turned-down mouth.

"Dear gentle soul," murmured Jik.

We drove away in the car we had hired at the airport.

"Where now?" Jik said.

"Shops." Sarah was adamant. "I must have some clothes."

The shops, it appeared, were in Queen Street, and still open for another half-hour. Jik and I sat in the car, waiting and watching the world go by.

"The dolly-birds fly out of their office cages about now," Jik said happily.

"What of it?"

"I sit and count the ones with no bras."

"And you a married man."

"Old habits die hard."

We had counted eight definites and one doubtful by the time Sarah returned. She was wearing a light olive skirt with a pink shirt, and reminded me of pistachio ice cream.

"That's better," she said, tossing two well-filled carriers onto the back seat. "Off we go, then."

The therapeutic value of the new clothes lasted all the time we spent in New Zealand and totally amazed me. She seemed to feel safer if she looked fresh and clean, her spirits rising accordingly. Armor-plated cotton, I thought. Drip-dry bullet-proofing. Security is a new pin.

We dawdled back to the hill overlooking the bay where Norman Updike's house stood in a crowded suburban street. The Updike residence was large but squashed by neighbors, and it was not until one was inside that one realized that the jostling was due to the view. As many houses that could be crammed onto the land had been built to share it. The city itself seemed to sprawl endlessly round miles of indented coastline, but all the individual building plots looked tiny.

Norman Updike proved as expansive as his wife was closed in. He had a round shiny bald head on a round short body, and he called his spouse Chuckles without apparently intending satire.

We said, Jik and I, that we were professional artists who would be intensely interested and grateful if we could briefly admire the noted picture he had just bought.

"Did the gallery send you?" he asked, beaming at the implied compliments to his taste and wealth.

"Sort of," we said, and Jik added: "My friend here is well known in England for his painting of horses, and is represented in many top galleries, and has been hung often at the Royal Academy."

I thought he was laying it on a bit too thick, but Norman Updike was impressed and pulled wide his door.

"Come in, then. Come in. The picture's in the lounge. This way, lass, this way."

He showed us into a large overstuffed room with dark ankle-deep carpet, big dark cupboards, and the glorious view of sunlit water.

Chuckles, sitting solidly in front of a television busy

160

with a moronic British comic show, gave us a sour look and no greeting.

"Over here." Norman Updike beamed, threading his portly way round a battery of fat armchairs. "What do you think of that, eh?" He waved his hand with proprietorial pride at the canvas on his wall.

We looked at it respectfully.

A smallish painting, fourteen inches by eighteen. A black horse, with an elongated neck curving against a blue-and-white sky; a chopped-off tail; the grass in the foreground yellow; and the whole covered with an old-looking varnish.

"Herring," I murmured reverently.

Norman Updike's beam broadened. "I see you know your stuff. Worth a bit, that is."

"A good deal," I agreed.

"I reckon I got a bargain. The gallery said I'd always make a profit if I wanted to sell."

"May I look at the brushwork?" I asked politely.

"Go right ahead."

I looked closely. It was very good. It did look like Herring, dead since 1865. It also, indefinably, looked like the meticulous Renbo. One would need a microscope and chemical analysis to make sure.

I stepped back and glanced round the rest of the room. There was nothing of obvious value, and the few other pictures were all prints.

"Beautiful," I said admiringly, turning back to the Herring. "Unmistakable style. A real master."

Updike beamed.

"You'd better beware of burglars," I said.

He laughed. "Chuckles, dear, do you hear what this young man says? He says we'd better beware of burglars!"

Chuckles's eyes gave me two seconds' sour attention and returned to the screen.

Updike patted Sarah on the shoulder. "Tell your friend not to worry about burglars."

"Why not?" I said.

"We've got alarms all over this house," he said. "Don't you worry, a burglar wouldn't get far."

Jik and Sarah, as I had done, looked round the room and saw nothing much worth stealing. Nothing, certainly, worth alarms all over the house. Updike watched them looking and his beam grew wider.

"Shall I show these young people our little treasures, Chuckles?" he said.

Chuckles didn't even reply. The television cackled with tinned laughter.

"We'd be most interested," I said.

He smiled with the fat anticipatory smirk of one about to show what will certainly be admired. Two or three steps took him to one of the big dark cupboards that seemed built into the walls, and he pulled open the double doors with a flourish.

Inside, there were about six deep shelves, each bearing several complicated pieces of carved jade. Pale pink, creamy white, and pale green, smooth, polished, intricate, expensive; each piece standing upon its own heavy-looking black base support. Jik, Sarah, and I made appreciative noises, and Norman Updike smiled ever wider.

"Hong Kong, of course," he said. "I worked there for years, you know. Quite a nice little collection, eh?" He walked along to the next dark cupboard and pulled open a duplicate set of doors. Inside, more shelves, more carvings, as before.

"I'm afraid I don't know much about jade," I said apologetically. "Can't appreciate your collection to the full."

He told us a good deal more about the ornate goodies than we actually wanted to know. There were four cupboardsful in the lounge and overflows in bedroom and hall.

"You used to be able to pick them up very cheap in Hong Kong," he said. "I worked there more than twenty years, you know."

Jik and I exchanged glances. I nodded slightly.

Jik immediately shook Norman Updike by the hand, put his arm round Sarah, and said we must be leaving. Updike looked inquiringly at Chuckles, who was now glued to commercials and still abdicating from the role of hostess. When she refused to look our way, he shrugged good-humoredly and came with us to his front door. Jik and Sarah walked out as soon as he opened it, and left me alone with him in the hall.

"Mr. Updike," I said. "At the gallery . . . which man was it who sold you the Herring?"

"Mr. Grey," he said promptly.

Mr. Grey . . . Mr. Grey . . . I frowned.

"Such a pleasant man." Updike nodded, beaming. "I

162

told him I knew very little about pictures, but he assured me I would get as much pleasure from my little Herring as from all my jade."

"You did tell him about your jade, then?"

"Naturally I did. I mean . . . if you don't know anything about one thing, well . . . you try and show you do know about something else. Don't you? Only human, isn't it?"

"Only human," I agreed, smiling. "What was the name of Mr. Grey's gallery?"

"Eh?" He looked puzzled. "I thought you said he sent you, to see my picture."

"I go to so many galleries, I've foolishly forgotten which one it was."

"Ruapehu Fine Arts," he said. "I was down there last week."

"Down?"

"In Wellington." His smile was slipping. "Look here, what is all this?" Suspicion flitted across his rounded face. "Why did you come here? I don't think Mr. Grey sent you at all."

"No," I said. "But, Mr. Updike, we mean you no harm. We really are painters, my friend and I. But—now we've seen your jade collection—we do think we must warn you. We've heard of several people who've bought paintings and had their houses burgled soon after. You say you've got burglar alarms fitted, so if I were you I'd make sure they are working properly."

"But . . . good gracious . . ."

"There's a bunch of thieves about," I said, "who follow up the sales of paintings and burgle the houses of those who buy. I suppose they reckon that if anyone can afford, say, a Herring, they have other things worth stealing."

He looked at me with awakening shrewdness. "You mean, young man, that I told Mr. Grey about my jade . . ."

"Let's just say, that it would be sensible to take more precautions than usual," I said.

"But . . . for how long?"

I shook my head. "I don't know, Mr. Updike. Maybe forever."

His round face looked troubled.

"Why did you bother to come and tell me all this?" he said.

"I'd do a great deal more to break up this bunch."

He asked "Why?" again, so I told him. "My cousin bought a painting. My cousin's house was burgled. My cousin's wife disturbed the burglars, and they killed her."

Norman Updike took a long slow look at my face. I couldn't have stopped him seeing the abiding anger, even if I'd tried. He shivered convulsively.

"I'm glad you're not after *me*," he said.

I managed a smile. "Mr. Updike . . . please take care. And one day, perhaps, the police may come to see your picture, and ask where you bought it. . . . Anyway, they will if I have anything to do with it."

The round smile returned with understanding and conviction. "I'll expect them," he said.

CHAPTER 14

Jik drove us from Auckland to Wellington, eight hours in the car.

We stopped overnight in a motel in the town of Hamilton, south of Auckland, and went on in the morning. No one followed us, molested us, or spied on us. I was sure, as far as I could be, that no one had picked us up in the northern city and no one knew we had called at the Updikes.

Wexford must know, all the same, that I had the overseas-customers list, and he knew there were several New Zealand addresses on it. He couldn't guess which one I'd pick to visit, but he could and would guess that any I picked with the prefix letter W would steer me straight to the gallery in Wellington.

So in the gallery in Wellington, he'd be ready. . . .

"You're looking awfully grim, Todd," Sarah said.

"Sorry."

"What were you thinking?"

"How soon we could stop for lunch."

She laughed. "We've only just had breakfast."

We passed the turning to Rotorua and the land of hot springs. Anyone for a boiling mudpack? Jik asked. There was a power station further on run by steam jets from underground, Sarah said, and horrid black craters stinking of sulfur, and the earth's crust was so thin in places that it vibrated and sounded hollow. She had been taken round a place called Waiotapu when she was a child, she told us, and had had terrible nightmares afterward, and she didn't want to go back.

"Pooh," Jik said dismissively. "They only have earthquakes every other Friday."

"Somebody told me they have so many earthquakes in Wellington that all the new office blocks are built in cradles," Sarah said.

"Rockabye, skyscraper," sang Jik, in fine voice.

The sun shone bravely, and the countryside was green with leaves I didn't know. There were fierce bright patches and deep mysterious shadows; gorges and rocks and heaven-stretching tree trunks; feathery waving grasses, shoulder high. An alien land, wild and beautiful.

"Get that chiaroscuro," Jik said, as we sped into one particularly spectacular curving valley.

"What's chiaroscuro?" Sarah asked.

"Light and shade," Jik said. "Contrast and balance. Technical term. All the world's a chiaroscuro, and all the men and women merely blobs of light and shade."

"Every life's a chiaroscuro," I said.

"And every soul."

"The enemy," I said, "is gray."

"And you get gray," Jik nodded, "by muddling together red, white, and blue."

"Gray lives, gray deaths, all leveled out into equal gray nothing."

"No one," Sarah said, sighing, "would ever call you two gray."

"Grey!" I said suddenly. "Of bloody course."

"What are you on about?" Jik said.

"Grey was the name of the man who hired the suburban art gallery in Sydney, and Grey is the name of the man who sold Updike his quote Herring unquote."

"Oh, dear." Sarah's sigh took the lift out of the spirits and the dazzle from the day.

"Sorry," I said.

There were so many of them, I thought. Wexford and Greene. The boy. The woman. Harley Renbo. Two toughs at Alice Springs, one of whom I knew by sight, and one (the one who'd been behind me) whom I didn't. The one

I didn't know might, or might not, be Beetle-brows. If he wasn't, Beetle-brows was extra.

And now Grey. And another one, somewhere.

Nine at least. Maybe ten. How could I possibly tangle all that lot up without getting crunched? Or worse, getting Sarah crunched, or Jik. Every time I moved, the serpent grew another head.

I wondered who did the actual robberies. Did they send their own two (or three) toughs overseas, or did they contract out to local labor, so to speak?

If they sent their own toughs, was it one of them who had killed Regina?

Had I already met Regina's killer? Had he thrown me over the balcony at Alice?

I pondered uselessly, and added one more twist. . . . Was he waiting ahead in Wellington?

We reached the capital in the afternoon and booked into the Townhouse Hotel because of its splendid view over the harbor. With such marvelous coastal scenery, I thought, it would have been a disgrace if the cities of New Zealand had been ugly. I still thought there were no big towns more captivating than flat old marshy London, but that was another story. Wellington, new and cared for, had life and character to spare.

I looked up the Ruapehu Fine Arts in the telephone directory and asked the hotel's reception desk how to get there. They had never heard of the gallery, but the road it was in must be up past the old town, they thought: past Thorndon.

They sold me a local area road map, which they said would help, and told me that Mount Ruapehu was (with luck) an extinct volcano, with a warm lake in its crater. If we'd come from Auckland, we must have passed nearby.

I thanked them and carried the map to Jik and Sarah upstairs in their room.

"We could find the gallery," Jik said. "But what would we do when we got there?"

"Make faces at them through the window?"

"You'd be crazy enough for that, too," Sarah said.

"Let's just go and look," I said. "They won't see us in the car if we simply drive past."

"And, after all," Jik said incautiously, "we do want them to know we're here."

"Why?" asked Sarah in amazement.

"Oh, Jesus," Jik said.

"Why?" she demanded, the anxiety crowding back.

"Ask Todd, it's his idea."

"You're a sod," I said.

"Why, Todd?"

"Because," I said, "I want them to spend all their energies looking for us over here and not clearing away every vestige of evidence in Melbourne. We do want the police to deal with them finally, don't we, because we can't exactly arrest them ourselves. Well, when the police start moving, it would be hopeless if there was no one left for them to find."

She nodded. "That's what you meant by leaving it all in working order. But . . . you didn't say anything about deliberately enticing them to follow us."

"Todd's got that list, and the pictures we took," Jik said, "and they'll want them back. Todd wants them to concentrate exclusively on getting them back, because if they think they can get them back and shut us up—"

"Jik," I interrupted. "You do go on a bit."

Sarah looked from me to him and back again. A sort of hopeless calm took over from the anxiety.

"If they think they can get everything back and shut us up," she said, "they will be actively searching for us in order to kill us. And you intend to give them every encouragement. Is that right?"

"No," I said. "Or, rather, yes."

"They'd be looking for us anyway," Jik pointed out.

"And we are going to say, 'Cooee, we're over here'?"

"Um," I said. "I think they may know already."

"God give me strength," she said. "All right. I see what you're doing, and I see why you didn't tell me. And I think you're a louse. But I'll grant you you've been a damn sight more successful than I thought you'd be, and here we all still are, safe and moderately sound, so all right, we'll let them know we're definitely here. On the strict understanding that we then keep our heads down until you've fixed the police in Melbourne."

I kissed her cheek. "Done," I said.

"So how do we do it?"

I grinned at her. "We address ourselves to the telephone."

In the end, Sarah herself made the call, on the basis

that her Australian voice would be less remarkable than Jik's Englishness, or mine.

"Is that the Ruapehu Fine Arts Gallery? It is? I wonder if you can help me," she said. "I would like to speak to whoever is in charge. Yes, I know, but it is important. Yes, I'll wait." She rolled her eyes and put her hand over the mouthpiece. "She sounded like a secretary. New Zealand, anyway."

"You're doing great," I said.

"Oh . . . Hello? Yes. Could you tell me your name, please?" Her eyes suddenly opened wide. "*Wexford*. Oh, er . . . Mr. Wexford, I've just had a visit from three extraordinary people who wanted to see a painting I bought from you some time ago. Quite extraordinary people. They said you'd sent them. I didn't believe them. I wouldn't let them in. But I thought perhaps I'd better check with you. Did you send them to see my painting?"

There was some agitated squawking from the receiver.

"Describe them? A young man with fair hair and a beard, and another young man with an injured arm, and a bedraggled-looking girl. I sent them away. I didn't like the look of them."

She grimaced over the phone and listened to some more squawks.

"No, of course I didn't give them any information. I told you I didn't like the look of them. Where do I live? Why, right here in Wellington. Well, thank you so much, Mr. Wexford; I am so pleased I called you."

She put the receiver down while it was still squawking.

"He was asking me for my name," she said.

"What a girl," Jik said. "What an actress, my wife."

Wexford. Wexford himself.

It had *worked*.

I raised a small internal cheer.

"So now that they know we're here," I said, "would you like to go off somewhere else?"

"Oh, no," Sarah said instinctively. She looked out the window across the busy harbor. "It's lovely here, and we've been traveling all day already."

I didn't argue. I thought it might take more than a single telephone call to keep the enemy interested in Wellington, and it had only been for Sarah's sake that I would have been prepared to move on.

"They won't find us just by checking the hotels by telephone," Jik pointed out. "Even if it occured to them

169

to try the Townhouse, they'd be asking for Cassavetes and Todd, not Andrews and Peel."

"Are we Andrews and Peel?" Sarah asked.

"We're Andrews. Todd's Peel."

"So nice to know," she said.

Mr. and Mrs. Andrews and Mr. Peel took dinner in the hotel restaurant without mishap, Mr. Peel having discarded his sling for the evening, on the ground that it was in general a bit too easy to notice. Mr. Andrews had declined, on the same consideration, to remove his beard.

We went in time to our separate rooms, and so to bed. I spent a jolly hour unsticking the Alice bandages from my leg and admiring the hemstitching. The tree had made tears that were far from the orderly cuts of operations, and as I inspected the long curving railway lines on a ridged backing of crimson, black, and yellow skin, I reckoned that those doctors had done an expert job. It was four days since the fall, during which time I hadn't exactly led an inactive life, but none of their handiwork had come adrift. I realized I had progressed almost without noticing it from feeling terrible all the time to scarcely feeling anything worth mentioning. It was astonishing, I thought, how quickly the human body repaired itself, given the chance.

I covered the mementos with fresh adhesive plaster bought that morning in Hamilton for the purpose, and even found a way of lying in bed that drew no strike action from mending bones. Things, I thought complacently as I drifted to sleep, were altogether looking up.

I suppose one could say that I underestimated on too many counts. I underestimated the desperation with which Wexford had come to New Zealand. Underestimated the rage and the thoroughness with which he searched for us.

Underestimated the effect of our amateur robbery on professional thieves. Underestimated our success. Underestimated the fear and the fury we had unleashed.

My picture of Wexford tearing his remaining hair in almost comic frustration was all wrong. He was pursuing us with a determination bordering on obsession, grimly, ruthlessly, and fast.

In the morning I woke late to a day of warm windy spring sunshine, and made coffee from the fixings provided by the hotel in each room; and Jik rang through on the telephone.

"Sarah says she *must* wash her hair today. Apparently it's sticking together."

"It looks all right to me."

His grin came down the wire. "Marriage opens vast new feminine horizons. Anyway, she's waiting down in the hall for me to drive her to the shops to buy some shampoo, but I thought I'd better let you know we were going."

I said uneasily, "You will be careful . . ."

"Oh, sure," he said. "We won't go anywhere near the gallery. We won't go far. Only as far as the nearest shampoo shop. I'll call you as soon as we get back."

He disconnected cheerfully, and five minutes later the bell rang again. I lifted the receiver.

It was the girl from the reception desk. "Your friends say would you join them downstairs in the car."

"O.K.," I said.

I went jacketless down in the lift, left my room key at the desk, and walked out through the front door to the sun-baked and windy car park. I looked around for Jik and Sarah; but they were not, as it happened, the friends who were waiting.

It might have been fractionally better if I hadn't had my left arm slung up inside my shirt. As it was, they simply clutched my clothes, lifted me off balance and off my feet, and ignominiously bundled me into the back of their car.

Wexford was sitting inside it: a one-man reception committee. The eyes behind the heavy spectacles were as hostile as forty below, and there was no indecision this time in his manner. This time he as good as had me again behind his steel-mesh door, and this time he was intent on not making mistakes.

He still wore a bow tie. The jaunty polka dots went oddly with the unfunny matter in hand.

The muscles propeling me toward him turned out to belong to Greene and to a thug I'd never met but who answered the general description of Beetle-brows.

My spirits descended faster than the Hilton lifts. I ended up sitting between Beetle-brows and Wexford, with Greene climbing in front into the driving seat.

"How did you find me?" I said.

Greene, with a wolfish smile, took a Polaroid photograph from his pocket and held it for me to see. It was a picture of the three of us, Jik, Sarah, and me, standing

171

by the shops in Melbourne Airport. The woman from the gallery, I guessed, had not been wasting the time she spent watching us depart.

"We went round asking the hotels," Greene said. "It was easy."

There didn't seem to be much else to say, so I didn't say anything. A slight shortage of breath might have had something to do with it.

None of the others, either, seemed overtalkative. Greene started the car and drove out into the city. Wexford stared at me with a mixture of anger and satisfaction; and Beetle-brows began twisting my free right arm behind my back in a grip that left no room for debate. He wouldn't let me remain upright. My head went practically down to my knees. It was all most undignified and excruciating.

Wexford said finally, "We want our list back."

There was nothing gentlemanly in his voice. He wasn't making light conversation. His heavy vindictive rage had no trouble at all in communicating itself to me without possibility of misunderstanding.

Oh, Christ, I thought miserably; I'd been such a bloody fool, just walking into it, like that.

"Do you hear? We want our list back, and everything else you took."

I didn't answer. Too busy suffering.

From external sounds, I guessed we were traveling through busy workaday Friday-morning city streets, but as my head was below window level, I couldn't actually see.

After some time, the car turned sharply left and ground uphill for what seemed like miles. The engine sighed from overwork at the top, and the road began to descend.

Almost nothing was said on the journey. My thoughts about what very likely lay at the end of it were so unwelcome that I did my best not to allow them houseroom. I could give Wexford his list back, but what then? What then, indeed.

After a long descent, the car halted briefly and then turned to the right. We had exchanged city sounds for those of the sea. There were also no more Doppler effects from cars passing us from the opposite direction. I came to the sad conclusion that we had turned off the highway and were on our way along an infrequently used side road.

The car stopped eventually, with a jerk.

Beetle-brows removed his hands. I sat up stiffly, wrenched and unenthusiastic.

They could hardly have picked a lonelier place. The road ran along beside the sea so closely that it was more or less part of the shore, and the shore was a jungle of sharply pointed rough black rocks with frothy white waves slapping among them, a far cry from the gentle beaches of home.

On the right rose jagged cliffs, steeply towering. Ahead, the road ended blindly in some workings that looked like a sort of quarry. Slabs had been cut from the cliffs, and there were dusty clearings, and huge heaps of small jagged rocks, and graded stones, and sifted chips. All raw and harsh and blackly volcanic.

No people. No machinery. No sign of occupation.

"Where's the list?" Wexford said.

Greene twisted round in the driving seat and looked seriously at my face.

"You'll tell us," he said. "With or without a beating. And we won't hit you with our fists, but with pieces of rock."

Beetle-brows said aggrievedly, "What's wrong with fists?" But what was wrong with Greene's fists was the same as with mine: I would never have been able to hit anyone hard enough to get the desired results. The local rocks, by the look of them, were something else.

"What if I tell you?" I said.

They hadn't expected anything so easy. I could see the surprise on their faces, and it was flattering, in a way. There was also a furtiveness in their expressions that boded no good at all. Regina, I thought. Regina, with her head bashed in.

I looked at the cliffs, the quarry, the sea. No easy exit. And behind us the road. If I ran that way, they would drive after me and mow me down. If I could run. And even that was problematical.

I swallowed and looked dejected, which wasn't awfully difficult.

"I'll tell you . . ." I said. "Out of the car."

There was a small silence while they considered it; but as they weren't going to have room for much crashing around with rocks in that crowded interior anyway, they weren't entirely against it.

Greene leaned over toward the glove compartment on

the passenger side, opened it, and drew out a pistol. I knew just about enough about firearms to distinguish a revolver from an automatic, and this was a revolver, a gun whose main advantage, I had read, was that it never jammed.

Greene handled it with a great deal more respect than familiarity. He showed it to me silently, and returned it to the glove compartment, leaving the hinged flap open so that we all had a clear view of his ultimate threat.

"Get out, then," Wexford said.

We all got out, and I made sure that I ended up on the side of the sea. The wind was much stronger on this exposed coast, and chilling in the bright sunshine. It lifted the thin carefully combed hair away from Wexford's crown, and left him straggly bald, and intensified the stupid look of Beetle-brows. Greene's eyes stayed as watchful and sharp as the harsh terrain around us.

"All right, then," Wexford said roughly, shouting a little to bring his voice above the din of sea and sky. "Where's the list?"

I whirled away from them and did my best to sprint for the sea.

I thrust my right hand inside my shirt and tugged at the sling-forming bandages.

Wexford, Greene, and Beetle-brows shouted furiously and almost trampled on my heels.

I pulled the lists of overseas customers out of the sling, whirled again with them in my hand, and flung them with a bowling action as far out to sea as I could manage.

The pages fluttered apart in midair, but the offshore winds caught most of them beautifully and blew them like great leaves out to sea.

I didn't stop at the water's edge. I went straight on into the cold inhospitable battlefield of shark-teeth rocks and green water and white foaming waves. Slipping, falling, getting up, staggering on, finding that the current was much stronger than I'd expected, and the rocks more abrasive, and the footing more treacherous. Finding I'd fled from one deadly danger to embrace another.

For one second, I looked back.

Wexford had followed me a step or two into the sea, but only, it seemed, to reach one of the pages, which had fallen shorter than the others. He was standing there with the frothy water swirling round his trouser legs, peering at the sodden paper.

Greene was beside the car, leaning in; by the front passenger seat.

Beetle-brows had his mouth open.

I reapplied myself to the problem of survival.

The shore shelved, as most shores do. Every forward step led into a stronger current, which sucked and pulled and shoved me around like a piece of flotsam. Hip-deep between waves, I found it difficult to stay on my feet, and every time I didn't I was in dire trouble, because of the black needle-sharp rocks waiting in ranks above and below the surface to scratch and tear.

The rocks were not the kind I was used to: not the hard familiar lumpy rocks of Britain, polished by the sea. These were the raw stuff of volcanoes, as scratchy as pumice. One's groping hand didn't slide over them; one's skin stuck to them, and tore off. Clothes fared no better. Before I'd gone thirty yards, I was running with blood from a dozen superficial grazes; and no blood vessels bleed more convincingly than the small surface capillaries.

My left arm was still tangled inside the sling, which had housed the overseas-customers list since Cup Day as an insurance against having my room robbed, as at Alice. Soaking wet, the bandages now clung like leeches, and my shirt also. Muscles weakened by a fracture and inactivity couldn't deal with them. I rolled around a lot from not having two hands free.

My foot stepped awkwardly on the side of a submerged rock and I felt it scrape my shin: lost my balance, fell forward, tried to save myself with my hand, failed, crashed chest-first against a small jagged peak dead ahead, and jerked my head sharply sideways to avoid connecting with my nose.

The rock beside my cheek splintered suddenly as if exploding. Slivers of it prickled in my face. For a flicker of time I couldn't undestand it; and then I struggled round and looked back to the shore with a flood of foreboding.

Greene was standing there, aiming the pistol, shooting to kill.

CHAPTER 15

Thirty to thirty-five yards is a long way for a pistol; but Greene seemed so close.

I could see his drooping mustache and the lank hair blowing in the wind. I could see his eyes and the concentration in his body. He was standing with his legs straddled and his arms out straight ahead, aiming the pistol with both hands.

I couldn't hear the shots above the crash of the waves on the rocks. I couldn't see him squeeze the trigger. But I did see the upward jerk of the arms at the recoil, and I reckoned it would be just plain silly to give him a stationary target.

I was, in all honesty, pretty frightened. I must have looked as close to him as he to me. He must have been quite certain he would hit me, even though his tenderness with the pistol in the car had made me think he was not an expert.

I turned and stumbled a yard or two onward, though the going became even rougher, and the relentless fight against current and waves and rocks was draining me to rags.

There would have to be an end to it.

Have to be.

I stumbled and fell on a jagged edge and gashed the inside of my right forearm, and out poured more good red life. Christ, I thought, I must be scarlet all over, leaking from a hundred tiny nicks.

It at least gave me an idea.

I was waist-deep in dangerous green water, with most of the shoreline rocks now submerged beneath the surface. Close to one side, a row of bigger rock teeth ran out from the shore like a nightmarish breakwater, and I'd shied away from it because of the even fiercer waves crashing against it. But it represented the only cover in sight. Three stumbling efforts took me nearer; and the current helped.

I looked back at Greene. He was reloading the gun. Wexford was practically dancing up and down beside him, urging him on; and Beetle-brows—from his disinclination to chase me—probably couldn't swim.

Greene slapped shut the gun and raised it again in my direction.

I took a frightful chance.

I held my fast-bleeding forearm close across my chest; and I stood up, swaying in the current, visible to him from the waist up.

I watched him aim, with both arms straight. It would take a marksman, I believed, to hit me with that pistol from that distance in that wind. A marksman whose arms didn't jerk upward when he fired.

All the same, I felt sick.

The gun was pointing straight at me.

I saw the jerk as he squeezed the trigger.

For an absolutely petrifying second I was convinced he had shot accurately; but I didn't feel or see or even hear the passing of the flying death.

I flung my own right arm wide and high, and paused there facing him for a frozen second, letting him see that most of the front of my shirt was scarlet with blood.

Then I twisted artistically and fell flat, face downward, into the water; and hoped to God he would think he had killed me.

The sea wasn't much better than bullets. Nothing less than extreme fear of the alternative would have kept me down in it, tumbling and crashing against the submerged razor edges like a piece of cheese in a grater.

The waves themselves swept me toward the taller

breakwater teeth, and with a fair amount of desperation I tried to get a grip on them to avoid being alternately sucked off and flung back, and losing a lot more skin.

There was also the problem of not struggling too visibly. If Wexford or Greene saw me threshing about, all my histrionics would have been in vain.

As much by luck as trying, I found the sea shoving me into a wedge-shaped crevice between the rocks, from where I was unable to see the shore. I clutched for a handhold, and then with bent knees found a good foothold, and clung there precariously while the sea tried to drag me out again. Every time a wave rolled in, it tended to float my foot out of the niche it was lodged in, and every time it receded, it tried to suck me with it in a siphonic action. I clung, and seesawed in the chest-high water, and clung, and seesawed, and grew progressively more exhausted.

I could hear nothing except the waves on the rocks. I wondered forlornly how long Wexford and Greene would stay there staring out to sea for signs of life. I didn't dare to look, in case they spotted my moving head.

The water was cold, and the grazes gradually stopped bleeding, including the useful gash on my forearm. Absolutely nothing, I thought, like having a young strong healthy body. Absolutely nothing like having a young strong healthy body on dry land with a paintbrush in one hand and a beer in the other, with the nice friendly airliners thundering overhead and no money to pay the gas.

Fatigue, in the end, made me look. It was either that or cling like a limpet until I literally fell off nervelessly, too weak to struggle back to life.

To look, I had to let go. I tried to find other holds, but they weren't as good. The first outgoing wave took me with it in no uncertain terms; and its incoming fellow threw me back.

In the tumbling interval I caught a glimpse of the shore.

The road, the cliffs, the quarry, as before. Also the car. Also people.

Bloody damn, I thought.

My hand scrambled for its former hold. My fingers were cramped, bleeding again, and cold. Oh, Christ, I thought. How much longer?"

It was a measure of my tiredness that it took the space

of three in-and-out waves for me to realize that it wasn't Wexford's car, and it wasn't Wexford standing on the road.

If it wasn't Wexford, it didn't matter who it was.

I let go again of the handhold and tried to ride the wave as far out of the crevice as possible, and to swim away from the return force flinging me back. All the other rocks were still there under the surface. A few yards was a heck of long way.

I stood up gingerly, feeling for my footing more carefully than on the outward flight, and took a longer look at the road.

A gray-white car. A couple beside it, standing close, the man with his arms round the girl.

A nice quiet spot for it, I thought sardonically. I hoped they would drive me somewhere dry.

They moved apart and stared out to sea.

I stared back.

For an instant it seemed impossible. Then they started waving their arms furiously and ran toward the water; and it was Sarah and Jik.

Throwing off his jacket, Jik plowed into the waves with enthusiasm, and came to smart halt as the realities of the situation scraped his legs. All the same, he came on after a pause toward me, taking care.

I made my slow way back. Even without haste driving like a fury, any passage through those wave-swept rocks was ruin to the epidermis. By the time we met, we were both streaked with red.

We looked at each other's blood. Jik said "Jesus," and I said "Christ," and it occurred to me that maybe the Almighty would think we had been calling for His help a bit too often.

Jik put his arm round my waist and I held on to his shoulders, and together we stumbled slowly to land. We fell now and then. Got up gasping. Reclutched, and went on.

He let go when we reached the road. I sat down on the edge of it with my feet pointing out to sea, and positively drooped.

"Todd," Sarah said anxiously. She came nearer. *"Todd."* Her voice was incredulous. "Are you *laughing?"*

"Sure." I looked up at her, grinning. "Whyever not?"

Jik's shirt was torn, and mine was in tatters. We took

179

them off and used them to mop up the grazes that were still persistently oozing. To judge from the expression on Sarah's face, we must have looked crazy.

"What a damn silly place to bathe," Jik said.

"Free back-scratchers," I said.

He glanced round behind me. "Your Alice Springs dressing has come off."

"How're the stitches?"

"Intact."

"Bully for them."

"You'll both get pneumonia, sitting there," Sarah said.

I took off the remnants of sling. All in all, I thought, it had served me pretty well. The adhesive rib-supporting cummerbund was still more or less in place, but had mostly come unstuck through too much immersion. I pulled that off also. That only left the plasters on my leg, and they, too, I found, had floated off in the melee. The trousers I'd worn over them had windows everywhere.

"Quite a dust-up," Jik observed, pouring water out of his shoes and shivering.

"We need a telephone," I said, doing the same.

"Give me strength," Sarah said. "What you need is hot baths, warm clothes, and half a dozen psychiatrists."

"How did you get here?" I asked.

"How come you aren't dead?" Jik said.

"You first."

"I came out of the shop where I'd bought the shampoo," Sarah said, "and I saw Greene drive past. I nearly died on the spot. I just stood still hoping he wouldn't look my way, and he didn't. . . . The car turned to the left just past where I was, and I could see there were two other people in the back . . . and I went back to our car and told Jik."

"We thought it damn lucky he hadn't spotted her," Jik said, dabbing at persistent scarlet trickles. "We went back to the hotel, and you weren't there, so we asked the girl at the desk if you'd left a message, and she said you'd gone off in a car with some friends. . . . With a man with a droopy mustache."

"Friends!" Sarah said.

"Anyway," Jik continued, "choking down our rage, sorrow, indignation, and whatnot, we thought we'd better look for your body."

"Jik!" Sarah protested.

He grinned. "And who was crying?"

"Shut up."

"Sarah hadn't seen any sign of you in Greene's car, but we thought you might be imitating a sack of potatoes in the boot or something, so we got out the road map, applied our feet to the accelerator, and set off in pursuit. Turned left where Greene had gone, and found ourselves climbing a ruddy mountain."

I surveyed our extensive grazes and scratches. "I think we'd better get some disinfectant," I said.

"We could bathe in it."

"Good idea."

I could hear his teeth chattering even above the din of my own.

"Let's get out of this wind," I said. "And bleed in the car."

We crawled stiffly into the seats. Sarah said it was lucky the upholstery was plastic. Jik automatically took his place behind the wheel.

"We drove for miles," he said. "Growing, I may say, a little frantic. Over the top of the mountain and down this side. At the bottom of the hill, the road swings round to the left, and we could see from the map that it follows the coastline round a whole lot of bays and eventually ends up right back in Wellington."

He started the car, turned it, and rolled gently ahead. Naked to the waist, wet from there down, and still with beads of blood forming and overflowing, he looked an unorthodox chauffeur. The beard, above, was undaunted.

"We went that way," Sarah said. "There was nothing but miles of craggy rocks and sea."

"I'll paint those rocks," Jik said.

Sarah glanced at his face, and then at me. She'd heard the fervor in that statement of intent. The golden time was almost over.

"After a bit we turned back," Jik said. "There was this bit of road saying 'No Through Road,' so we came down it. No you, of course. We stopped here on this spot and Sarah got out of the car and started bawling her eyes out."

"You weren't exactly cheering yourself," she said.

"Huh," he said, smiling. "Anyway, I kicked a few stones about, wondering what to do next, and there were those cartridges."

"Those what?"

"On the edge of the road. All close together. Maybe

181

dropped out of one of those spider-ejection revolvers, or something like that."

"When we saw them," Sarah said, "we thought . . ."

"It could have been anyone popping off at sea birds," I said "And I think we might go back and pick them up."

"Are you serious?" Jik said.

"Yeah."

We stopped, turned again, and retraced our tire treads.

"No one shoots sea birds with a revolver," he said. "But bloody awful painters of slow horses, that's different."

The quarry came in sight again. Jik drew up and stopped, and Sarah, hopping out quickly, told us to stay where we were, she would fetch the bullet cases.

"They really did shoot at you?" Jik said.

"Greene. He missed."

"Inefficient." He shifted in his seat, wincing. "They must have gone back over the hill while we were looking for you round the bays." He glanced at Sarah as she searched along the side of the road. "Did they take the list?"

"I threw it in the sea." I smiled lopsidedly. "It seemed too tame just to hand it over . . . and it made a handy diversion. They salvaged enough to see that they'd got what they wanted."

"It must all have been a bugger."

"Hilarious."

Sarah found the cases, picked them up, and came running back. "Here they are. I'll put them in my handbag." She slid into the passenger seat. "What now?"

"Telephone," I said.

"Like that?" She looked me over. "Have you any idea—" She stopped. "Well," she said, "I'll buy you each a shirt at the first shop we come to." She swallowed. "And don't say what if it's a grocery."

"What if it's a grocery?" Jik said.

We set off again, and at the intersection turned left to go back over the hill, because it was about a quarter of the distance.

Near the top there was a large village with the sort of store that sold everything from hammers to hairpins. Also groceries. Also, upon inquiry, shirts. Sarah made a face at Jik and vanished inside.

I pulled on the resulting navy T-shirt and made wobbly tracks for the telephone, clutching Sarah's purse.

"Operator . . . which hotels have a telex?"

She told me three. One was the Townhouse. I thanked her and rang off.

I called the Townhouse. Remembered, with an effort, that my name was Peel.

"But, Mr. Peel," said the girl, sounding bewildered. "Your friend—the one with the mustache, not the one with the beard—he paid your account not half an hour ago and collected all your things. . . . Yes, I suppose it is irregular, but he brought your note asking us to let him have your room key. . . . I'm sorry but I didn't know you hadn't written it. . . . Yes, he took all your things: the room's being cleaned at this minute."

"Look," I said, "can you send a telex for me? Put it on my friend Mr.—er—Andrews's bill."

She said she would. I dictated the message. She repeated it, and said she would send it at once.

"I'll call again soon for the reply," I said.

Sarah had bought jeans for us, and dry socks. Jik drove out of the village to a more modest spot, and we put them on: hardly the world's best fit, but they hid the damage.

"Where now?" he said. "Intensive Care Unit?"

"Back to the telephone."

"Jesus God Almighty."

He drove back, and I called the Townhouse. The girl said she'd received an answer, and read it out. "Telephone at once, reverse charges," she said. "And there's a number. . . ." She read it out, twice. I repeated it. "That's right."

I thanked her.

"No sweat," she said. "Sorry about your things."

I called the international exchange and gave them the number. It had a priority rating, they said. The call would be through in ten minutes. They would ring back.

The telephone was on the wall of a booth inside the general store. There was nothing to sit on. I wished to God there was.

The ten minutes dragged slowly by. Nine and a half, to be exact.

The bell rang, and I picked up the receiver.

"Your call to England . . ."

The modern miracle. Halfway round the world, and I was talking to Inspector Frost as if he were in the next room. Eleven-thirty in the morning at Wellington: half past midnight in Shropshire.

"Your letter arrived today, sir," he said. "And action has already been started."

"Stop calling me sir. I'm used to Todd."

"All right. Well, we telexed Melbourne to alert them, and we've started checking on all the people on the England list. The results are already incredible. All the crossed-out names we've checked so far have been the victims of break-ins. We're alerting the police in all the other countries concerned. The only thing is, we see the list you sent us is a photocopy. Do you have the original?"

"No . . . Most of it got destroyed. Does it matter?"

"Not really. Can you tell us how it came into your possession?"

"Er . . . I think we'd better say it just did."

A dry laugh traveled twelve thousand miles.

"All right. Now what's so urgent that you're keeping me from my bed?"

"Are you at home?" I said contritely.

"On duty, as it happens. Fire away."

"Two things. One is, I can save you time with the stock-list numbers. But first . . ." I told him about Wexford and Greene being in Wellington, and about them stealing my things. "They've got my passport and traveler's checks, and also my suitcase which contains painting equipment."

"I saw it at your cousin's," he said.

"That's right. I think they may also have a page or two of the list. . . ."

"Say that again."

I said it again. "Most of it got thrown into the sea, but I know Wexford regained at least one page. Well . . . I thought they'd be going back to Melbourne, probably to-day—any minute, really—and when they land there, there's a good chance they'll have at least some of those things with them."

"I can fix a customs search," he said. "But why should they risk stealing?"

"They don't know I know," I said. "I think they think I'm dead."

"Good God. Why?"

"They took a pot shot at me. Would bullet cases be of any use? Fortunately I didn't collect a bullet, but I've got six shells."

"They may be. . . ." His voice sounded faint. "What about the stock list?"

"In the shorter list . . . Got it?"

"Yes, in front of me."

"Right. The first letter is for the city the painting was sold in: M for Melbourne, S for Sydney, W for Wellington. The second letter identifies the painter: M for Munnings, H for Herring, and I think R for Raoul Millais. The letter C stands for copy. All the paintings on that list are copies. All the ones on the longer list are originals. Got that?"

"Yes. Go on."

"The numbers are just numbers. They'd sold fifty-four copies when I—er—when the list reached me. The last letter R stands for Renbo. That's Harley Renbo, who was working at Alice Springs. If you remember, I told you about him last time."

"I remember," he said.

"Wexford and Greene have spent the last couple of days chasing around in New Zealand, so with a bit of luck they will not have destroyed anything dodgy in the Melbourne gallery. If the Melbourne police can arrange a search, there might be a harvest."

"It's their belief that the disappearance of the list from the gallery will have already led to the immediate destruction of anything else incriminating."

"They may be wrong. Wexford and Greene don't know I photocopied the list and sent it to you. They think the list is floating safely out to sea, and me with it."

"I'll pass your message to Melbourne."

"There's also another gallery here in Wellington, and an imitation Herring they sold to a man in Auckland."

"For heaven's sake."

I gave him the Ruapehu address, and mentioned Norman Updike.

"There's also a recurring B on the long stock list, so there's probably another gallery. In Brisbane, maybe. There may also be another one in Sydney. I shouldn't think the suburban place I told you about had proved central enough, so they shut it."

"Stop," he said.

"Sorry," I said. "But the organization is like a mushroom. It burrows along underground and pops up everywhere."

"I only said stop so I could change the tape on the recorder. You can carry right on now."

"Oh." I half laughed. "Well . . . did you get any answers from Donald to my questions?"

"Yes, we did."

"Carefully?"

"Rest assured," he said dryly. "We carried out your wishes to the letter. Mr Stuart's answers were 'Yes, of course' to the first question, and 'No, whyever should I' to the second, and 'Yes' to the third."

"Was he absolutely certain?"

"Absolutely." He cleared his throat. "He seems distant and withdrawn. Uninterested. But quite definite."

"How is he?" I asked.

"He spends all his time looking at a picture of his wife. Every time we call at his house, we can see him through the front window, just sitting there."

"He is still . . . sane?"

"I'm no judge."

"You can at least let him know that he's no longer suspected of engineering the robbery and killing Regina."

"That's a decision for my superiors," he said.

"Well, kick them into it," I said. "Do the police positively yearn for bad publicity?"

"You were quick enough to ask our help," he said tartly.

To do your job, I thought. I didn't say it aloud. The silence spoke for itself.

"Well . . ." His voice carried a mild apology. "Our cooperation, then." He paused. "Where are you now? When I've telexed Melbourne, I may need to talk to you again."

"I'm in a phone booth in a country store in a village on the hills above Wellington."

"Where are you going next?"

"I'm staying right here. Wexford and Greene are still around in the city, and I don't want to risk the outside chance of their seeing me."

"Give me the number, then."

I read it off the telephone.

"I want to come home as soon as possible," I said. "Can you do anything about my passport?"

"You'll have to find a consul."

Oh, ta, I thought tiredly. I hung up the receiver and wobbled back to the car.

"Tell you what," I said, dragging into the back seat, "I

186

could do with a double hamburger and a bottle of brandy."

We sat in the car for two hours.

The store didn't sell liquor or hot food. Sarah bought a packet of biscuits. We ate them.

"We can't stay here all day," she said explosively, after a lengthy glum silence.

I couldn't be sure that Wexford wasn't out searching for her and Jik with murderous intent, and I didn't think she'd be happy to know it.

"We're perfectly safe here," I said.

"Just quietly dying of blood poisoning," Jik agreed.

"I left my pills in the Hilton," Sarah said.

Jik stared. "What's that got to do with it?"

"Nothing. I just thought you might like to know."

"*The* pill?" I asked.

"Yes."

"Jesus," Jik said.

A delivery van struggled up the hill and stopped outside the shop. A man in an overall opened the back, took out a large bakery tray, and carried it in.

"Food," I said hopefully.

Sarah went in to investigate. Jik took the opportunity to unstick his T-shirt from his healing grazes, but I didn't bother.

"You'll be glued to those clothes, if you don't," Jik said, grimacing over his task.

"I'll soak them off."

"All those cuts and things didn't feel so bad when we were in the sea."

"No."

"Catches up with you a bit, doesn't it?"

"Mmm."

He glanced at me. "Why don't you just scream or something?"

"Can't be bothered. Why don't you?"

He grinned. "I'll scream in paint."

Sarah came back with fresh doughnuts and cans of Coke. We made inroads, and I at least felt healthier.

After another half-hour, the storekeeper appeared in the doorway, shouting and beckoning.

"A call for you . . ."

I went stiffly to the telephone. It was Frost, clear as a bell.

187

"Wexford, Greene, and Snell have booked a flight to Melbourne. They will be met at Melbourne Airport."

"Who's Snell?" I said.

"How do I know? He was traveling with the other two."

Beetle-brows, I thought.

"Now, listen," Frost said. "The telex has been red-hot between here and Melbourne, and the police there want your cooperation, just to clinch things. . . ." He went on talking for a long time. At the end he said, "Will you do that?"

I'm tired, I thought. I'm battered, and I hurt. I've done just about enough.

"All right."

Might as well finish it, I supposed.

"The Melbourne police want to know for sure that the three Munnings copies you—er—acquired from the gallery are still where you told me."

"Yes, they are."

"Right. Well . . . good luck."

CHAPTER 16

We flew Air New Zealand back to Melbourne, tended by angels in sea-green. Sarah looked fresh, Jik definitely shopworn, and I apparently like a mixture (Jik said) of yellow ocher, Payne's gray, and white, which I didn't think was possible.

Our passage had been oiled by telexes from above. When we arrived at the airport after collecting Sarah's belongings in their carrier bags from the Townhouse, we found ourselves whisked into a private room, plied with strong drink, and subsequently taken by car straight out across the tarmac to the airplane.

A thousand miles across the Tasman Sea and an afternoon tea later, we were driven straight from the aircraft's steps to another small airport room, which contained no strong drink but only a large hard Australian plainclothes policeman.

"Porter," he said, introducing himself and squeezing our bones in a blacksmith's grip. "Which of you is Charles Todd?"

"I am."

"Right on, Mr. Todd." He looked at me without favor. "Are you ill, or something?" He had a strong rough voice and a strong rough manner, natural aids to putting the fear of God into the chummy and bringing on breakdowns in the nervous. To me, I gradually gathered, he was grudgingly offering the status of temporary inferior colleague.

"No," I said, sighing slightly. Time and airline schedules waited for no man. If I'd spent time on first aid, we'd have missed the only possible flight.

"His clothes are sticking to him," Jik observed, giving the familiar phrase the usual meaning of being hot. It was cool in Melbourne. Porter looked at him uncertainly.

I grinned. "Did you manage what you planned?" I asked him. He decided Jik was nuts and switched his gaze back to me.

"We decided not to go ahead until you had arrived," he said, shrugging. "There's a car waiting outside." He wheeled out of the door without holding it for Sarah and marched briskly off.

The car had a chauffeur. Porter sat in front, talking on a radio, saying in stiltedly guarded sentences that the party had arrived and the proposals should be implemented.

"Where are we going?" Sarah said.

"To reunite you with your clothes," I said.

Her face lit up. "Are we really?"

"And what for?" Jik asked.

"To bring the mouse to the cheese." And the bull to the sword, I thought; and the moment of truth to the conjurer.

"We got your things back, Todd," Porter said with satisfaction. "Wexford, Greene, and Snell were turned over on entry, and they copped them with the lot. The locks on your suitcase were scratched and dented but they hadn't been burst open. Everything inside should be O.K. You can collect everything in the morning."

"That's great," I said. "Did they still have any of the lists of customers?"

"Yeah. Damp but readable. Names of guys in Canada."

"Good."

"We're turning over that Yarra gallery right this minute, and Wexford is there helping. We've let him overhear what we wanted him to, and as soon as I give the go-ahead we'll let him take action."

"Do you think he will?" I said.

"Look, Mister, wouldn't you?"

190

I thought I might be wary of gifts from the Greeks, but then I wasn't Wexford, and I didn't have a jail sentence breathing down my neck.

We pulled up at the side door of the Hilton. Porter raised himself agilely to the pavement and stood like a solid pillar, watching with half-concealed impatience while Jik, Sarah, and I eased ourselves slowly out. We all went across the familiar red, purple, and blue opulence of the great entrance hall, and from there through a gate in the reception desk, and into the hotel manager's office at the rear.

A tall dark-suited member of the hotel staff there offered us chairs, coffee, and sandwiches. Porter looked at his watch and offered us an indeterminate wait.

It was six o'clock. After ten minutes, a man in shirt and neck-tie brought a two-way personal radio for Porter, who slipped the earplug into place and began listening to disembodied voices.

The office was a working room, lit by neon strips and furnished functionally, with a wallpapering of charts and duty rosters. There were no outside windows: nothing to show the fade of day to night.

We sat, and drank coffee, and waited. Porter ate three of the sandwiches simultaneously. Time passed.

Seven o'clock.

Sarah was looking pale in the artificial light, and tired also. So was Jik, his beard on his chest. I sat and thought about life and death and polka dots.

At seven-eleven, Porter clutched his ear and concentrated intently on the ceiling. When he relaxed, he passed to us the galvanic message.

"Wexford did just what we reckoned he would, and the engine's turning over."

"What engine?" Sarah said.

Porter stared at her blankly. "What we planned," he said painstakingly, "is happening."

"Oh."

Porter listened again to his private ear and spoke directly to me. "He's taken the bait."

"He's a fool," I said.

Porter came as near to a smile as he could. "All crooks are fools, one way or another."

Seven-thirty came and went. I raised my eyebrows at Porter. He shook his head.

"We can't say too much on the radio," he said. "Because you get all sorts of ears listening in."

Just like England, I thought. The press could turn up at a crime before the police; and the mouse might hear of the trap.

We waited. The time dragged. Jik yawned and Sarah's eyes were dark with fatigue. Outside, in the lobby, the busy rich life of the hotel chattered on unruffled, with guests' spirits rising toward the next day's race meeting, the last of the carnival.

The Derby on Saturday, the Cup on Tuesday, the Oaks (which we'd missed) on Thursday, and the International Day on Saturday. No serious racegoers went home before the end of things if they could help it.

Porter clutched his ear again, and stiffened.

"He's here," he said.

My heart, for some unaccountable reason, began beating overtime. We were in no danger that I could see, yet there it was, thumping away like a steam organ.

Porter disconnected himself from the radio, put it on the manager's desk, and went out into the foyer.

"What do we do?" Sarah said.

"Nothing much except listen."

We all three went over to the door and held it six inches open. We listened to people asking for their room keys, asking for letters and messages, asking for Mr. and Mrs. So-and-So, and which way to Toorak, and how did you get to Fanny's.

Then, suddenly, the familiar voice, sending electric fizzes to my fingertips. Confident: not expecting trouble. "I've come to collect a package left here last Tuesday by a Mr. Charles Todd. He says he checked it into the baggage room. I have a letter here from him authorizing you to release it to me."

There was a crackle of paper as the letter was handed over. Sarah's eyes were round and startled.

"Did you write it?" she whispered.

I shook my head. "No."

The desk clerk outside said, "Thank you, sir. If you'll just wait a moment, I'll fetch the package."

There was a long pause. My heart made a lot of noise, but nothing much else happened.

The desk clerk came back. "Here you are, sir. Paintings, sir."

"That's right."

There were vague sounds of the bundle of paintings and the print folder being carried along outside the door.

"I'll bring them round for you," said the clerk, suddenly closer to us. "Here we are, sir." He went past the office, through the door in the desk, and round to the front. "Can you manage them, sir?"

"Yes. Yes. Thank you." There was haste in his voice, now that he'd got his hands on the goods. "Thank you. Goodbye."

Sarah had begun to say "Is that all?" in disappointment when Porter's loud voice chopped in to the Hilton velvet like a hatchet.

"I guess we'll take care of those paintings, if you don't mind," he said. "Porter, Melbourne city police."

I opened the door a little more, and looked out. Porter stood foursquare in the lobby, large and rough, holding out a demanding hand.

At his elbows, two plainclothes policemen. At the front door, two more, in uniform. There would be others, I supposed, at the other exits. They weren't taking any chances.

"Why—er—Inspector . . . I'm only on an errand—er—for my young friend Charles Todd."

"And these paintings?"

"I've no idea what they are. He asked me to fetch them for him."

I walked quietly out of the office, through the gate, and round to the front. I leaned a little wearily against the reception desk. He was only six feet away, in front of me to my right. I could have stretched forward and touched him. I hoped Porter would think it near enough, as requested.

A certain amount of unease had pervaded the Hilton guests. They stood around in an uneven semicircle, eyeing the proceedings sideways.

"Mr. Charles Todd asked you to fetch them?" Porter said loudly.

"Yes, that's right."

Porter's gaze switched abruptly to my face.

"Did you ask him?"

"No," I said.

The explosive effect was all that the Melbourne police could have asked, and a good deal more than I expected. There was no polite quiet identification followed by a polite quiet arrest. I should have remembered all my own theories about the basic brutality of the directing mind.

I found myself staring straight into the eyes of the bull. He realized that he'd been tricked. Had convicted himself out of his own mouth and by his own presence on such an errand. The fury rose in him like a geyser and his hands reached out to grab my neck.

"*You're dead!*" he yelled. "*You're fucking dead!*"

His plunging weight took me off balance and down onto one knee, smothering under his choking grip and two hundred pounds of city suiting; trying to beat him off with my fists and not succeeding. His anger poured over me like lava. Heaven knows what he intended, but Porter's men pulled him off before he did bloody murder on the plushy carpet. As I got creakily to my feet, I heard the handcuffs click.

He was standing there, close to me, quivering in the restraining hands, breathing heavily, disheveled and bitter-eyed. Civilized exterior all stripped away by one instant of ungovernable rage. The violent core plain to see.

"Hello, Hudson," I said.

"Sorry," Porter said perfunctorily. "Didn't reckon he'd turn wild."

"Revert," I said.

"Uh?"

"He always was wild," I said. "Underneath."

"You'd know," he said. "I never saw the guy before." He nodded to Jik and Sarah and finally to me, and hurried away after his departing prisoner.

We looked at each other a little blankly. The hotel guests stared at us curiously and began to drift away. We sat down weakly on the nearest blue velvet seat, Sarah in the middle.

Jik took her hand and squeezed it. She put her fingers over mine.

It had taken nine days.

It had been a long haul.

"Don't know about you," Jik said. "But I could do with a beer."

"Todd," said Sarah, "start talking."

We were upstairs in a bedroom (mine) with both of

them in a relaxed mood, and me in Jik's dressing gown, and he and I in a cloud of Dettol.

I yawned. "About Hudson?"

"Who else? And don't go to sleep before you've told us."

"Well . . . I was looking for him, or someone like him, before I ever met him."

"But why?"

"Because of the wine," I said. "Because of the wine which was stolen from Donald's cellar. Whoever stole it not only knew it was there, down some stairs behind an inconspicuous cupboardlike door—and I'd stayed several times in the house and never knew the cellar existed—but, according to Donald, they would have had to come prepared with proper cases to pack it in. Wine is usually packed twelve bottles in a case, and Donald had two thousand or more bottles stolen. In bulk alone it would have taken a lot of shifting. A lot of time, too, and time for house-breakers is risky. But also it was special wine. A small fortune, Donald said. The sort of wine that's bought and sold as an asset and ends up at a week's wage a bottle, if it's ever drunk at all. Anyway, it was the sort of wine that needed expert handling and marketing if it was to be worth the difficulty of stealing it in the first place . . . and as Donald's business is wine, and the reason for his journey to Australia was wine, I started looking right away for someone who knew Donald, knew he'd bought a Munnings, and knew about good wine and how to sell it. And there, straight away, was Hudson Taylor, who matched like a glove. But it seemed too easy . . . because he didn't *look* right."

"Smooth and friendly," said Sarah, nodding.

"And rich," Jik added.

"Probably a moneyholic," I said, pulling open the bed and looking longingly at the cool white sheets.

"A what?"

"Moneyholic. A word I've just made up to describe someone with an uncontrollable addiction to money."

"The world's full of them," Jik said, laughing.

I shook my head. "The world is full of drinkers, but alcoholics are obsessive. Moneyholics are obsessive. They never have enough. They *cannot* have enough. However much they have, they want more. And I'm not talking about the average hard-up man, but about real screwballs. Money, money, money. Like a drug. Moneyholics will do anything to get it. Kidnap, murder, cook the computer, rob banks, sell their grandmothers—you name it."

I sat on the bed with my feet up, feeling less than fit. Sore from too many bruises, on fire from too many cuts. Jik, too, I guessed. They had been wicked rocks.

"Moneyholism," Jik said, like a lecturer to a dimmish class, "is a widespread disease easily understood by everyone who has ever felt a twinge of greed, which is everyone."

"Go on about Hudson," Sarah said.

"Hudson had the organizing ability. . . . I didn't know when I came that the organization was so huge, but I did know it was *organized,* if you see what I mean. It was an overseas operation. It took some doing. Know-how."

Jik tugged the ring off a can of beer and passed the can to me, wincing as he stretched.

"But he convinced me I was wrong about him," I said, drinking through the triangular hole. "Because he was so careful. He pretended he had to look up the name of the gallery where Donald bought his picture. He didn't think of me as a threat, of course, but just as Donald's cousin. Not until he talked to Wexford down on the lawn."

"I remember," Sarah said. "When you said it had ripped the whole works apart."

"Mmm . . . I thought it was only that he had told Wexford I was Donald's cousin, but of course Wexford also told *him* that I'd met Greene in Maisie's ruins in Sussex and then turned up in the gallery looking at the original of Maisie's burnt painting."

"Jesus Almighty," Jik said. "No wonder we beat it to Alice Springs."

"Yes, but by then I didn't think it could be Hudson I was looking for. I was looking for someone brutal, who passed on his violence through his employees. Hudson didn't look or act brutal." I paused. "The only slightest crack was when his gamble went down the drain at the races. He gripped his binoculars so hard that his knuckles showed white. But you can't think a man is a big-time thug just because he gets upset over losing a bet."

Jik grinned. "I'd qualify."

"In spades, redoubled," Sarah said.

"I was thinking about it in the Alice Springs Hospital. . . . There hadn't been time for the musclemen to get to Alice from Melbourne between us buying Renbo's picture and me diving off the balcony, but there

196

had been time for them to come from *Adelaide,* and Hudson's base was at Adelaide. . . . But it was much too flimsy."

"They might have been in Alice to start with," Jik said reasonably.

"They might, but what for?" I yawned. "Then on the night of the Cup you said Hudson had made a point of asking you about me . . . and I wondered how he knew you."

"Do you know," Sarah said, "I did wonder, too, at the time, but it didn't seem important. I mean, *we'd* seen *him* from the top of the stands, so it didn't seem impossible that somewhere he'd seen you with us."

"The boy knew you," I said. "And he was at the races, because he followed you, with Greene, to the Hilton. The boy must have pointed you out to Greene."

"And Greene to Wexford, and Wexford to Hudson?" Jik asked.

"Quite likely."

"And by then," he said, "they all knew they wanted to silence you pretty badly, and they'd had a chance and muffed it. . . . I'd love to have heard what happened when they found we'd robbed the gallery." He chuckled, tipping up his beer can to catch the last few drops.

"On the morning after," I said, "a letter from Hudson was delivered by hand to the Hilton. How did he know we were there?"

They stared. "Greene must have told him," Jik said. "We certainly didn't. We didn't tell anybody. We were careful about it."

"So was I," I said. "That letter offered to show me round a vineyard. Well, if I hadn't been so doubtful of him, I might have gone. He was a friend of Donald's . . . and a vineyard would be interesting. From his point of view, anyway, it was worth a try."

"Jesus!"

"On the night of the Cup, when we were in that motel near Box Hill, I telephoned the police in England and spoke to the man in charge of Donald's case, Inspector Frost. I asked him to ask Donald some questions . . . and this morning outside Wellington I got the answers."

"This morning seems several light-years away," Sarah said.

"Mmm . . ."

"What questions and what answers?" Jik said.

"The questions were, did Donald tell Hudson all about the wine in his cellar, and did Donald tell *Wexford* about the wine in the cellar, and was it Hudson who had suggested to Donald that he and Regina should go and look at the Munnings in the Arts Centre. And the answers were 'Yes, of course,' and 'No, whyever should I,' and 'Yes.' "

They thought about it in silence. Jik fiddled with the dispenser in the room's in-built refrigerator and liberated another can of Fosters.

"So what then?" Sarah said.

"So the Melbourne police said it was too unsubstantial, but if they could tie Hudson in definitely with the gallery they might believe it. So they dangled in front of Hudson the pictures and stuff we stole from the gallery, and along he came to collect them."

"How? How did they dangle them?"

"They let Wexford accidentally overhear snippets from a fake report from several hotels about odd deposits in their baggage rooms, including the paintings at the Hilton. Then, after we got here, they gave him an opportunity to use the telephone when he thought no one was listening, and he rang Hudson at the house he's been staying in here for the races, and told him. So Hudson wrote himself a letter to the Hilton from me, and zoomed along to remove the incriminating evidence."

"He must have been crazy."

"Stupid. But he thought I was dead . . . and he'd no idea anyone suspected him. He should have had the sense to know that Wexford's call to him would be bugged by the police . . . but Frost told me that Wexford would think he was using a public phone booth."

"Sneaky," Sarah said.

I yawned. "It takes a sneak to catch a sneak."

"You'd never have thought Hudson would blaze up like that," she said. "He looked so—so dangerous." She shivered. "You wouldn't think people could hide such really frightening violence under a friendly public face."

"The nice Irish bloke next door," Jik said, standing up, "can leave a bomb to blow the legs off children."

He pulled Sarah to her feet. "What do you think I paint?" he said. "Vases of flowers?" He looked down at me. "Horses?"

We parted the next morning at Melbourne Airport,

where we seemed to have spent a good deal of our lives.

"It seems strange, saying goodbye," Sarah said.

"I'll be coming back," I said.

They nodded.

"Well . . ." We looked at watches.

It was like all partings. There wasn't much to say. I saw in their eyes, as they must have seen in mine, that the past ten days would quickly become a nostalgic memory. Something we did in our crazy youth. Distant.

"Would you do it all again?" Jik said.

I thought inconsequentially of surviving wartime pilots looking back from forty years on. Had their achievements been worth the blood and sweat and risk of death; did they regret?

I smiled. Forty years on didn't matter. What the future made of the past was its own tragedy. What we ourselves did on the day was all that counted.

"I guess I would."

I leaned forward and kissed Sarah, my oldest friend's wife.

"Hey," he said. "Find one of your own."

CHAPTER 17

Maisie saw me before I saw her, and came sweeping down like a great scarlet bird, wings outstretched.

Monday lunchtime at Wolverhampton races, misty and cold.

"Hello, dear, I'm so glad you've come. Did you have a good trip back, because of course it's such a long way, isn't it, with all that wretched jet lag?" She patted my arm and peered acutely at my face. "You don't really look awfully well, dear, if you don't mind me saying so, and you don't seem to have collected any suntan, though I suppose as you haven't been away two weeks it isn't surprising, but those are nasty gashes on your hand, dear, aren't they, and you were walking very *carefully* just now."

She stopped to watch a row of jockeys canter past on their way to the start. Bright shirts against the thin gray mist. A subject for Munnings.

"Have you backed anything, dear? And are you sure you're warm enough in that anorak? I never think jeans are good for people in the winter—they're only cotton, dear, don't forget—and how did you get on in Australia? I mean, dear, did you find out anything useful?"

"It's an awfully long story. . . ."

"Best told in the bar, then, don't you think, dear?"

She bought us immense brandies with ginger ale and settled herself at a small table, her kind eyes alert and waiting.

I told her about Hudson's organization, about the Melbourne gallery, and about the list of robbable customers.

"Was I on it?"

I nodded. "Yes, you were."

"And you gave it to the police?" she said anxiously.

I grinned. "Don't look so worried, Maisie. Your name was crossed out already. I just crossed it out more thoroughly. By the time I'd finished, no one could ever disentangle it, particularly on a photocopy."

She smiled broadly. "No one could call you a fool, dear."

I wasn't so sure about that. "I'm afraid, though," I said, "that you've lost your nine thousand quid."

"Oh, yes, dear," she said cheerfully. "Serves me right, doesn't it, for trying to cheat the customs, though frankly, dear, in the same circumstances I'd probably do it again, because that tax makes me so mad, dear. But I'm ever so glad, dear, that they won't come knocking on my door this time—or, rather, my sister Betty's, because of course I'm staying with her again up here at the moment, as of course the Beach told you, until my house is ready."

I blinked. "What house?"

"Well, dear, I decided not to rebuild the house at Worthing, because it wouldn't be the same without the things Archie and I bought together, so I'm selling that plot of seaside land for a fortune, dear, and I've chosen a nice place just down the road from Sandown Park Racecourse."

"You're not going to live in Australia?"

"Oh, no, dear, that would be too far away. From Archie, you see, dear."

I saw. I liked Maisie very much.

"I'm afraid I spent all your money," I said.

She smiled at me with her well-kept head on one side, and absentmindedly stroked her crocodile handbag.

"Never mind, dear. You can paint me *two* pictures. One of me, and one of my new house."

I left after the third race, took the train along the main line to Shrewsbury, and from there traveled by bus to Inspector Frost's official doorstep.

He was in an office, chin-deep in papers. Also present,

the unblinking Superintendent Wall, who had so un-
nerved Donald, and whom I'd not previously met. Both
men shook hands in a cool and businesslike manner,
Wall's eyes traversing the anorak, jeans, and desert boots,
and remaining unimpressed. They offered me a chair:
molded plastic and armless.

Frost said, faintly smiling, "You sure kicked open an
ant hill."

Wall frowned, disliking such frivolity. "It appears you
stumbled on an organization of some size."

The gaze of both men swept the mountain of paper.
"What about Donald?" I asked.

Frost kept his eyes down. His mouth twitched.

Wall said, "We have informed Mr. Stuart that we are
satisfied the break-in at his house and the death of Mrs.
Stuart were the work of outside agencies, beyond his
knowledge or control."

Cold comfort words. "Did he understand what he was
hearing?"

The Wall eyebrows rose. "I went to see him myself, this
morning. He appeared to understand perfectly."

"And what about Regina?"

"The body of Mrs. Stuart," Wall said correctively.

"Donald wants her buried," I said.

Frost looked up with an almost human look of compassion. "The difficulty is," he said, "that in a murder
case one has to preserve the victim's body in case the defense wishes to call for its own post-mortem. In this case,
we have not been able to accuse anyone of her murder,
let alone get as far as them arranging a defense." He
cleared his throat. "We'll release Mrs. Stuart's body for
burial as soon as official requirements have been met."

I looked at my fingers, interlacing them.

Frost said, "Your cousin already owes you a lot. You
can't be expected to do more."

I smiled twistedly and stood up. "I'll go and see him,"
I said.

Wall shook hands again, and Frost came with me
through the hall and out into the street. The lights shone
bright in the early-winter evening.

"Unofficially," he said, walking slowly with me along
the pavement, "I'll tell you that the Melbourne police
found a list of names in the gallery which it turns out
are of known house-breakers. Divided into countries, like
the overseas customers. There were four names for Eng-

land. I suppose I shouldn't guess and I certainly ought not to be saying this to you, but there's a good chance Mrs. Stuart's killer may be one of them."

"Really?"

"Yes. But don't quote me." He looked worried.

"I won't," I said. "So the robberies were local labor?"

"It seems to have been their normal method."

Greene, I thought. Greene could have recruited them. And checked afterward, in burned houses, on work done.

I stopped walking. We were standing outside the flower shop where Regina had worked. Frost looked at the big bronze chrysanthemums in the brightly lit window, and then inquiringly at my face.

I put my hand in my pocket and pulled out the six revolver shell cases. Gave them to Frost.

"These came from the gun which the man called Greene fired at me," I said. "He dropped them when he was reloading. I told you about them on the telephone."

He nodded.

"I don't imagine they're of much practical use," I said. "But they might persuade you that Greene is capable of murder."

"Well . . . what of it?"

"It's only a feeling."

"Get on with it."

"Greene," I said, "was in England at about the time Regina died."

He stared.

"Maybe Regina knew him," I said. "She had been in the gallery in Australia. Maybe she saw him helping to rob her house—supervising, perhaps—and maybe that's why she was killed, because it wouldn't have been enough just to tie her up and gag her. . . . She could identify him for certain if she was alive."

He looked as if he were trying to draw breath.

"That's all . . . guessing," he said.

"I know for certain that Greene was in England two weeks after Regina's death. I know for certain he was up to his neck in selling paintings and stealing them back. I know for certain that he would kill someone who could get him convicted. The rest—well, it's over to you."

"My God," Frost said. "My God."

I started off again, toward the bus stop. He came with me, looking glazed.

"What everyone wants to know," he said, "is what put you on to the organization in the first place."

I smiled. "A hot tip from an informer."

"What informer?"

A smuggler in a scarlet coat, glossy hairdo, and crocodile handbag. "You can't grass on informers," I said.

He sighed, shook his head, stopped walking, and pulled a piece of torn-off telex paper out of his jacket.

"Did you meet an Australian policeman called Porter?"

"I sure did."

"He sent you a message." He handed me the paper. I read the neatly typed words: "Tell that Pommy painter Thanks."

"Will you send a message back?"

He nodded. "What is it?"

"No sweat," I said.

I stood in the dark outside my cousin's house, looking in.

He sat in his lighted drawing room, facing Regina, unframed on the mantelshelf. I sighed and rang the bell.

Donald came slowly. Opened the door.

"Charles!" He was mildly surprised. "I thought you were in Australia."

"Got back yesterday."

"Come in."

We went into the kitchen, where at least it was warm, and sat on each side of the table. He looked gaunt and fifty, a shell of a man, retreating from life.

"How's business?" I said.

"Business?"

"The wine trade."

"I haven't been to the office."

"If you didn't have a critical cash-flow problem before," I said, "you'll have one soon."

"I don't really care."

"You've got stuck," I said. "Like a needle in a record. Playing the same little bit of track over and over again."

He looked blank.

"The police know you didn't fix the robbery," I said.

He nodded slowly. "That man Wall . . . came and told me so. This morning."

"Well, then."

"It doesn't seem to make much difference."

"Because of Regina?"

He didn't answer.

"You've got to stop it, Donald," I said. "She's dead. She's been dead five weeks and three days. Do you want to see her?"

He looked absolutely horrified. "No! Of course not."

"Then stop thinking about her body."

"Charles!" He stood up violently, knocking over his chair. He was somewhere between outrage and anger, and clearly shocked.

"She's in a cold drawer," I said, "and you want her in a box in the cold ground. So where's the difference?"

"Get out," he said loudly. "I don't want to hear you."

"The bit of Regina you're obsessed about," I said, not moving, "is just a collection of minerals. That . . . that *shape* lying in storage isn't Regina. The real girl is in your head. In your memory. The only life you can give her is to remember her. That's her immortality, in your head. You're killing her all over again with your refusal to go on living."

He turned on his heel and walked out. I heard him go across the hall, and guessed he was making for the sitting room.

After a minute, I followed him. The white paneled door was shut. I walked across the hall. Opened the door. Went in.

He was sitting in his chair, in the usual place.

"Go away," he said.

What did it profit a man, I thought, if he got flung over balconies and shot at and mangled by rocks, and couldn't save his cousin's soul.

"I'm taking that picture with me to London," I said.

He was alarmed. He stood up. "You're *not.*"

"I am."

"You can't. You gave it to me."

"It needs a frame," I said. "Or it will warp."

"You can't take it."

"You can come as well."

"I can't leave here," he said.

"Why not?"

"Don't be stupid," he said explosively. "You know why not. Because of . . ." His voice died away.

I said, "Regina will be with you wherever you are. Whenever you think of her, she'll be there."

Nothing.

"She isn't in this room. She's in your head. You can go out of here and take her with you."

Nothing.

"She was a great girl. It must be bloody without her. But she deserves the best you can do."

Nothing.

I went over to the fireplace and picked up the picture. Regina's face smiled out, vitally alive. I hadn't done her left nostril too well, I thought.

Donald didn't try to stop me.

I put my hand on his arm.

"Let's get your car out," I said, "and drive down to my flat. Right this minute."

A little silence.

"Come on," I said.

He began, with difficulty, to cry.

I took a long breath and waited. "O.K.," I said. "How are you off for petrol?"

"We can get some more," he said, sniffing, ". . . on the motorway."

Bestselling Novels From POCKET BOOKS